LOCK IT DOWN

Bonnie,
I hope this book
is cozy company for a
day or Two!
Gently Forward Movement
Susan James

LOCK IT DOWN

SUSAN JAMES

Daily Pages Press / Waterloo, NY

Daily Pages Press books may be purchased for educational, business, or sales promotional use.

For information, contact:
Daily Pages Press
PO Box 89
Waterloo, NY 13165

DailyPagesPress.com
SusanJamesWriter.com

First Daily Pages Press Trade Paperback published 2014.

Book Layout © 2014 TheBookMakers.com

Lock It Down/ Susan James. – 2nd ed.
ISBN 978-0692349526

For my husband, Dennis Benjamin, for bringing me to the stunning Finger Lakes and introducing me to the richest landscape I have ever known and for giving me the life and the love to enable me to sit down and write my stories from beginning to end.

ACKNOWLEDGMENTS

This book was inspired by the rich history and beauty the Finger Lakes Region has to offer. Originally from the valley and the shores of California, this book has firmly rooted me to bloom where I am planted.

I offer my deepest thanks first to my fellow readers, writers, and editors who offered both encouragement and brilliance in working out conundrums in the manuscript both large and small: Susan Gold, Holly Clancy, Nicola Stewart, Annette Van, Caroline Upcher, Barbara Sotcan, and Ann Ealy.

Full gratitude to the production team who made this book a reality: Design and Layout done expertly by the team at The Book Makers, proofreading by Melissa Gilbert and my longest-loved Eagle Eye, Bill Molesky.

I thank Janet Ridgeway who guided the genius who watched over every single page of the first draft as much as the pages of the final book. Any rendering of non-genius on the pages here is purely my own.

I forever thank Joe Duemer, who originally gave me this interminable contagion called the need to write, for which writing is the only cure.

CHAPTER 1

THE LAST BIRTHDAY PARTY Cady Colette had attended was her own, six years ago. That day had dissolved into terror when her husband mysteriously disappeared. *Why did I agree to do this?* Cady thought as Sara set her birthday cake down in front of her. Cady regretted agreeing to let her friends throw her a party for her thirty-second birthday. But she also felt gratitude for having these people in her life who cared so deeply for her—something she couldn't have imagined half a decade ago. Cady lived her life, now, in quiet. In small groups. One on one. Eric had lit the candles and there were people everywhere. The people, the food, the love—all of it mixed together in the park as the high summer sun edged toward the horizon.

"Happy birthday to you," they all trailed off in clumsy harmony. Cady's big brown eyes sparkled in the light of the colored flames of the candles. Blue, red, green. Her cheeks were rosy from the heat. She sat at the end of the picnic table and made a wish—the same wish she'd wished for the last five birthdays. Her two best friends, Sara and Rosalind, and Eric, the man she'd recently started dating, a picnic table full of friendly eyes—everyone's eager face on. They were all waiting for her to blow out her candles. Her performance skills were rusty and she wanted them all to look away.

"What did you wish for?" Eric asked. He placed the matches on the picnic table and beamed his warm, kissable smile at her.

"Now if I told you . . ." Cady blinked hard, gathered focus, and let a smile form as she lifted a tiny creamy white rose with her finger and swooped it into her mouth. Rusty, but her people brought the oil can.

"Hey, no fair. You said the roses were mine," Natalie laughed from the bench next to her.

"All but the first one, Teenager," Cady said, nudging her shoulder against Natalie's. "You can have the first piece. Your mom has got that knife and she means to do business."

"First piece goes to the birthday girl," Sara said from behind Cady. "Here, let me cut. Natalie, grab those plates and pass."

"But of course," Natalie put on her public voice to her mom. Then she turned to her boyfriend as she stood up. "Chris, get up and help."

Rosalind knelt next to Cady. The petticoats of her period costume fluffed around her. "Thanks for doing this," she whispered into Cady's ear. "I know it's hard but it's good. And no matter what happens tonight, you remember this party was good. Okay?"

Cady tilted her head and kissed Rosalind on the cheek. "I wish you didn't have to leave."

"I'll be back before the fireworks," Rosalind said. "I just have to go introduce the keynote speaker." She stood up. "I confess, though, that I'd rather be wearing the little sundress you've got on than all these layers. I know. I say it every year. If I were as young as you and Sara, I could stand this heat better and maybe this high collar wouldn't choke me half to death."

"You do," Cady laughed, "say it every year. And I swear you're younger than all of us."

"Now that you're back to celebrating birthdays, we'll have to do something big for my fiftieth. Thirty-two really does seem like just yesterday."

"Hurry back," Cady said. "I promise not to have any fun without you."

"I'll tell Sara you are forbidden to crack a smile until I return." Rosalind gave Cady's hand a squeeze and made a quiet escape to resume her duties as organizer of the yearly festival commemorating the first convention on women's rights, held in the 19th century on the very block where they had set up their picnic.

Sara had arranged for the Harbor House Cone and Grill to cater the little party inside of the big party. The trick was to get there early to stake out one of the ten picnic tables at People's Park. Sara laid blankets on the grass next to the table to further delineate their party from the larger festival. Cady's friends filtered in and out of the picnic site all evening.

The Harbor House had provided dinner for the guests and they were feeling gluttonous even before they cut the cake. The Harbor House cooked simple picnic fare better than anyone in the Finger Lakes. Pulled BBQ pork on seeded buns, homemade baked beans with crispy bacon chunks all through, corn on the cob, roasted with the shucks on, salt potatoes crusted like a salt lick. Fresh green salad, without a sliver of cabbage or carrot. Ice cold lemonade from Lauralei's grandmother's recipe. They weren't big enough to cater an entire festival like Convention Days, but small weddings and birthday parties were their specialty. And Lauralei was a master baker. She made Cady's favorite, lemon cake with sweet lemon sugar frosting on top and in the middle. Lauralei dotted the cake with tiny white roses because Cady had a romance with the beautiful rose-covered frosted cakes her mom used to buy her at the grocery store for her birthdays.

"I knew this cake was coming out," Eric said. "I'm glad I made my rounds down here before it was all gone." He grinned and accepted a slice from Chris, who was dutifully serving.

"Who made this food?" said Mulligan. "It's like an ad for the perfect summer picnic." Mulligan had become friends with Cady when he was doing some construction at her apartment.

"You know the Harbor House?" said Sara. "It's that little porch restaurant next door to the state trooper's house on the canal." She handed a plate of food to Eric, who took it in addition to the cake.

"Yeah," said Mulligan, "that trooper who parks his patrol car at the edge of the canal to slow boats down to a no wake?" He nodded to his wife. "I know him. He gave me a ticket once."

"I'm sure he's given everyone around here a ticket at one time or another," said Cady.

"No. Get this," said Mulligan, as he put his plate on the picnic table so he could illustrate with his hands. "I'm flying down the river, minding my own business, and I come up on the trooper's house. It's the middle of the day on like a Wednesday. I catch him out of the corner of my eye, standing at the end of his dock waving me over. He's all geared up with his Stetson and he's packing. He's got this hairy eye so I say screw him, flip him off, and step on the gas even faster as I fly by his dock. I mean, what's he gonna do, jump in and swim me down? Doesn't that son of a bitch meet me in his troop car down at the marina. He gets on his speaker and yells out my name and says I can either come get my tickets now or I can get them and a few more at my house later. Bastard took down my hull number and looked me up in the three miles between his dock and the marina. It was so good I couldn't even fault him. I never do make a wake going down the canal anymore. That's how I first met him. Nicest guy to know around here." He had the whole table laughing.

"Eric, you ever met that guy?" asked Mulligan, picking up his cake.

"Sam Baldwin?" said Eric. "Of course. I know all the troopers. He's the one who trained Blue."

Cady winced at Blue's name—the trooper who couldn't solve the mystery of what happened to her husband. She knew he and Eric were friends and roommates because Eric had mentioned it on their first date. Hearing his name on her birthday stole away some of the easy joy she was starting to allow herself as the party progressed. She visibly shook it off in an effort to stay in the moment.

"He's cool as the lake is wet," Eric went on, "but even I don't want to get on his wrong side. Black ops type. He's a lawyer now, you know. With the DA's office. Now he's the one prosecuting all those tickets instead of writing them." Eric took a huge bite of his sandwich and wiped his mouth with a paper napkin. He'd started with the cake and eaten the meal backwards. "Damn this food is good," he said. "I've never been to the restaurant, but if they are half as good as this pulled pork is, I might have to bet on them to win."

Cady and Sara moved with their cake to sit together on one of the blankets on the grass.

"Pay Lauralei extra for this, would you?" Cady said as she leaned down on her elbow, vintage U2 playing low on the small boom box Sara had brought. Cady had swept up her shoulder-length chestnut hair in a couple of bobby pins, and the effect was both elegant and casual at the same time. Cady's high cheekbones were sun-kissed from her late morning walk by Seneca Lake.

"I'm paying Harbor House for this?" Sara feigned surprise.

"Put it on Rosalind's tab." Cady crinkled her nose and giggled at herself. "Seriously, though. Thanks so much for all this. I'm not going to lie. I'm actually feeling festive." She looked over at the people there to celebrate with her. A few of her book club kids, the kids she got attached to during the couple of years they spent with her at her library, reading and loving books. A few of their parents who had become her friends. Mulligan and his crew. Eric Peterman. He was working security for the festival but came down to patrol People's Park as the cake was being unveiled.

"You deserve it. We all do. Nice party. Good food. I'm stuffed," Sara said.

"I haven't seen Kiery," Cady said. "Her parents didn't make it either. Maybe they're still up on Fall Street." Cady was grateful more people hadn't shown up. "Can you believe her painting? Who would know from the book club that she'd be so brilliant with a paintbrush?" Cady had started a painting group on Friday evenings for local residents. Kiery was the only teenager in it. She was also the only one of them with real talent.

"I know. Gifted," Sara said. "She rode down here on her bike this morning. She was up at the Visitor Center doing face painting with the Children's Program. She said she was coming with her parents tonight. I haven't seen her, though."

"She could paint a Monet on the side of a kid's face," Cady said.

"What about Jonathan?" Sara said.

"He came for a minute right when I showed up," said Cady. "He said he was going up to Fall Street." Cady paused. "I have to confess, I'm glad he didn't stay. He's not my favorite. Rosalind can't make heads out of him either. He failed her senior English class. He's in summer school because he just wouldn't write the last paper. I understand procrastination, but that's a bit much. She said he had no excuses about why he didn't finish but he went steely cold on her when he found out. I think she's the only one who holds his feet to the fire. My sense is that the rest of them just want to be rid of him."

"He's never missed a book club meeting, though, has he?" said Sara.

"Not a one. He doesn't say much when we meet, but it's clear he's always read the book. I don't know. He's nice enough, but I'm glad to be phasing him out of the club. I can't dislodge him until he finishes summer school because he's technically still in high school until then. But at that point, I am going to throw a little party for him as a reminder of his last meeting. He'd be just the type to keep coming even after the new school year started up."

"Natalie says there's something strange about him, too," Sara said. "Can't you take applications and screen for people to be in the book club?"

Cady laughed out loud. "You're assuming there's enough interest for there to be competition. With the smallest library in all of New York State," she said with her usual flourish, "I'm lucky to have any interest at all. No, any high schooler who wants to read what we're reading and talk about it over water and wafers is welcome. If he were a real problem I'd ask him to leave, but he's not. He just creeps me out a little."

Cady laid back on the blanket and looked up at the darkening summer sky. Sara was picking grass absently as she rested on her elbow. A late summer firefly blinked into Cady's view, a last dozy male searching for a mate. Natalie and Chris had pulled out their pack of Uno cards and a few people settled onto the benches while Chris dealt the cards.

"Hey, ladies," Eric drawled as he stepped into view, "I have to go make my rounds. See what the hoodlums are doing up on the main drag. Radio's been quiet but I got to earn my pay. Rosalind wouldn't like it if I were hanging around partying all night." He rubbed his hands together like he was warming them over a fire. He ran one hand over his shaggy blond hair, gelled back more conservatively for his work hours.

"Sure you can't stay?" Sara asked as she heaved herself up off the blanket.

"You throw a mighty soiree, Sara Jane," he said as he kissed her on the cheek. "But I'm senior security officer tonight so I need to keep moving. And my uniform buttons are bulging after all this good food. Got to walk it off."

"Your uniform knows nothing of bulging, pretty boy," Sara said as she tapped him on his flat stomach.

"Happy birthday, Cady," he said, smiling and grabbing onto the hand she'd offered to him to lift her up. He gave her a hug and said, "I left a little something for you on the picnic table."

"No," Cady protested. "You weren't supposed to bring presents."

"It's just a trinket." He gently squeezed her hand. "I picked it up for you last weekend." He turned his focus to the phone clipped on his belt. "Hang on. Duty calls." He stepped away to check the text he'd just received. A second later, he rejoined Sara and Cady.

"Come here. Walk me to the road." He took her hand and started walking toward Water Street at the edge of the park that led up to Fall Street where the festival was getting into full swing now that the keynote address was over. His hand had turned a little clammy since he'd helped her up off the blanket but Cady found that sweet. Eric was a small town boy, grown into a small town man. He was gregarious and shy all at the same time. He introduced himself as "Deuce" and preferred to be called by his nickname, but no one she knew actually did.

"Thanks for the trinket," she said as they reached the road and she dropped her hand from his. "And thanks for coming down. We'll be here at least until after the fireworks so feel free to patrol down here again. We could use the protection. And when you see Rosalind up there, tell her to come down and eat cake. I know she's exhausted and could probably use a sugar lift."

"Yeah. I'll tell my boss to come down and eat cake," Eric said.

"She's not your boss," Cady said.

"She is for this weekend," Eric said.

"What-ev," Cady said as she held up her hand.

"You're hanging around those kids too much," he teased.

"You just come back for the fireworks. If you want," she said as she started walking backward toward her party.

He watched her go and when she noticed, she turned around and started a little jog back to the picnic table.

"Did he mention another date?" Sara said as Cady made her way back onto the blanket.

"No." She shifted her mouth to the side trying not to smile. "I can't even decide if I want him to," she said. "Maybe he'll ask at the fireworks. Maybe I will."

Sara blew out between her lips.

"I mean, I want him to." She fanned herself. "Supposed to, right? He came out of nowhere. A man who reads. I am so not ready for this. And something about a man so pretty makes me a little nervous." She smiled. "And he can't be away from his phone for two seconds."

"You can tick off the 'faults' all you want," she used air quotes, "but it does not change the fact that a handsome stranger stumbled into your library—not mine, I note—

and is courting you like a soap opera ingénue. And you know there are no supposed tos."

"Maybe his phone is the Kryptonite to those Hollywood good looks," Cady smiled.

"He *is* working tonight," Sara said. "They probably communicate with their phones as much as by radio. Here, open his present. I swiped it before anyone noticed it was there. It wasn't wrapped."

Cady opened the hinge-top box. Inside was a wooden circle with a web of thread woven through it. Dangling from the bottom of the circle were three feathers. Cady straightened the feathers inside the box.

Sara said, "It's a dream catcher. Beautiful. Native Americans say they can catch any bad feelings in the air." Cady handed it over as Sara reached for it. The thread matched the color of Cady's dress, a shimmering blue halter that bared her olive-skinned summer shoulders and skimmed her knees.

Cady picked it up out of the box. "Best place to get these around here would be the Turning Stone Indian Casino."

They looked at each other. Both knew of Eric's rumored gambling problems but neither knew him well enough to know the extent of the problem or even if the rumors were true.

"You might be able to pick one up at the gas station down at the reservation," Sara offered. "We shouldn't be so quick to worry. I've never seen one this beautiful."

"Or the internet," Cady said. "You're right. There are a million places to get a dream catcher. He could have bought it at a craft fair in Canandaigua for all we know."

"It's sweet, Cady. And I did tell him not to bring any gifts. He's a good egg."

"I know he is." Cady smiled at the dream catcher.

"Ms. Colette," Natalie called over her shoulder, "I need help whipping the Uno off of Chris. Come help." She laughed as Chris nuggied her head.

"Enough about Dreamboat," Cady said and tucked the trinket back into its box. "Let's focus and get to the real party." They stood up and squeezed in at the picnic table.

As the sky lit up with fireworks, most of the crowd from the main festival had funneled down one of the two sets of stone stairs to People's Park and were planted somewhere along the canal's edge or on the grass facing Bailey Bridge. The stairs kept the foot traffic off the roadway that wound down from Fall Street. During the festival weekend, they created the effect of a two-story outdoor party.

"You know that's the *It's a Wonderful Life* bridge?" Eric said to Cady as they were gathering up the blankets to make room for the surge of people.

"Yeah. I've heard that." Cady looked at the bridge. She invited no explanation. Cady had met Victor during the yearly Christmas celebration in Seneca Falls. He had told her that night they first met that it was long rumored, and now firmly believed by everyone who lived there, that

Bedford Falls was designed after Frank Capra visited the sleepy mill town of Seneca Falls in 1945 on his way to visit his aunt in nearby Auburn. The bridge over the canal is virtually identical to the bridge George Bailey jumps off of to save Clarence the guardian angel on Christmas Eve. At Christmas time, Bailey Bridge is lit with thousands of little white lights. Seneca Falls is transformed into Bedford Falls. In July, the bridge serves as the fireworks station for the Convention Days.

Among the oohs and aahs of the crowd at the glittering fireworks shooting up over the bridge, Cady and Eric, who had come back to keep an eye on the crowd, stood in back of the picnic table, side by side. Sara sat on the table top with her feet on the bench. Mulligan, his crew, and his wife had left right after the cake. With every few sprinkles of colored light in the sky, Eric tilted toward Cady with an exaggerated "Ooh."

"All right, Officer," she said before too long, "nudge me again and I'll file a complaint for excessive force against a citizen."

He put his arm around her and pulled her close. "I'm a citizen just like you," he whispered in her ear over the pops and cracks of the fireworks. "Who you gonna complain to?"

"Ha," she said and leaned into him. "I'll tell Rosalind on you. You do not want to come under her wrath and you know it."

He snapped his hands up like she was holding a gun to him. "I'm innocent. Don't rat me out. I'll behave. Promise." He aimed his perfect smile at her.

"Just remember who holds all the power here," she said, relenting and coming back to his side, almost cuddling in.

As the finale began, he stepped behind her and placed his hands on her shoulders. Everyone was looking up. The sky was on fire. Roaring. As the last firework exploded and the applause erupted from the crowd, that magical moment of total silence that follows the applause after a spectacular finale was interrupted by a horrifying scream that was working its way from the lock toward Bailey Bridge.

Cady and Eric turned away from the bridge to follow the scream. It didn't seem real. Like someone had a party favor that they kept blowing into over and over. The crowd parted and Cady saw Natalie running at her full speed, grabbing the sides of her head and screaming. At first Cady was stunned into stillness. Her brain didn't connect that this sound was coming from Natalie. It wasn't until Chris ran up behind her, panting, that Cady thought to move. Sara was at Natalie's side in seconds. Natalie collapsed into her mother's arms and her screams turned to hoarse, desperate sobs. It was Chris who was able to speak.

"It's Ms. M'Clintock," he said almost in a whisper. Doubled over with his hands on his knees, catching his breath. He hadn't run far but something had stolen his breath. "It's Ms. M'Clintock," he said again.

"What?" Cady asked, moving to Chris. "Where is she?"

"It's Ms. M'Clintock," he said again.

"Chris," snapped Eric. "What's Ms. M'Clintock? Where is Rosalind?"

"She's dead," Natalie screamed with renewed horror. Her mother held her as they both sat on the grass. Natalie shook out of her mother's arms and stood up. "She's dead!" Everyone was silent for a split second before the crowd flared and seemed on the verge of losing control.

"God, where?" Cady grabbed Natalie's shoulders.

Natalie turned and pointed to the lock. Instinctively, Eric and Cady started off at a trot in the direction Natalie was pointing. Chris ran after them, followed by everyone in Cady's party except Natalie and her mother. The crowd parted once again and filled in after them like water.

CHAPTER 2

WHEN BLUE PULLED up in his black Crown Victoria, the onsite security officers and two Seneca Falls police officers who were patrolling the fireworks crowd were directing the crowd back and masking off the area with crime scene tape. His car sputtered to a stop. He'd been meaning to take the unmarked police car in for servicing. Although the state troopers were not particular about the cars they assigned to the BCI units—whatever dark color make and model New York State could buy or seize cheap—they were militant about requiring regular maintenance. Blue was behind on the maintenance schedule. He pulled up just ahead of the coroner and the two walked up to the scene together. Eric was standing with Cady and Sara.

"Deuce, what's the story here?" Blue said to Eric as he walked up on the crime scene.

Eric turned around and said, "Hey, glad you're on this weekend. It's Ms. M'Clintock. You know, Rosalind? She's dead, Blue." Even in the dim light of the globe lanterns at the edge of the canal, Blue could see that Eric's face was pale. Rosalind M'Clintock had been both Eric and Blue's English teacher in high school. She was the beautiful teacher with the soft, wavy blond hair that she wore back in a clip every day but that anyone could tell would fall lazily around her shoulders if let down. All the boys had a crush on her, but Eric had been particularly drawn to her in high school. Neither of them liked English as their favorite subject, but Eric had failed a class in his senior year because of Rosalind M'Clintock. He delayed college admissions to attend summer school. In reality, he could have started in the fall, but the combination of mediocre grades in his senior year along with the F that landed him in summer school choked what little enthusiasm he had for college out of him. Blue knew that, even if it was still hard for Eric to admit.

"Jeff, you need help getting her out of the water?" Blue called to Jeff Chapman, the coroner.

"Not yet, but in a minute," Jeff called back to Blue over his shoulder as he made his way to the water's edge.

"Blue, you know Cady," Eric said. "And this is Sara. She helped organize the festival. They both knew Rosalind very well."

"Ladies. How are you?" Blue said.

"Well, let's see," Cady started in, shaking. "One of my best friends is lying dead in the blackness of the canal, another of my friends is sitting over there still near hysterics because she discovered her teacher floating face up. One hell of a birthday, you could say. As always."

Cady's birthday fell during the Seneca Falls Women's Rights Convention Days festival, and since Rosalind and Sara were part of the planning committee, they needed to be at the festival for the whole weekend. They also used the backdrop of the established event to convince Cady to have a little birthday party. Just some food and a cake.

All around the festival, there were people dressed in authentic mid-19th century costumes, as true to the period as was practical. Even the purists were loath to wander around Seneca Falls in the 21st century with ten pounds or more of dresses and petticoats like they did in 1848 on any regular day. While Cady and Sara did not dress up, Rosalind trolled vintage shops and online stores for period clothes. Her favorite were bloomers—billowy pants under a mid-calf-length dress, usually split in the front. The style of dress, popularized by Amelia Bloomer, allowed Rosalind to get around the festival she organized every year and still be in period style. Although the feminist reformers eventually abandoned wearing bloomers in public because they brought such vicious ridicule by men that their message would get lost at any public gathering, Rosalind wore them on the first day of the festival every year as a tribute to the dress reform that was such a critical piece of the women's rights movement.

Rosalind had convinced Cady that since she was named after Elizabeth Cady Stanton, and since her namesake was also thirty-two at the time she launched the women's rights movement that the festival was celebrating, having her birthday party during the festival would be a fitting tribute to both Cadys. Cady had agreed partly because her friends were convincing and partly because she was making a genuine effort to open up and live a life.

"Cady," Sara said, "I'm so sorry. I should never have made you do this."

"Oh, Sara," Cady turned Sara to face her, "I didn't mean that." She brought Sara into her arms. "I'm not fit for public consumption right now," she said to Sara but looked right at Blue over Sara's shoulder.

Blue stared at her. His black eyes were fixed on her. His eyes were normally dark brown but when his blood pressure rose, they turned an onyx black. His jaw tightened but he did not respond.

Blue was tall, 5'11". In better humor, he would tease that he always fell short because he was not the full six foot. He had deep, pronounced cheekbones, a slender face with a five o'clock shadow by 5:01. He had dark brown hair, cut close to the scalp. He was not in the military but wore his hair high and tight as though he were.

"She's shaken up," Eric said. "Why don't you come sit down. Both of you." He led Cady and Sara away from Blue and over to where Natalie was sitting with Chris.

The officer who had taken Natalie and Chris's statements approached Blue.

"Hey, Paine," Blue said quietly as he watched Cady walk away in the dark. "Give me the run down."

"The girl says they were making out under the lock bridge over there where the lamp is out, and in between the firework pops, they heard a banging at the edge of the dock. At first they ignored it. They both said they were trying to hurry before the fireworks were over." Officer Paine paused and tilted his head at Blue. "But it was an odd muffled sound that didn't stop. The girl says she thought it might be an animal in trouble. The girl," he glanced at his notes, "Natalie Cross, says she left the boy-friend at the bench and tiptoed up to the water. She didn't want to scare the animal. Between the fireworks it was dark so at first she didn't know what she was looking at. She called him over," he looked at his notes again, "Chris Temple is his name. One of the fireworks went off," he read directly from his notes, "and she 'saw it was a hard-soled shoe that was bumping up against the cement wall of the dock.' It took them a minute to understand what they were looking at and when another firework lit up the sky, they both said," again he read straight from his notes, "they 'saw her eyes staring straight out into the middle of the canal.' Her back was up against the cement wall and her face and body were nearly submerged. That's when Natalie ran like hell toward her mother who was attending the birthday party of Ms. Colette here." He pointed his pencil toward Cady. "They were all watching the fire-works." He looked up at Blue who was taking it all in, watching the coroner examine the body as best he could from the dock without moving her.

"Can I let the girl go?" Officer Paine asked Blue. "She's still really shaken up and her mother wants to get her home."

"If she's signed a statement, that'll do for now, but give me a minute to sort things out here before you let her go. We're cool with this, right?" said Blue.

"Absolutely. I was the first on the scene after your security buddy here but my boss already cleared calling you in. BCI homicide resources trump ours any day on something like this."

"Thanks. Go ahead and finish getting statements and then let these people go home. Let me just have a minute with Jeff first," said Blue as he was making his way toward the water. "What does it look like, Jeff?"

"Hard to say. There doesn't seem to have been any blood lost but I won't know for sure until we get the autopsy results. The water may have washed it away. Looks like she fell in. Maybe she hit her head on the edge there. I'm taking samples of the water right next to her but not sure what it will tell me yet. The belt loop of her costume got caught on this dock hook here, which is why she didn't sink. She might have oohed and aahed at one too many fireworks and slipped off the dock. I don't know why she would have been watching from this far back. If she fell, she must have been by herself, or whoever was with her would have helped. I need to get her to Geneva General for the medical examiner to do a full autopsy, but it seems like foul play is a logical conclusion until I can tell you otherwise." He stood up and moved aside as Blue directed the ID technicians to capture the crime scene.

"We had one like this around the time of the actual Women's Rights Convention over a hundred and fifty years ago," Jeff said.

"Happy fact at the tip of your brain?" Blue asked.

"Death is my business. A lot of people have died in or near this water over the years. Since we've been keeping records, I could probably tell you each one and the cause of death. It's almost never drowning. Sometimes, but not as often as you'd think."

"Blue, what can I do?" Eric said from behind him.

"Nothing, man," Blue said as he pulled the lobe of his ear absently and turned away from Jeff. "Actually, yes. Could you organize your guys to direct people out of here and clear this area," Blue said, not framing it as a question. "Anyone who says they saw anything, have them sit over there and give a statement to Paine. I'll get a trooper to secure Fall Street with Sara. She can help with the festival business. You help keep an eye up there, too. We don't need any more trouble tonight."

One of Rosalind's responsibilities as festival chair was hiring the additional security for the festival. Several years ago, the festival had devolved into a bawdy, drunk-fest of a weekend for anyone who was feeling rowdy on a hot July weekend. The normal patrolling of the local law enforcement proved to be insufficient and the people most interested in celebrating the birth of the women's rights movement started staying away. The festival was now under new management. The organizers got together and decided to restore the family and community atmosphere to the weekend. They hired Eric's private security firm to enhance the local law enforcement presence and eliminated the beer tent, although they didn't prohibit anyone from bringing their own alcohol to their private picnics. They encouraged all the local businesses on Fall Street to stay open until midnight so that the street was lit and active. She was strict with the security officers and wanted them to be as professional as the local police department and the state troopers who patrolled.

"Will do," Eric said as he radioed some instructions to his team and started off toward the stone stairs.

"Sara," Blue walked over to her, "we're going to need to cancel the rest of this festival. We have no idea what happened here. If she fell, or if she was pushed, we don't want anyone else getting hurt. Can you go up and tell the store owners and get on the website and put up a cancellation notice?"

"Sure, sure. Whatever I can do," Sara said. Absently, "Charlotte."

"Pardon?" Blue said.

When Sara didn't respond, Cady offered, "Charlotte Woodward. Rosalind was dressed up like Charlotte Woodward. Charlotte was the only member of the original convention to survive to see the amendment pass in 1920 giving women the right to vote. Rosalind always honored Charlotte at the keynote event for being the sole survivor."

Cady and Sara stood next to the bench where Natalie sat after Chris's parents had come for him. They stood outside the police tape watching them pulling Rosalind out of the water. Cady's face was tortured into a grimace of both revulsion and grief. She was not connecting the body coming out of the water with that of her friend, but she was also clear that her friend was gone.

Rosalind was dressed in her costume of mid-19th century gown with many petticoats, all adhering now to her slender legs with the weight of the water. She had on brown leather ankle boots with low heels, laced up tight. She always saved her finest costume for the evening of the keynote address she would be announcing. She tried every year to come as close to authentic 1848 costuming as she could but was not rigid. If it were miserably hot, she would wear her crinoline instead of her starched petticoats even though crinoline was not developed until the late 1850s. It was cooler and that mattered in the humid Central New York heat. To find the proper attire, she tracked down skirts from Sears, Roebuck and Co. and chemises and slips from the National Cloak and Suit Company. She even found a corset with silk laces, although she didn't tighten it beyond what was comfortable. She wanted to be authentic, but one of the triumphs of feminism over the years was the abolishment of the corset. Women could thank Coco Chanel for that, Rosalind always said, but that revelation, even though not completely attributable to Coco Chanel, didn't come until well after the original Women's Rights Convention was held in Seneca Falls.

Rosalind had even told Cady and Sara that she wore authentic dressing sacques and gowns of fine French Cambric and German Val lace and eyelet embroidery to bed during the festival. She still cooked on her GE stove and drank vintage wine from their wine cellar, but everything she wore was as authentic as was practical during those three days each July.

Her hair had been parted down the middle with long row curls in the front, but as she was being lifted out of the water, it was trailing her in a sheet of dark blond. Every year she cut her hair for Locks of Love right after the Convention festival. She would then let it grow out for the year so it would be long enough to wear in the spaniel curls fashion of 1848. When she was Eric and Blue's teacher, she had long, flowing blond hair. She always tied it back during school days, but the satiny quality was unmistakable. These days she kept it shorter because of the yearly donations and she had stopped adding the subtle blond highlights that turned her already golden hair a particular shade of morning sunlight. It was only in recent years that strands of gray had begun to sneak in. The effect was shimmery rather than dulling. She wanted healthy tresses to go to the charity so she took good care of her hair. Natural, like an Ivory Girl.

"Sara is in no condition to close this festival," Cady said, more biting than she intended. "Might there be a uniform around here who could handle that? Not only is

Rosalind one of Sara's best friends—was—but this is her daughter here waiting to be delivered from this nightmare."

Before Blue could respond, they all zoned in at the same time. Silence fell. Then the sound of an industrial zipper. Rosalind's lifeless body was being zipped into a body bag. Horrified, Cady came to her senses, "Where's Ron? Dear God, where's Ron?" She turned to Sara and then Blue. "Where's Ron? I never saw him here today. I never went up to Fall Street so he might have been up there, but I never saw him." They had found Rosalind's body over an hour ago and Cady had not thought to notify Ron or even wonder where he was.

Ron M'Clintock and Rosalind had been married for their entire adult lives. He was a history professor at Hobart and William Smith Colleges in Geneva, the town that butted Waterloo to the west. He was as passionate about his Civil War reenactments as Rosalind was about her Women's Rights activities in the community. He and Rosalind never had children. They were both career teachers and felt about many of their students like they were surrogate children. They had full, happy lives together and separately. He had been considering retirement lately. It was just as likely that Ron was down South at a reenactment as that he was home preparing his syllabus for the coming semester.

"Take it easy, Cady," Paine said from behind her as he put his hand on her arm. She turned to him. "We sent a car over to him a little while ago. As soon as we had a pos-

itive ID we mobilized the notification team. Blue wanted
to go himself but thought it was more important that Ron
know sooner rather than later. We've got a car taking him
to the morgue to meet Rosalind's body." There was no official notification team, but Blue had dispatched one of
the troopers on duty that night to make sure Ron heard
from an official source before any rumors started to trickle out. "And we'll send someone up to Fall Street to shut
everything down. You going to be okay?" he asked.

"God, I'm losing my mind," Cady said, crossing her
arms and holding her hand to her throat. "This just can't
be happening."

Ever since Sara had brought up the idea of a birthday
party, Cady had been dreaming of the last birthday she
had celebrated with a party. She was turning 26, still rel-
ishing the idea of being married. Cady had spent the
morning with Sara and Rosalind riding their bikes down
Lower Lake Road and absorbing the breathtaking vistas of
Seneca Lake. The three parted ways and Cady went for a
massage. It was a birthday tradition. When she returned,
Victor's sister Alexa and her partner Michelle were just
getting out of the inground pool and were about to shower. When all three women were ready, they decided to
head to the restaurant together. Victor wasn't home. Cady
hadn't heard from him all day. She assumed he'd meet her
at The Pier. It was the nicest restaurant on the lake and
the three had dressed for the event. Cady wore her new
charcoal three-quarter sleeve slinky dress that hugged all
her right places. She'd bought it for her birthday and was

going to entice Victor from across the table. She'd planned an elaborate unveiling of the new lingerie underneath at the end of the night.

Alexa and Michelle were all linen pants and bare backs and bare shoulders. They had walked in fashionably late to kisses and cheers from Rosalind and Ron, Sara and Marshall, Victor's brother, Clint, and his girlfriend, Blair. Victor was not there. When they settled in and Cady realized Victor was not on the premises, she gave her drink order to Clint and texted Victor. Clint hadn't seen him all day. He thought he was with Cady.

After her drink was more or less gone and she'd still received no response from him, she let a tiny strand of worry in. Of all things Victor was, he was never late. She called him. The buzz of activity, the massage, the glass of wine—it was all wearing off. She got his voicemail and left a coquettish message and told him to get his fine ass to The Pier before she started to pout. They ordered some appetizers at the bar. Another round of drinks.

They never were seated that night. They never ate anything beyond clams casino and black bean and steak quesadillas. They had waited two hours. In a dull panic, everyone went back to Victor and Cady's house. Clint called the police. Michelle and Sara divvied up the local hospitals and called them all. The police stopped in because it was a slow night and Victor's family was well known in the area because of their world-class winery, but other than taking a report, there was nothing to be done on a missing person until sufficient time had passed for them to be officially determined missing. Before midnight on the night of Cady's 26th birthday, she knew in her gut that her life had changed forever.

"Paine," Blue said, "let's move everyone back from this tape. I'm sure Delaney will be here any minute so there'll be a notice in tomorrow's paper—along with her above-the-fold story chocked full of rich details."

Jeff called Blue over. "It's too early to be sure, but she's got a knot on the back of her head. Couldn't see it in the water. I'll know more in a couple of hours, but it doesn't look like she fell." Jeff unzipped the body bag down to her neck. "It looks like her head hit something round." Jeff turned Rosalind's head so that Blue could see the nearly perfectly round indentation in the back of her skull.

"Oh, Rosalind," Blue said as he knelt down next to her. They weren't close, but he had known her for years. As adults, they were part of the same community. She had long ago stopped being Ms. M'Clintock to him and had become Rosalind, the one who organized the festival every year, who sat on the Waterloo Town Board, who he ran into grocery shopping at Wegmans every Sunday with her newspaper and Seattle Roast coffee. She and Ron had even invited Blue and Delaney to a party or two in an effort to become friends. The effort faded when Delaney and Blue started to fade, but the good intention was always there. "Somebody did this to you," he said. "I hate doing the ones I know," he said to no one in particular as he stood up.

"You need to go back to Fishkill, my friend," said Jeff, "where you don't know absolutely everybody."

"Call me when you know something," Blue said and walked back to the edge of the police tape. Cady was visibly shaking.

"Maybe you should take Cady home," Blue said to Officer Paine as he approached him standing with Cady and Sara. "A few more minutes and the others can go as well."

"I will," Paine said. "No problem."

"Cady can take herself home," Cady snapped. "I'm the least of the worries around here tonight." She stopped herself. She didn't need to make any of this worse. Calmer, "I'll wait with Sara until Natalie can go home. We'll all go together."

Blue nodded once, his eyes landing on Cady's a second too long, and turned around to walk away.

CHAPTER 3

"DAN!" DELANEY BARKED as she dropped her bag onto the bench next to where Natalie was sitting. Blue whipped around at the sound of his name. "Tell me everything, stat. I have to get this story filed ASAP to make the Sunday paper if I don't want to be relegated to online coverage only."

"Delaney," Blue spoke in measured tones. "Where is Mollie?"

"She's in the car," Delaney said. "Of course she's not in the car." Her tone was caustic. "She's with Aunt Jessica." A little softer, "Aunt Jess was there so I never even had to wake Mollie up. Do we have to go through this every time? I'm on a deadline here."

"As always," Blue said. "You know I can't tell you anything, Lane. And neither can the District Attorney," he added when he saw her glance at Sam Baldwin, the retired state trooper, now assistant DA, on the scene. He slipped under the police tape and led her to a park bench one down from where Cady stood. He spoke quietly, calmly. "Stay behind the police tape to observe anything. I'll call you personally when we've set up a press conference. You will be the first to know, okay?"

Cady paced behind the police tape near Sara and Natalie who were sitting on a park bench waiting for the all-clear sign. Cady saw Blue lead Delaney by the elbow toward the bench. There was a tenderness there she hadn't expected. Blue and Delaney had been divorced for over a year. Cady had met Blue six years ago when her husband first went missing. Blue had helped her in her search for him when all the official leads had gone cold. She had met Delaney then, but mainly knew of her by reputation. She read Delaney's stories in the local paper every day. Rosalind had thought highly of Delaney's reporting. They'd both praised her as fair and impartial. Privately, Rosalind confided she believed it was because Delaney didn't care enough about the local scene to take a side. Back when Cady came to know them, she knew Blue had only been back in Waterloo with his new wife for a year or so at that point. Now, she could see a lifetime had passed between them in that touch on Delaney's elbow. It was soft and familiar but not intimate. There was no tenderness like a lover's touch. More like a sense of belonging and surety. He would lead her by the elbow and she would follow. There was no question in the touch. There was assumption and compliance. Cady had never known of Delaney West to be compliant in any other context.

Blue looked past Delaney to where Cady was pacing. Having these two women in his proximity flashed him back to a time when both women were squarely in his life. His life had seemed simple back then. His beautiful bride. His solid job. Cady's husband's disappearance still plagued him to this day as one of his biggest failures on the job. It seemed since that time, his life had been a downward spiral from the idyllic to the rote and often lonely. Delaney, his recently exed wife, represented his biggest personal failure.

Delaney was the crime beat reporter for the *Finger Lakes Times*, and she went anywhere and did anything to get her story. She longed for the old school of journalism where reporters dug up stories and exposed truths. She probably wouldn't have been allowed on the paper as anything but a secretary in those old school days, but the hard-nosed world of investigative journalism drew her in anyway.

Delaney was an infamous paradox in the Waterloo area. She was a fierce career woman and a loving mother to the daughter she and Blue had while they were married. She was the toast of the town and knew all the right people but openly mocked small town life. Blue had learned to accept her mocking because he had come to feel guilty for bringing her here. She was from downstate and was working in New York City when Blue showed up at a 4th of July picnic thrown by her parents in Fishkill. She was bunking at her parents' house for the holiday weekend for some much needed quiet and rest from the bustle of the big city. She'd told him later that she could only stand it for a day or two and then she longed to be back in the midst of the people.

When they met, Blue was a road trooper in Fishkill, stationed downstate for his first tour as nearly all New York State troopers are when freshly minted from the academy. He was fighting crime and she was reporting all the news fit to print. She was standing by the pool when he came through the gate of her parents' back yard with a take-out box of barbequed ribs in his hands. The afternoon sun was bright and hot. He was wearing camp cargo shorts and a slim fit golf shirt. His tanned legs were muscled. He had the long, lanky look of a swimmer but with the strength and definition to his muscles of a climber. Blue never lifted weights. He lifted his body. He used his muscles and they showed well for the wear.

Delaney walked over to him and introduced herself as she took the take-out box off his hands. "This will go great with a beer. Thanks. Can I get you one? A beer, I mean. The food will be ready in a minute. You're just in time for that."

Delaney's father, Frank, came up and patted Blue on the back. "Delaney, I'd like you to meet Labatt. Labatt, this scarlet-haired beauty is Princess Delaney, the fairest lady in all of Duchess County."

Blue spoke up when he saw Delaney's confused expression. "I'm Blue." He shook her hand. "Well, Dan. Dan Emerson. Everyone calls me Blue. Everyone but Frank. He's called me Labatt since I started here downstate."

"I suppose if your sergeant names you after his favorite beer, you must be doing something right," Delaney said to the both of them. She held up the back of her hand to the side of her mouth like she was pretending to tell Blue a secret she didn't want her dad to hear, "I think Dad's got an affinity for the Canadians."

Frank handed Blue an ice cold Labatt Blue beer. "Bought this just for you."

"But, downstate?" Delaney asked. "Now I'm totally confused."

"Yeah, your father tells me you work in New York City. I know you Manhattanites consider all of New York outside the City to be upstate."

"So you're from farther upstate than Fishkill?" she said with faux incredulousness. "I will not believe such fairy tales."

"Ah, dear princess," Blue said, "'twas a land far, far away called Central New York . . ." He swept the sky like he was painting her a picture.

They all three laughed. Delaney put her arm through Blue's bent arm holding the beer and led him to the food tables. They spent the rest of the party within reach of each other and their whirlwind romance began in earnest that night.

Blue kept erratic hours as a trooper relatively new to the force. Delaney was on call most of the time and when a story was there, she needed to be available to cover it. They spent most of their relationship in New York City. He would take the train in for the night or a couple of days if he had a few off in a row. She would drive out to Fishkill, less often, and spend the weekend with him in his apartment. She would write him letters during the week, and he felt like a soldier fighting a war when he would go to his mailbox and a scented letter from Delaney would be there. He was many miles from home and although he'd made somewhat of a life in Fishkill, he worked most of the time and had always planned to settle in Waterloo, with his family.

Central New York had space and air and quiet. There were farms and cows that he would drive by on his way to the grocery store. The neighbor on the end of his block growing up had loose chickens that somehow stayed in his property line and never roamed out into the road. Blue's mother bought eggs from him during his entire childhood until one week when a pair of foxes picked off the entire flock. The owner was so upset by the violent loss that he never replaced the birds and Blue's mother had to buy eggs at the farmer's market from then on. Even so, he thought of home as a place where chickens roamed free in the yard.

There was crime in Waterloo. There was a trooper station, a Waterloo Village police force, a Seneca County Sheriff and his deputies, all of whom had jurisdiction to protect and serve the 5,000 people in the town of Waterloo. The troopers could patrol anywhere in New York State. The Sheriff's deputies could patrol anywhere in Seneca County, a county in the Finger Lakes Region made up of some 30,000 people. But there were patrol routes that they all followed and their jurisdiction overlapped with only minor disturbances to life and limb.

When Blue proposed to Delaney, he did so in her parents' back yard next to the pool where they had first met. It was the 4th of July weekend exactly one year after they had met and the site of her parents' annual barbeque. He knew she loved him. He knew she wanted to be with him forever. He was not at all sure she would marry him and agree to move upstate and live her life in the snow belt. They had talked about a future together, but it had always seemed somehow academic because Delaney was addicted to the hustle of New York City. Even the intensity of Fishkill was wearing on Blue. He needed breathing space. He was sure that he would not be able to live his career as a trooper if he had to do it in Fishkill or any other downstate city. He had put in his transfer request the day he arrived in Fishkill. During his fourth year in Fishkill, he was promoted to the Bureau of Criminal Investigations unit. The BCI handled everything from homicides, sex crimes, and gang assaults to perjury, prostitution, and prison escapes. Any case involving extensive investigation or a felony was the domain of the BCI unit.

He had met Delaney the month before he was promoted. Even though it took him a year to propose, he knew from early on that he was ready to make a life with Delaney. He was always clear with her that he was still trying to transfer back home, but that if the right transfer didn't come about, he would stay put. When they got married, they kept Delaney's apartment in Manhattan and his in Fishkill and they both made the one-hour commute more regularly. His hours as an investigator evened out somewhat, but he was always subject to the standard two-hour recall that confines all state troopers without pre-approved leave to a two-hour radius even on their off-duty hours. The Metro-North commuter line became a daily route for at least one of them.

In retrospect, he was sure Delaney never believed him about moving back to Waterloo. When it happened, they had just gotten married. He was finishing his second year as an investigator and his sixth year as a trooper. Even he had begun to think a transfer wasn't going to happen. He had been offered many transfers since landing in Fishkill, but he was waiting to go home. Spots at the Waterloo station didn't open up often. People transferred in but didn't leave unless they retired or died.

They decided that Delaney would write for the *Finger Lakes Times*, which was headquartered in Geneva. Her commute to work dropped from over an hour when she'd stayed at Blue's to less than ten minutes. Blue's parents were able to help her secure a position on the crime beat and she rose to senior reporter in no time. Blue's father was a retired trooper who had lived his entire life in Waterloo and was well-connected in the community.

Delaney was excited about the move because she was able to get excited about almost any change, but the peace and quiet worked to unnerve her within the first few months. She contracted with her paper in New York City to write some feature pieces that didn't require on-site reporting because the pace she was used to working at wasn't the pace of upstate New York. She tried to learn to cook. She planted a vegetable garden. She tried to make some friends. She took on the political beat as well as the crime beat and started attending all the local town and Village Board meetings. She traveled to New York City every six weeks to get her hair cut and meet with her editor to hand in the feature pieces she had finished, an excuse because she could email the pieces in seconds.

Blue settled into small town life like he had never left. The first night they spent in their new home on Center Street, Blue exhaled the air of all the noise and congestion and slept a full night's sleep for the first time since graduating Buffalo State and heading off to the Police Academy in Albany. And the party to welcome home the prodigal son rivaled the Biblical version. Blue's parents rented out the Elks Club and invited anyone and everyone Blue had ever known. It wasn't the first time he'd brought Delaney to Waterloo, but it was their first extended time in the area. They'd enjoyed the party. They were in love.

After three years in Waterloo, Delaney got pregnant. They both had high hopes that a baby would save them and give Delaney some peace and somewhere to direct her immense energies. Mollie was born in the winter and Delaney took six weeks off of work to be home with her. Blue took vacation time and the three of them snuggled in while the harsh dark heart of winter raged on for the first months of Mollie's life.

When spring finally broke, so did Delaney. Blue's Aunt Jessica, who lived next door to them, became a daily fixture at their house while Delaney went into the paper for a few hours. Aunt Jessica was Blue's father's sister. All of Blue's aunts and uncles lived within a ten-block radius in the Village of Waterloo. Blue and Delaney had bought the house next door to Aunt Jessica because she had known the couple who lived there for 45 years. She had been like a nurse maid to the man after his wife had died, and when he was starting to decline and wanted to move to an assisted living facility, Aunt Jessica put Blue in touch with him so Blue could buy his house. Aunt Jessica said the house was blessed—45 Center Street matched the 45 years she had been friends with the previous owners and living on Center Street would put Blue and Delaney in the center of their community.

Aunt Jessica was in her 60s but other than her gray hair, one would never know it. Her energy rivaled Delaney's except that Aunt Jessica had a calmness about her that drew people in like a campfire on a cold night. Her own children were older than Blue and she kept herself busy, more and more with tending to Mollie while Delaney wrote or went to New York City for the weekend.

Blue worked normal hours as an investigator—until he didn't. At any point and at any time, he would be called out with the District Attorney or the coroner to investigate a suspicious death or a violent crime. Most of the legwork happened during the day, but most of the crime happened in the middle of the night. Blue spent his time with Mollie when he wasn't working. He didn't ask Aunt Jessica to babysit unless he had to work. He would take Mollie on errands with him. They'd play with her Duplos on his porch as the sun set.

Summer in the Finger Lakes region was a magical time. It used to get hot enough to melt make-up, Blue's mother would always say, but in the last few years, the temperatures had evened out some. There were a few too-hot-to-move days, but they were fewer and farther between every year. During those few days, the humidity would saturate the air and the heat would lay on the surface of the world like a wet electric blanket. On those days, the lakes or the canal were the only refuge. Few people had air conditioning in their homes. All the new construction, of which there was little, had central air. Most people had window air conditioners in one room. Mostly Central New Yorkers flocked to the water for relief.

Blue would take Mollie out on the lake while he sat and read the paper. That was their Sunday routine during the first summer of her life. Delaney didn't like boating because she got bored, but Blue would head to Wegmans, buy the Sunday paper and a cup of coffee, off-load his 19-foot speed boat into Seneca Lake and drive just far enough to let her float without having to drop the anchor. He would read the paper from cover to cover playing with Mollie's toes or watching her sleep between stories, many of which had been written by Delaney.

Delaney loved Mollie but never settled into being a full-time mom. She was a do-it-all woman. Blue's mother had been a stay-at-home mom. The role fit her easily and well. Blue's father's career as a state trooper kept him away from home at odd hours and random holidays. Blue's mother was always there. They worked well as a team. She never resented him for working hard and he appreciated everything she did to make their life a family and a home and not just a place where they all lived. Blue didn't particularly need Delaney to be his wife in that same way. One of the benefits of having a strong mother and so many brothers and sisters is that she taught her children to fend for themselves. Blue knew how to do laundry and wash dishes and fix anything in sight by the time he started middle school. She taught all her children to be self-sufficient and together they ran a fun, bustling home.

The greatest sadness in Blue's marriage had been Delaney's inability to adjust to life with him. He never could ease the restlessness she always felt. By the time Mollie turned one, Delaney had filed for divorce and bought a house two streets over. Blue was sure she was going to try to take Mollie back downstate but she didn't. She knew her best chance of getting help with raising Mollie was with Aunt Jessica rather than her parents. And with a small child, she could never go back to the hour-long commute if she were to live in Fishkill. If she lived in New York City, Mollie would spend most of her time with babysitters and nannies. Delaney did not want that for her daughter. And she never wanted to take Mollie away from her father. Even after she'd told him all of this, he always had the uneasy feeling she'd take flight out of a desperate need to touch the sky.

Blue and Delaney never had a big blow up. She quietly said one day that she needed her own breathing space and wanted a divorce. They hadn't been intimate since before Mollie was born. They had landed in a kind of celibate roommate, rotating-scheduled life. Blue could hardly protest when she approached him. They worked out the terms of the divorce amicably and she moved into a little two-story house in the neighborhood. They shared custody of Mollie, and Aunt Jessica was instrumental to the both of them in making sure Mollie was always with family even when both of her parents had to work.

Delaney became even more hostile toward small-town life after the separation. She became snide and sarcastic about "Mayberry." The town residents called their piece of heaven Mayberry because it gave them that feeling where everyone was friendly and life was simple. When Delaney said "Mayberry" it sounded like an epithet. She always said it with a smile on her face but Blue knew her well enough to know she was seething inside.

It was this seething that he had to deal with anytime Delaney felt there was something Blue could do for her that he wasn't doing.

CHAPTER 4

AS THEY WAITED for the final okay to go home after Natalie's statement had been taken, Sara sat with her daughter. She'd wrapped her Beach Wonder Blanket around Natalie because she couldn't stop shivering, even though the night air seemed overheated. Sara was the product researcher of the group. Sara bought and tested almost all the As Seen on TV gadgets and reported to anyone who would listen on the ones that lived up to the hype and the ones that weren't worth the postage or the trip to the local Wal-Mart. She had gadgets like the Beach Wonder Blanket on hand at all times. Cady stood nearby, wanting to help them both get home. She felt the charge in the air as the two finally had a little space to talk.

"Nat," said Sara, "what on earth were you doing under the bridge?"

"God, Mom," Natalie said between sniffles, her straight blond hair sticking to her cheek. "You do realize that I am seventeen years old? Really? This is what you want to talk about right now?"

Cady saw Sara look straight ahead at the scene in front of her at the water's edge. Sara said nothing. She imagined Sara wanted to both comfort her daughter and wring her neck for being the one who found Rosalind, a vision they all knew Natalie would never get out of her memory.

"Chris and I have been dating for over two years," Natalie continued when her mother didn't answer.

Natalie and Cady had started the book club three years ago when Natalie was about to start high school. Cady and Sara were already good friends, and when Natalie had asked Cady to help her start the club, they all decided that it would be better to have the monthly meeting at the local library where Cady was the Executive Director than at the high school where her mom was the resident librarian. Natalie was about to start 9th grade then and Cady knew Sara's relationship with her daughter had been strained since Marshall had left. Now the book club had five members in it—including Natalie's boyfriend, Chris, who attended just to hang out with Natalie.

Now, every month, Cady brought in orange creamsicle ice water, which she made by floating a sliced navel orange and a fresh vanilla bean, slit down the center, in a pitcher of water overnight, and a different kind of cookie to every meeting. Oreos were the hands-down favorites, but the kids liked iced oatmeal and chocolate chip as well. During the two summer months, she splurged and brought in lunch since they moved their meetings from after school to noon on Mondays. She had pizza delivered as an extra incentive to entice them away from other summer fun, or for most of them, work. She always held the book club meetings during regular library hours and it was budgeted in as an official duty of hers, but the food budget came out of her own pocket. She purposefully didn't get too elaborate with the food. Just a nibble to keep their stomachs from rumbling. Truth was, she was always amazed when any kids showed up. There were so many activities for kids to choose from at their age. She always lost one here and there to football season or the spring musical, but they would usually come back, often having read the books they missed anyway.

Since Natalie had come to Cady to start the book club and now that Natalie worked for Cady, Cady had gotten to know Natalie separate and apart from Sara. When Sara and Natalie were together, their interactions were always the same. They never out and out fought in front of Cady. Instead, Sara asked for information. Natalie questioned her mother's need for the information. There was a pause and then Natalie told her mother what she wanted to know. It played out here as it always did.

"We were about to have sex. We were trying to get in a quickie while the fireworks were going on. Happy? You happy you know?" Natalie was sobbing again. "We're practically adults, Mom. This isn't something you want to know so why are you even asking?"

Cady knew Sara well enough to know Sara wasn't sure why she was asking at this point. She would want to comfort her daughter. She would want to hold her while she cried. Why didn't she just do that? Cady was pretty sure Sara knew what Natalie was doing under the bridge. Even Cady had hoped it wasn't so lurid as full-blown sex in such a public place, but it hardly surprised her when she heard it was. Natalie worked for Cady at the library and Cady saw her as an adult, even though she was still in some ways a child. Cady liked Chris but she knew Sara was not impressed by him. Maybe the trauma Natalie had just suffered would bring her closer to Sara and drive her from Chris. Not likely. Chris had been there with her. He had not let go of her hand until his parents had shown up to take him home. And it was Sara now who was making Natalie cry all over again.

"Shh," Sara said as she put her arm around Natalie and tried to rock her on the bench. Natalie was shivering. "We don't need to talk about that now. I shouldn't have brought it up."

Natalie tensed and pulled away. "Seriously? You want to be a mom now? I should have gone home with Chris." She yanked herself out of her mother's arms and moved over to the end of the bench. Cady moved far enough away to be out of earshot. She began to feel like she was spying on her friends. As she moved off, she saw Sara let out a deep sigh full of resignation. Sara lifted herself heavily off the bench and started toward the police officer to say she was taking her daughter home.

*   *   *

As Cady and Sara and Natalie walked the length of the park back to their original picnic table, Cady said, "Can I drive you guys home? We can come pick up your car tomorrow."

"Thanks, but I'm okay to drive," said Sara. Natalie said nothing.

"You sure?" She willed Sara to look her in the eyes. She needed to see if Sara needed help with Natalie or if they needed a little time alone.

"Yeah." Sara took Cady's hand, assuring Cady she could handle the rest of the night.

"Okay. We'll talk tomorrow then." Cady gave her hand a squeeze. "Nat," Cady leaned past Sara, "try to sleep, okay? Take as much time as you need. Don't worry about coming back to work quickly."

Natalie nodded and continued to stare at the ground as they walked to the picnic table.

Someone had cleaned up all the party supplies and taken the food away. Cady noticed that everything was gone but didn't give it a second thought. She grabbed her little backpack and Sara's purse, which were both sitting on the picnic table. As she hooked her arm through Sara's arm and started walking toward the cement stairs, Cady was not thinking about going home. She was thinking about how Rosalind died. An accident? How? She was practically in charge of this whole festival. When would she have ever been alone today? How would she not have been seen down by the lock? Could she have fallen? And how would this mystery ever get solved with Blue in charge?

CHAPTER 5

"LOOK, BLUE," DELANEY SAID, "I just got the call about this incident and I had to haul myself out of deep sleep to come down here and cover this story and find out it's Rosalind M'Clintock. At least you were already on duty."

"I wasn't on duty, Lane," he said. "I was on call. I wasn't sleeping at 10:00 on a Saturday night, but I wasn't working either." Blue had called Delaney *Lane* since their first meeting at the summer barbeque. When he was being more playful, he called her *Lois* to tease her about how although she was a tenacious reporter, her exotic beauty did not match the pedestrian name for her comic book namesake. When she was being more loving, she called him *Superman* because he fought crime and always seemed to bring order and safety wherever he went. She hadn't called him *Superman* in years.

Delaney raised one eyebrow. "Not sleeping. Not working. That doesn't leave a whole lot of options."

"I was in the shop," he said flatly. He always promised himself he would not exchange personal information with Delaney when he saw her, but somehow he always let her in. They used to tease that he interrogated her and she interviewed him. Since their divorce, there was little more than that between them. Most of the information about Mollie floated back and forth through Aunt Jessica. It seemed more and more that Delaney and Blue only saw each other at crime scenes.

"I thought Eric was living in your shop," she said, arching one eyebrow.

"He is. Don't worry. I haven't let him sleep inside. I closed in the loft and he put his futon up there. I've tried not to use as many power tools but sometimes he just has to live with the wood dust."

"I'm sure he doesn't mind, sponge that he is." Eric was a sore spot between Delaney and Blue. He and Blue had been friends most of their lives. Delaney always saw Eric as a hanger-on. The security guard to Blue's state trooper. The perpetual adolescent to Blue's manhood. The little brother who never quite got it together. Where Blue was successful and rose through the ranks of the state trooper organization, Eric floundered. He was a fun guy and was always around to lend a helping hand, but Blue knew Delaney always felt like he was working for his place. Like he never felt secure enough to just be friends. He felt threatened by Delaney. When Blue brought her to live in Waterloo, he was like sulking cousin Clyde. He acted like he was happy for Blue and he acted like he was accepting of Delaney, but she never felt it. Blue accepted Eric where he lay but he could never explain to Delaney exactly why. With so many brothers and sisters, Blue had always found solace in Eric's only-child quiet. They required virtually nothing from each other. There was always an easy presence with no effort. Blue never could effectively explain the draw to Delaney.

When she moved out, Eric needed a place to stay within the month. He claimed he had had a little trouble with some gambling debts. Nothing he couldn't deal with but needed to move from his apartment. He was bunking on Blue's couch before all of Delaney's things were fully moved out. Delaney put her foot down. Absolutely not. When Blue tried to tell her she had no say over who he lived with now that she had moved out, she told him he couldn't be more wrong. Where Mollie was concerned, she had all the say in the world. As long as Blue was running a boarding house for wayward grown men, Mollie was not allowed to stay overnight. When Blue argued that she had no right to dictate the terms of their custody agreement, she threatened to take him to family court to let the judge decide whether it would be in Mollie's best interest to grow up in a house with Eric Peterman. Blue knew the family court system well. He knew she would never prevail and that Eric was a perfectly fine roommate, but what he knew about family court was enough for him to cave to her wishes. If she filed a petition, all of his colleagues in the courthouse would know his business. They would see him there appearing in front of the judge. The same judge who presided over the trials of the people Blue arrested would be deciding who was fit to live in his home with him and his daughter. He couldn't do it. Delaney knew that and she used it as a weapon any time Blue did not comport himself according to her wishes.

When she threatened the family court action, he negotiated with her to allow Eric to move into his detached garage that he had turned into a workshop. It was a two-story garage that he had converted into a clean, finished workshop where he made furniture. He had installed a small, full bathroom with a shower, sink, and commode during their first year of living there. He had collected the tools and the cabinets and work benches over the years. He did all the finish work with hand tools, but he loved to start a project with loud, humming power tools. It gave him the same sense of power as being on the firing range. He liked quiet most of his day but sometimes his own energy backed up on him so fiercely that the only thing that could relieve him besides sex was discharging a weapon or running a power tool.

Eric had taken up residence in the shop. It was fully heated and had powerful fan lights in the ceiling for the hot summer days and nights. It had all the comforts of home—full bathroom, his own futon and flat screen TV, a beer fridge that he had converted into a half beer/half leftovers from takeout fridge. It even came equipped with a small microwave, which Blue used for popcorn he always bought from the local Boy Scout troop but that Eric used for warming up leftovers. What was Blue's man cave had become Eric's home. After a few months, Blue made Eric help him finish off the loft area and put Eric's futon and TV upstairs. A full-grown man could only stand up in the center few feet of the loft, but it was good enough to get dressed in. While Eric was at work patrolling the Outlet Mall for shoplifters and forgers, Blue was able to reclaim his shop.

He had less spare time now that he spent most of his nonworking hours with Mollie, but the occasional few hours would be gifted to him and as long as Eric wasn't sleeping, Blue felt comfortable working in his shop. He had minored in Wood/Furniture at Buffalo State. He majored in Criminal Justice. He had known he would be a trooper from his first career day assignment in eighth grade.

He had asked his father if he could do a ride-along with him. His father was still a road trooper at the time. He secured a day shift and was proud to show off his son around town and was even more proud to show his son what he had dedicated his life's work to—protecting and serving. Blue's father showed him how the car radio transmitted and how the sirens worked. He fingerprinted Blue and handcuffed him to the desk while he took Blue's statement of why he wanted to be a cop. They ate lunch at the Sunshine Diner and even stopped for donuts just before the shift ended. It was the best day of Blue's life and he'd never wavered from that day on about what he wanted to be when he grew up.

Still, he always liked working with wood. He used to whittle sticks in his backyard. He started carving them into figurines. Eventually, he started constructing miniature furniture. Chairs with interconnecting slats and joints. Bookcases that looked like miniature prototypes for assembly line models. In college, he made his first piece that he exhibited and sold. He had made a side table out of dark cherry with inlaid carving covered with glass. It was an exquisite piece. He received an A and a place in the semester's exhibition as well as a few hundred dollars from the sale. He was sure he never wanted to be a furniture maker by trade, but as a hobby, it provided him with a creative outlet that paid him a little on the side. He always said any money he made from furniture would go toward his children's college fund. Between that and his regular savings, if Mollie followed him to his alma mater, she would graduate with no student loan debt.

Delaney had reluctantly agreed not to pursue legal action if Eric were confined to the garage. Mollie adored her "Uncle Dooz." Delaney knew that to be true. Blue was never going to abandon Eric. She also knew that to be true. Blue knew she was never afraid to play the shrew when it suited her needs, but relegating Eric to the garage was the best she was going to get without making good on her threat to go to court. Even Delaney did not want to go through that public humiliation. She knew it was a quality threat because Blue's stakes in the community were so much deeper than her own. Everyone knew him. But most of what anyone knew of her was through her connection to Blue. Hauling him into court would hurt her already precarious reputation. She was aware that Blue was a favorite son in Waterloo. She was a favorite daughter, but only by marriage and when the marriage was over, she believed, everyone assumed she was at fault and the squeeze began. Blue hadn't believed Delaney when she related the first few instances of her being subtly snubbed. He thought she was imagining it. She fought her way into covering the good stories and knew the influential people, but she didn't interact in many other ways with the community. Her city was 200 miles away. Her family was 200 miles away. She had friends in Waterloo, but they were all "their" friends and had been Blue's friends since childhood. None had really survived the divorce, except Aunt Jessica. Blue knew that was as much her fault as theirs, but also knew she didn't have it in her to pursue them. He had come to realize that she was here, rootless, because of him and that made him more accommodating than he otherwise might have been.

To divert Delaney's attention from taking Eric apart at the seams, Blue would do just about anything.

"All right," Blue said. "Moving on." He loosened his tie. "What do you need here?"

"Facts. I've got the who. What is time of death? Cause of death?"

"I don't know any of that yet," said Blue. "Maybe you should follow Jeff to the morgue and wait for the autopsy."

"I don't have time for that. What *can* you tell me?"

"Nothing."

"Blue." She tilted her head, gently pleading with her eyes.

He cursed himself for giving into her. Times like these he hated her. But he had loved her for a long time and when she needed something from him, he still felt all but powerless to refuse.

"She died tonight. Jeff is sure of that at this point. He's not sure what time tonight. We're still trying to piece together the last time anyone saw her here at the festival. I'll have to review all the statements before I'll have a timeline. She seems to have suffered blunt force trauma to the back of her head, but Jeff couldn't tell yet if that was as a result of her falling into the water or if someone hit her on the head. That's all I know. You cannot confirm this from any official source. Got it?" He was glaring at her, putting his foot down on this one point.

"Can I read the statements?"

"Of course not. I'll let you know more as soon as I know. Call me tomorrow. I've got to finish up here." He started to walk away.

"Are you confirming Rosalind was murdered? Who are you looking at for it?" When he didn't answer, "This isn't going to make a complete story for the Sunday edition," she called after him.

"Really not my problem," he said into the air.

*   *   *

Delaney wrote in her notebook that Rosalind's death was being seen as a possible murder. As she did so, sweat dripped down her neck and pooled around her waistband.

CHAPTER 6

SUNDAY MORNING BROKE early for Cady. Blue knocked on her door at 7:00 a.m. She had been up for a half hour after falling asleep sometime after 3:00 a.m. Blue knocked quietly. He knew he had to wake her but didn't want to jolt her out of bed.

"Blue," Cady said as she slid open the door, "what's going on?"

"I'm sorry for coming by so early," he said leaning his shoulder against the screen doorjamb, holding up a waxy bag.

"No, of course. Come in. Are you working?" As she let Blue in, Hero, her fluffy muted-gray striped cat, slid in between his feet.

"Yes. I left my jacket in the car. It's already blistering hot outside." He rolled up his sleeves on his light gray collared shirt as he entered her flat. "I was talking to your cat for the last ten minutes," Blue said. "I couldn't bring myself to wake you before 7:00. I brought donut holes, though."

She twitched, almost imperceptibly. "I've been up. I didn't know you were out there." She picked up Hero and cuddled him close. She held him straight up against her and cupped her arm around his hind legs. He laid a paw on either side of her neck. "This is Hero Sizemore. He hugs me," she said to Blue. "Can't start my day without it."

"Is he?" Blue said.

"Hmm?" she said as she nuzzled Hero.

"A hero?"

"He certainly is. He saves me from the dark side every day."

"He's got some Maine coon in him? I can tell by the tufts in the ears. He's also got that soft cat hair, not fur," said Blue.

"I don't know. He's the most beautiful mutt I've ever seen. You know a lot about cats?" She put him down and took a packet of cat food out of her lower cupboard and ripped the top off. Hero began meowing in full conversation with Cady.

"That's funny. Sounds like a real conversation," said Blue. "Maine coons are also mouthy cats. I don't know a lot. Maybe a little."

"I'm pretty sure we communicate on a level way beyond 'I'm hungry, feed me.'" She could tell Blue was stalling so she let him. One-on-one conversations were easy for Cady, and Hero was an effortless topic. She told Blue that Hero had come to her at the library during the yearly January thaw. There was still snow on the roads, and even though the snow was melting, it was still cold. He was a kitten of about six months. He was so perfectly groomed she couldn't believe he was an abandoned stray. She put an ad in the paper to find his family but no one ever stepped forward, so she kept him. And other than food and water, he was the least demanding roommate she'd ever had. She washed her hands. "Here." She handed him a coffee cup. "Just made a pot."

"Expecting company?" he asked taking the cup.

They were supposed to go swimming today. She and Sara. Probably even Rosalind if she could dial herself down after the festival wrapped up. Cady lived in Waterloo, which neighbors Seneca Falls like a Hatfield and a McCoy, although the community rivalry didn't extend beyond football season at the two local high schools. Together they span a total of about twelve miles from east to west and if all the traffic lights align just right, they can both be driven in twenty minutes. The two towns are butted by Cayuga Lake on the east side of Seneca Falls and Seneca Lake on the southwest side of Waterloo.

Since she'd moved to the area from Syracuse, Cady had spent as much free time as she could during the summer in one of the two lakes or floating in an inner tube down the canal between them. Especially since Victor, it was one of her alone-time or small group activities she relished. The Seneca and Cayuga Lakes, the two biggest lakes of the glacier-created Finger Lakes in Central New York, are connected by the Seneca-Cayuga Canal. The fourteen foot difference in elevation between the two lakes is managed by a series of locks that control the rush of water and regulate boat traffic. The canal runs through Waterloo and Seneca Falls. They share the water. Back when water ran the towns, controlled access to the water made for deadly political rivalries. The opening of the Erie Canal all but shut down the towns of Seneca Falls and Waterloo, and the control of the water no longer made or broke fortunes. Now the towns are known simply by their most famous parentage—Waterloo as the congressionally recognized birthplace of Memorial Day and Seneca Falls as the birthplace of the American Women's Rights Movement.

Cady fell in love with Victor Nicholas on Seneca Lake. They had been dating for about six months when he took her out on his boat. It was a sweltering day. They didn't have a third person to spot for skiing so they just lolled in the water on noodles. He dipped under the cool water and came up spouting water like a whale. He turned upside down and did a handstand on the noodle. He was playful where he had usually been suave and unbelievably hot. He always smiled easily, but it was that day in the cool lake water in the baking heat that he melted her. When she saw his feet plunge out of the water and tip over immediately from lack of a steady platform, she was head over from that point on.

They spent many weekend afternoons on Seneca Lake. They would most often weigh anchor at Boater's Beach and they would play the day away. They would set out from the vineyards with Victor driving the boat and Cady and Sara following on the jet skis. Natalie would snorkel in the shallows while the adults broke the water at high speeds. If they timed it right, they would all wade ashore for the ice cream truck where they got Drumsticks, ice cream sandwiches, or Creamsicles, Cady's pick. They would as often as not go back to the house, bronzed and sun weary, for a light dinner before dispersing with relaxed good cheer.

"Not that it's any of your business," she brought herself back to the man in her home, "but no. I was up all night. I slept for about three hours and then up again." She put out a small pitcher with a flip top lid of cream and a matching sugar bowl. "It's the real stuff so if you're watching your figure, you may want to go easy."

"I like my coffee light and sweet," he said doctoring his coffee.

"Sissy. How do you make it at the trooper station with tastes like that?" She put the donut holes on a plate and she sat at the bar stool at the edge of the kitchen counter. He sat at the stool in the middle of the counter facing her and drank deeply of the dark, strong coffee. She remembered the way he took his coffee. She remembered the easy way they had of communicating, even in the midst of her trauma. He was always like a neutral oasis in the middle of her storm.

"If anyone there made coffee this good, I might actually be able to drink it black."

Cady smiled. "If you're gonna drink swill, you may as well pop a No Doze and avoid the trips to the bathroom."

"Yeah." He took another drink. "That's a good idea. What's the music?" He had noticed the soft music she had playing. It had distinct French undertones.

"Blue. What are you doing here?" When she saw him at her door, she had the momentary hope that he was there with news about Victor. The last time Cady had had any meaningful contact with Blue was when her husband had disappeared six years ago. Blue knew Victor long before Cady ever met and married him. Blue had worked for Victor for two years in high school and then during the summers while in college. He had been almost as invested in finding out what happened to Victor as Cady was.

Blue sighed. He hadn't slept in over 24 hours. "I need your help."

"Mine? Help with what?" She twirled her wedding ring around on her finger.

"I need someone with your research skills. I know what I'm looking for but our damn crime lab has been on complete shut down for the last three weeks with no end in sight."

"I read about that. Forensic scientist being investigated for falsifying results?"

"It's a nightmare. The state inspector general is all over the place. Nothing comes out of the lab until they determine how far-reaching the problem is and the lab can be recertified. I have put in a request for some forensic computer expert help but it could be weeks before anything

materializes. I know you control a brain trust of computers and databases downstairs at the library."

"You want me to help with Rosalind's case?" Cady
leaned forward, contemplating him.

"Yes," he said. "I helped you and now I want to call in
the favor."

"Favor?" Cady stood up. "It was your *job* to investigate
Victor's disappearance. And some job you did, too, right?
Do any of us have one clue as to where he is? Even all
these years later?" Her voice was rising and her eyes were
going steely cold.

"I know," he stood up. "Poor choice of words. I didn't
mean favor. I need your help and I'm asking as a friend."

"God, Blue. We're not even friends. We don't do *this*
anymore." She waved her hand at the coffee and donuts.
"What do you want from me?" Her nerves were fraying
and the normal control she held over her emotions was
disappearing inside of her grief and lack of sleep. They
had once done *this*. They'd worked together like a TV
crime-fighting team. He treated her and her case as top
priority until he couldn't anymore. He'd come in two
hours earlier than his normal shift every day to greet her
with coffee and donut holes and his full attention. She'd
come to the station every day before she opened the library to go over the details one more time. They'd pored
over the missing persons file. They'd talk about that last
day. The day before that last day. It was a cycle that
seemed never-ending. When it was clear they were not
coming upon any new information, Blue had encouraged

her to move on. He'd almost touched her once. He'd almost hugged her when she'd almost cried. She'd bristled and rounded her shoulders. She didn't go to the station the next day. Or the next.

"I need you to find out some information for me."

"This must be illegal. Why not use the power of the state of New York otherwise?"

"It's not illegal. I told you. I'm short on time. New York State can't help me right now."

"What about Delaney?" Cady asked. "She is the media queen in these parts. You're still friends with her, aren't you?"

"Of course I am. Cady, look. I need *your* help. I don't need this information splattered all over the newspaper and internet. I need someone I can trust. I'll always protect my source."

Hero wrapped himself in and around the bar stool Blue was standing next to and nudged the tips of Blue's shoes. He lay down with his warm body across the bridge of Blue's foot.

Cady and Blue considered each other. "I don't know how you do these things when you have an actual body you're working with. What would you need from me?" she said coolly as she settled back on her bar stool.

Cady had come to Blue the previous winter with a lead she thought was viable. She had shared it with him and when he questioned how she came across it, she had reluctantly shared with him that she had been boning up on her computer skills since their first attempts when Victor disappeared. He'd been impressed and had followed the lead. Like all the others, it went cold. But he hadn't forgotten the secret agent operating in her quiet little library down the street from him.

"I don't need help with the investigation into Rosalind's murder. I need information."

"Murder?" Cady stopped cold. "Rosalind was murdered? How do you know?"

"I can't discuss the case at this point," Blue said picking up his coffee cup and sliding his foot out from under a lounging Hero so he could sit back down.

"I don't think so," Cady said. "You want my help, you tell me what's going on with my best friend's murder."

"Cady."

"That's my price. Take it or leave it. I'll eventually find out what I need to know. Will you?"

He leaned forward on his elbows. "This is going to be one of those relationships that I will reflect back on someday down the road and say, 'I should have known right then,' isn't it?"

Cady sighed. "I'm not trying to be an ass ache. You came to me. Rosalind was my friend."

"She was my friend, too," Blue said, staring into his coffee cup like he wanted to read the coffee swirls like tea leaves.

"I'm sorry. You're right. What can I do to help?" Hero lay at the edge of Blue's bar stool, cleaning his face with his paw.

"She was hit on the back of the head," Blue said after taking another drink. She gave. He gave. "That's not even what killed her. Someone hit her in the head and left her to die. She died from drowning. Although, mercifully, she was unconscious by then. Jeff puts the time of death at around 8:30 on Saturday night."

Cady pushed herself up from the bar stool and took her cup to the sink. As she propped herself against the sink, she dropped her head. The thought of Rosalind being attacked. Being beaten. Taking in her last breath on this earth, unconscious and under water. The violence assaulted Cady's senses.

Blue stepped up behind her and laid his hands on her shoulders softly. When she didn't move, he gently turned her around and brought her into his arms. She buried her face in his shirt where his shoulder met his broad chest. Her arms were folded in on herself. His arms enveloped her, one hand around her body and one hand cupped on the back of her head. He didn't stroke her hair. He didn't say, "Shh," or "It'll be all right." He didn't say anything. He held her with no hint of needing to break the embrace.

It was Cady who finally patted him on the chest. Two soft pats near his breastbone and he knew to let her go. She took a deep breath. She swept her hands across her morning face, dry eyes. "Yeah, no." She waved him away. "I can't believe this is happening. It just hit me all at once."

"Sissy," Blue said as he leaned back against the kitchen counter.

She smiled at him. He looked tired. His eyes were sunken. "You haven't been to bed yet, have you?"

"No." He drug his hand across his stubbled jaw. "Pour me another cup of that glug and I'll name my next born after you."

CHAPTER 7

BLUE SAT IN Cady's love seat with his second cup of coffee while she took a quick shower. He had made a quick tour of the living room and looked at her CD collection, reggae, French, Caribbean, Van Morrison. All of them were library issue. He asked her why she didn't have an iPod, but the water was already running and she didn't hear him. When he had finally sat down, Hero had crawled up and made a perfectly round kitty circle in Blue's lap. He scratched Hero behind the ears and then lay his hand on the cat's soft back cupping his belly.

Cady lived in the flat above the Waterloo Library in the center of Downtown Waterloo. She had moved into the flat a year after Victor had disappeared without a trace. Her bedroom spanned the northwest third of the apartment. The one piece of furniture she kept from the house that she and Victor had lived in was their king-sized bed. She had shared it only with Hero since.

Her apartment was shaped like a rectangle cut into rough thirds. Her bedroom took up one third. A living room and a bathroom took up the middle third and the southeast third was made up of a kitchen and dining area combination across from a second bedroom that Cady had turned into an art studio. There was a door leading to the bathroom from both the living room and her bedroom. When there was no one there, as there usually was no one there, she left all the doors open except for the ones that led to the staircase taking her downstairs to the library. Hero liked to roam the apartment at will. No need to shut doors.

Next to the bathroom was the second bedroom of the original flat. The first year Cady lived in the flat, she began to use the second bedroom as an art studio. She had stacks and stacks of books in every other corner of the flat, but in this room, she kept easels and canvases and paints at the ready. She also set up a beading table to nurture a hobby she had loved since she was a child. Victor's sister, Alexa, was a jewelry designer. Before his disappearance, she had taught Cady some tricks for securing her findings so that her work looked professional instead of like it did when she was ten. She kept a boom box in the studio so she could play music while she painted.

The painting class she ran met in her studio. Although she had never studied painting, she loved it. She did not teach painting to the participants, but she provided a space for them to play on canvas each week. Sometimes she arranged for a guest teacher to come in and give them pointers. Cady loved the feel of the brush on the canvas, but she felt no real calling. It soothed her and she was getting better at her realism, but she painted mostly landscapes with deep, bright colors of the season she was in at the moment. Sara joined because it was a perfect way to end the week—relaxing, colorful, utterly unlike her job. Sara's natural tendency was to go home and sit in front of the TV all night trying to downshift from the week. She saw the painting class, as did everyone who gave their Friday evening to it, as a perfect transition to the weekend.

When Cady had first decided to use the room as an art studio, she felt like a dilettante, indulgent. But she had to keep moving at that point in her life. She needed to keep her mind engaged. Any stillness then and she felt her mind would spin right out of her head. She bought one easel and a few paints from a craft store. She also bought a set of mid-priced brushes. She knew nothing about painting.

At first she was too intimidated to put a brush stroke on a canvas so she started off with a project. She painted Tinkerbelle dust around the top of the room like a wallpaper border. She used the tiniest brushes to paint glittering gold and silver specs from the top of the wall to about eight inches down. Every few inches, she would add a Tink star, which was a long cross with four little slivers of gold or silver shooting out of the intersection. It took her over a month to circle the room in gold and silver. When she was done, she began again at the beginning with fine-point marker pens in sparkling blue, pink, and purple. After she'd enhanced a few feet with color, she knew this would be the most special detail in her home. She always invited guests of the art studio to wish upon a star as they entered the room.

Blue sat in the living room, which was a spacious, open room with a long couch on the wall shared by the bedroom, a love seat that looked out the sliding glass door and two square, cushy club chairs facing the long couch. She'd covered the chairs and the couch in celery green and soft white striped slipcovers and the love seat was a sage green chenille. She had found a small square coffee table at a yard sale and that, along with end tables and a few lamps, completed the conversation pit.

One evening a month, Cady hosted a book club for adults in her flat. The book club for the teenagers met in the library, but her friends whom she read books with met in her home. Each month somebody brought snacks, but they always met at Cady's apartment. She was the only one who lived alone and didn't have to maneuver around a spouse or kids to get the house for the evening. This book club was purely for pleasure. They drank good wine and stayed, sometimes for hours after they were done discussing the book, talking about life and art and politics. Rosalind was in the evening book club as were Sara; Alice, who worked with Cady; and Amanda, who was the mother of one of her current teen book clubbers. They had never lost a member. Until now. Theirs was a special group of women—smart, funny, engaged. They had added a few over the years. Amanda was newer than the rest. But once someone got in, they never wanted to leave.

Cady's kitchen was a small U-shaped room with a stove and counter space on the far northeast wall. Her sink overlooked her deck and what was technically her back yard. Around the U from the sink and across from the stove was an attached island that overlooked the living room. A small wooden dining room table sat between the island and the living room, delineating an informal dining area.

Next to the sliding glass door and overlooking the table was a waist-high window with a ten-inch sill and a cat window mounted into it. Hero came and went as he pleased. He spent most of his nights wandering around the backyards of the Village of Waterloo. He came home every morning at the sound of Cady's Zen chime alarm clock. She always knew he wasn't far. He came home sometimes in the middle of the night and curled up on her head to sleep. Sometimes he would knead her hair while she slept and her hair would look like a mass of pony tail gone wild in the morning.

The one enhancement she had made since she had arrived five years ago was the addition of a second-story deck off the back side of the flat. She spent the money out of her own paycheck. The library, and her flat, were privately owned by a corporation with an active board of directors. Enhancing the aesthetic appeal of her apartment was not in the budget, in any year. There had been a rickety but safe landing outside the living room sliding glass door with a set of fire escape stairs leading to the path that took her to the empty grassy lot behind the library and then out on to Elisha Street. She loved the view out her sliding glass door. She could see straight down the street that dead-ended at the grassy lot behind her. She hoped no one would ever build on the lot and block her view.

When she had lived there a year and Victor had been gone for two, she began to settle into the thought of living there indefinitely. The apartment itself was plenty big enough for one person. Her rent was paid as a stipend attached to her salary so she thought of it as rent-free. She paid for heat and electric, but her monthly expenses were virtually nonexistent. One day she looked around and decided to spruce the place up. Until then, she had been living there "temporarily." Even if she were only to be there a short while more, she decided to bud where she had been planted. She hired a local contractor and his team to build the deck and cut a sliding glass door into her bedroom to add more light and a way to get out to the deck straight from her bedroom in the morning.

Mulligan and his crew built the deck during her second summer there and by the end of July, she was drinking her coffee on her new deck in her lounge chair and letting the warmth of the morning sun wake her up. The deck faced northeast so she got direct morning light on it. The shade on summer afternoons when the sun dipped behind the library was a blessing.

Mulligan's crew had become a familiar comfort to her in the short time they were building her deck. There was a sound and a rhythm to her days when they were there. Company of a sort. There were four of them including Mulligan himself. She noticed right off the good natured comradery between the team members and a genuine gratitude toward her for being a kind and patient home-owner to work for in the blazing heat. They had shown up every morning before 8:00 to get in as much work as they could before the afternoon sun baked their workplace for that day. Even with the sun slipping over the library in the late afternoons, the heat could be relentless. She made them coffee every morning. It was how she perfected her famous brew. She tried out different recipes on them every day until they all agreed that she had hit on the secret to gourmet coffee. Every morning she set out the thermal pot for them and cups, cream, and sugar. They finished the pot before 10:00 and always came into the library to say hello and thank you on their way to use the facilities. She enjoyed having them there during the day. Aside from the pounding of the hammers and the whirring of the saws cutting the wood for the decking, they were good company.

She usually crept up the library stairs for a quiet lunch. They always walked one block over to Main Street and had lunch. Two slices of pizza and a Coke. At night she baked them muffins or cupcakes or something sweet to go with their morning coffee. She liked having someone to cook for. Someone to make coffee for. They never expected it, but she knew once she started, they would be disappointed if she ever stopped.

When they had nailed their last board into place and had packed up all their tools, making a final sweep for nails on the ground, she felt lonely. It was too quiet. She loved the quiet, but she had gotten used to having company during the day. She worked at the library. They worked around back on her deck. They would always be gone by the time she closed up the library for the night. Even if she were not closing herself, they would be packed up and gone by 4:00. The baking sun drove them out in the late afternoons. But they would always leave evidence of having been there. A soda cup or a box of screws. They were not messy and they took time every afternoon to clean up after themselves, but there was always some telltale sign they'd been there. It comforted her. When they were gone, she felt a hole. She baked that night and took the muffins into the library, but the people who came in that day were on a diet or even if they ate, they did so with guilt and regret. She didn't bake again for anyone else.

She enjoyed living alone. She always had. But she had married Victor for life. She made that transition to a wife and partner and when it was revoked without warning or explanation, it took her a long time to adjust. She never fully had.

Her apartment was nearly as big as the library and with the two sliding glass doors that opened out on to the deck, it was always filled with bright daylight. The deck itself spanned the length of her apartment, which was the length of the library. She had them build it extra wide so she felt like it was another room. The new outside stairs that led up to her flat came up the front and then rounded at the top to a landing that switched back to the deck itself.

In the late spring, she filled pots with flowers she bought at the farmer's market. She had petunias in every corner and colorful pansies and trailing vines. Once a month, she would replace any plants that didn't fare well but other than that, she watered the plants and let them be. She wasn't a big fan of gardening, but she was a huge fan of being smothered in blooming flowers.

She had strung little white fairy lights along the edge of the entire deck and down the railing. They were plugged into a timer so they served as a porch light when she came home late enough to have missed turning on her deck lights to guide her. She parked under her deck in a private space she created as a result of the deck renovation. She joked that she now had covered parking, but in truth, she still had to trudge through the snow to get upstairs in the winter. And she shoveled the snow off the deck and stairs herself. Through her budget, she hired a guy to shovel the snow around the library, front and back, but that privilege didn't extend to her private stairs.

All year long, her fairy lights made her happy. They were a personal touch and she didn't have to consult anyone before she put them up. One of the advantages of living alone. In the beginning, she had been so traumatized by Victor's sudden disappearance that she found nothing comforting about living alone. She had spent a year living in the house she had shared with Victor. They called it a house, but it was more accurately a villa or an estate. Alone, it swallowed her up. When no one could pick up a single trace of where he might have gone or what might have happened to him, she decided to relinquish the house to Victor's younger brother, Clint, who moved in as soon as Cady had moved out. He had already been running the family winery since Victor disappeared. His entrenchment as the patriarch of the family was completed by his living in the family home attached to the vineyards. She hadn't seen Clint since. Nor had she seen Alexa. She and Michelle traveled most of the year aboard various cruise liners selling Alexa's custom made jewelry. The Nicholas family was like a whisper to her now.

"Blue," Cady whispered as she touched his shoulder. She was standing behind the love seat. Blue started awake. "Did I take that long?" she asked.

"No." He lifted Hero off his lap and started to stand up. "Sorry, I drifted off."

"Stay sitting," she said as she came around to sit in the chair closest to Blue while she was twisting her towel-dried hair up into a clip that would leave her hair softly wavy when it dried fully. Hero climbed back into his lap. "Want some more coffee?"

"No thanks. I think I'm beyond help at this point." He yawned. Hero yawned.

"I know. Too much coffee has the opposite effect on me. Okay. I'm showered, shampooed, and shined. I'm all yours. Should I take notes?"

"Okay. Notes? No. Maybe. You can decide. Okay." He was still shaking the nap off. "I need some information about the Convention Days festival."

"What kind of information?"

"I need to know who was organizing it, who used to organize it, what the finances are like, who signs the checks, who made the final decisions on booths and exhibitors and bands. That kind of stuff."

"Sara was on the organizing committee," said Cady. "She could probably tell you most of that."

"I thought of that. But I need to find this information out discreetly. I also need the history. I need to know what's happened over the years. This festival used to be a rowdy brawl of a weekend. It was cancelled for a number of years. Then it came back as a major community event. I need the history of all that and what was happening in the last few years, too."

"Are you thinking Rosalind's death . . . murder had something to do with the festival?"

"I can't rule it out. She was a prominent organizer. It happened at the festival. These are all public facts," said Blue. "It's the obvious first place to look."

"If it's so obvious, why the need for discretion?"

"It's protocol for one. And for two, it might have nothing to do with the festival. Somebody killed Rosalind. I don't want that person to know which angle we're pursuing and which angle we haven't thought of yet."

"Okay." She sat forward and patted her thighs. "What can I do?"

"Can you get access to that kind of information?" Blue asked.

"If it's there to be known, I can know it. But if you say that in public, I will disavow all knowledge of computers beyond my own bank account's password and my little old databases full of book titles."

"Hey, I thought I was the covert operator here," Blue smiled.

"There are lots of things I know and lots of things I *can* know if the need presents itself," she said.

"Everything but the one thing." He met her eyes.

"Everything but the one thing. Yes." She never could figure out the one thing she most needed to know. She had accepted Victor's disappearance after all these years. She knew he was not coming back. She had told herself dozens of stories about what happened. Each one gave her less comfort than the last, but each brought her closer to moving on with her life without him. In one more year, she could declare him dead with all the benefits and emotional turmoil that would bring. She could have legally done it after three years because she lived in New York State, but she knew in her heart that she would need to wait the typical seven years before she could allow herself to be sure.

"This isn't illegal, is it?" she asked again to change the subject. She never blamed Blue for not figuring out the mystery or for turning the case back to missing persons. Blame was not what she felt. Numb and alone was a clearer description. She interacted with Blue intensely for a couple of months and then had not seen him for more than a passing moment standing in line for coffee at Wegmans or when he was out mowing his lawn while she was walking in the neighborhood they shared since she moved into the library apartment.

"I honestly don't know," he said, rubbing Hero's tummy. "It depends on where we have to look. Who ever heard of a cat letting you rub his belly?" He fluffed Hero's belly like a dog's. "I imagine everything I'm asking for is public record because this festival is a public event put on by the Seneca Falls Community somebody. I just don't have time to draw in the resources I would need to get the information. Subpoenas and all that. If I find anything I need to know, I can go through proper channels to secure it for the D.A., but I need to know if this is even an angle worth pursuing. Shit. I need a tech guy. I should be a tech guy. Instead you're my go-to 7:00 a.m. on a Sunday."

"What if I turn up nothing? Or what if it has nothing to do with the festival?" Cady asked.

"Then I follow lead number two."

"And what's that?"

"Cady." He tilted his head.

"Okay. Okay. I don't even want to know anymore. This is just horror come to visit and I want to change the channel. That's a crazy mixed metaphor. Let's go downstairs. The library is closed on weekends all summer so we've got the place to ourselves."

Sitting at her desk in the morning light that was streaming in through the window, Cady was clicking through various sites she had access to as the Executive Director and house librarian. Blue sat next to her in a wooden chair he had pulled up to her desk. They clicked through page after page. She found the page set up by the festival organizers to record the financial and structural matters year after year.

"See. This is a public page," Cady said and turned the monitor slightly so he had a better angle. "And see this page." She clicked through. "It gives a history of the event. You can see, no discussion of the reasons for the brief hiatus. Probably trying to be politically correct. Rosalind could have given you chapter and verse on that. Sara can, too, I'm sure."

After they'd read the short history, Cady clicked on the financial page. "All their finances are public." She let Blue look through the financials to see if there was anything out of sync.

"These records are not totally up to date," Blue said. "It looks like the last week's entries haven't yet been made. Everything else looks in order, but I'll need to see what's happened in the last week. That could prove valuable."

"Sara is the financial head of state when it comes to the festival," Cady said. "I'm sure she could tell you anything you need to know."

"I don't want to ask her just yet," Blue said.

Cady knew that meant Sara was as much a suspect as anyone else at this point. "Sara was with me all night on Saturday night. You know that, right? Maybe you haven't asked her for an alibi yet but she was with me. We'd just cut the cake at my birthday party. We cut the cake at 7:45 sharp. I know because I remember thinking if the keynote speaker were short-winded, Rosalind would make it for the candles. She never did make it, of course. Sara never left my side for that entire night. We were hot and heavy in a battle of Uno with the kids by 8:30."

Blue took in what she was saying. He made no comment. He was happy to have an alibi for both of the women. He trusted Cady's word. He wasn't entirely sure why but for now, he did.

They continued to poke around in the online presence of the festival. They clicked through every link, which Blue could have done on his own, and then Cady took him into the one encrypted page, which he couldn't have gone into on his own. The security barriers were low and a simple HTML hack deleting JavaScript and saving a chan.html file for a password capture was all she needed. They found meeting notes and security schematics. It proved interesting enough that he would go ahead and file his subpoena request, but he did not find anything that screamed motive to him.

When they had gone as far as they could go based on what they knew, Blue stood up and stretched.

"You didn't even bring me anything hard. You could have found most of this with a simple Google search. You going to get some rest now?" Cady asked.

"No, I wish. I'm going to head to Ron's house to see how he's doing and ask him some questions," Blue said.

"Really? He's not going to be up for that. You can't wait?"

"No. I wish I could wait. I wish I never had to go see him. I would do any part of this job over having to talk to the surviving family members of a murder victim."

Cady winced.

"Sorry. I know. It doesn't sound right to me either. But I'm not going to let this bastard get any distance from me on this. I want to catch whoever did this by the end of the day."

"Can you really do that?" Cady asked with all sincerity.

"Not likely. But if I sleep, he gets that much more time to live free and clear of paying for what he's done."

"Can I go with you?"

"To Ron's? Why?" he asked.

"He's going to be in bad shape. We're good friends. Not as close as Rosalind and I are. Were. But I want to be there to help him. They don't have kids. They don't have family around here. Their friends are their family."

He sighed.

"I won't interfere," she said. "I'll just hold his hand while he answers your questions. Or make him some breakfast if he can stomach eating anything. I can't bear that he's there all alone and then he'll have to answer questions about his wife's murder alone. Let me do this."

CHAPTER 8

WHEN CADY AND BLUE arrived at the M'Clintock's house on Virginia Street, the morning was unrolling hot and sultry. Blue was wearing the same black suit he'd worn to the crime scene the night before. Cady had put on a white cotton sleeveless button-up shirt that fitted close on her slim frame. She wore cargo pants made of breathable Flight Cloth. She wore the shoes she almost always wore on weekends, and often during the week—a pair of flirty flat sandals with straps that crisscrossed over the bridge of her foot that functioned like fashionable approach shoes. The barefoot style insoles were made of Memory Foam so it was like she was walking on clouds. They had fast become her go-to shoes and she had a pair in several different colors. Especially on days where the heat was such a presence, she needed to be dressed in clothes that felt light as air.

She wore no jewelry except for a pair of delicate emerald studs that her mother had given her when she left the east coast to live and teach English in California. And her wedding ring. Cady had long ago taken off her engagement ring. Even when Victor was still with her, she would often bench her engagement ring in her jewelry box because of its size. The 1.5 carat Asscher-cut diamond solitaire felt heavy on her ring finger. She was always afraid she would catch it on something and lose the stone. She felt like a fairy princess wearing it, but for her daily rounds, she felt a little ostentatious. She mostly saved it for special occasions even then and never wore it now.

Victor thought it was sweet that she was a little overwhelmed by the ring. He had it designed for her. He'd proposed to her in a delicate snowfall on Bailey Bridge. When he opened the ring box, kneeling in front of her, she thought she saw a snowflake melting on his cheek. His eyes were tearing and he was blinking more than usual. His big, open smile, cheeks flushed. That he would be nervous at this moment captivated her. He had to ask her twice, "Will you marry me?" before she snapped to and covered him in yesses and kisses.

He hadn't meant to give her something that made her feel uncomfortable, but when she asked if he would mind if she didn't wear it daily after they were married, he thought she was dear for not being the kind of woman who loved him for his money. She was the exact opposite of a gold digger. She never felt like she belonged at the mansion overlooking the vineyards. She took to learning about wines and became a connoisseur almost immediately. That was something she could learn. Something she could earn. The lavish lifestyle that Victor had provided for her when they fell in love always seemed like a gift she could never reciprocate.

The streets of Waterloo were deserted save for the occasional die-hard weekend gardener getting in some weeding or lawn mowing before the afternoon heat drove even them indoors. The local churches would be letting out after the morning sermons and the Village would come alive again. Ron's car was in the driveway but there were no other signs that anyone was home. Blue stepped to the side of the front door on the roomy front porch and held out his hand in an offer to let Cady ring the doorbell.

"No way," she said. "I don't want him to feel ambushed. If he sees you and doesn't want to come to the door, so be it. I don't want him to open the door for me and then find you here." Cady gathered up her hair, which was now dry and falling in waves, and fanned the back of her neck.

Blue nodded and knocked on the door. Cady stood to the side. No sound was coming from inside the house. They looked at each other. Blue rang the doorbell. Silence.

Cady stepped up to the door. She knocked on one of the glass window panes that made up the top half of the front door. "Ron? Are you in there? It's me. Cady. I've got Detective Emerson here with me." No sound. "Ron?"

They heard heavy footsteps coming down the staircase that led to the front door. Ron opened the door in his bathrobe. A wave of cold air came pouring out of the house.

"Ron," Cady said and moved to hug him. They stood like that for a long moment. When they broke their embrace, his eyes were wet. Cady asked, "I can't think of a worse time for you and I'm sorry we even have to be here." Ron clasped Cady's hands as if to comfort her. "But do you think we could come in so Blue could talk to you for a minute?"

He seemed disoriented but nodded his head. "Come in. Out of the heat. Hello, Blue. Come in."

"Ron," he said as he shook Ron's hand and stepped into the foyer of their stately Victorian house, "I'm sorry." He looked Ron in the eye. "I will find out how this happened," he promised.

When they were seated in the front-room turret, Blue asked Ron how the chair was holding up. The chair Blue sat in was the one he had made for Rosalind. She had loved it but had asked for it to be altered in small ways several times. It was more ornate than he usually created but to match the old Victorian stylings of the particular room she had in mind for it, he added extra routing and details into the arms and legs and recovered the back and seat with the fabric she had changed her mind about. It was a beautiful chair, sturdy and wide for the modern age but with a delicate look to match the room. Ron did not respond. He seemed beyond small talk.

Cady asked, "Can I make some coffee? Can I scramble you up some eggs?" As the only woman there, she felt uncomfortable volunteering for the domestic chores, but she wanted to help Ron in any way she could and couldn't imagine a homicide detective feeding his subject while he questioned him.

"Thank you, Cady. I couldn't eat. Maybe some coffee, though. I haven't slept all night. The police came. I was sitting right there, where you are, Cady." Cady sat in a Caper Elliot wingback chair with high arms. The matching footstool was pushed to the side. "I was reading. That's what I was doing when Rosalind. . . ." He trailed off. To Cady, he said, "The coffee is right in here." He got up and started in toward the kitchen. They both followed.

"I know where everything is. You just sit." She guided him to a seat at the island. Blue sat across from him. Cady busied herself with the coffee. Ron stared at his hands. He worried his knuckles with the tips of his fingers.

"I'm as sorry as I can be to be the one here today," Blue said.

"No. I'm glad it's you," said Ron. "I mean I'm not glad. I'm not glad of anything, but at least if I know you're handling this, I can trust. I can trust. You know."

"Of course," said Blue. "And I'm sorry to bring you more bad news this morning. Ron, Rosalind was murdered." Blue always felt it was better to just say what needed to be said rather than beating around a hollow bush. Let the information out as gently as he could and then let the reactions be what they would be.

"What?" Ron lifted his head. "She fell. They told me last night she fell into the canal."

"She did. But she had help." Ron would have access to the autopsy results if he wanted them so Blue felt no need to go into the details of her murder unless Ron asked for them. And even then he would use as many euphemisms as he could think of. Ron didn't ask. Blue didn't offer.

Cady had started the coffee maker and sat down next to Ron and put her hand on his. She said nothing. He looked at her and then back at Blue, tears filled his eyes. The doorbell rang.

"Let me get it," Cady jumped up. She glanced pleadingly at Blue as if to ask that he hold the questions until she got back.

A minute later, Cady came back into the kitchen with Eric following her. He had changed from his security officer's uniform into a broken-in V-neck T-shirt and flat-front chinos. He was clean shaven but for his sideburns to his ear lobes and the loosely curled ends of his ungelled hair were still damp. The hair that just reached the base of his neck could have been damp from the muggy air and heat. Nothing dried in wet air like the air that was hanging outside heavy and thick. The air conditioning in the M'Clintock's house provided a respite from the heat already so heavy it made you feel drunk, even on a Sunday morning.

"Deuce," Blue stood up. "What are you doing here?" Ron sat at the island dazed by the news he had just received.

"Hey, man," said Eric. "I stopped by to see how Ron is doing. I wanted to see if he needed anything."

Ron stood up. "Eric, my boy," he said as Eric shook his hand and put an arm around him. "Thank you for stopping by. There's coffee." He indicated that Eric should sit.

Blue looked at Eric as they both sat down. Eric said quietly to Blue as though it were just between the two of them, "Aunt Jessica took Mollie to church with her. She's going to take her swimming at Vince's Park this afternoon." Blue nodded, grateful for the information. Having Eric as a tenant of sorts was useful in some respects.

Cady poured Ron a cup of coffee and put the insulated pot down in front of Eric with a carton of milk. He stood up, offering Cady his chair.

"Here, I took your chair, Cade. Sorry." He put his hand on her elbow and led her back into her chair at the island.

"No problem. Thanks," she said. "No assigned seats. I can sit there." She indicated the chair across from her. He said he'd be just as happy to stand and she stayed where she was.

Eric and Blue selected mugs off the mug tree next to the sugar bowl on the island and poured themselves a cup. Eric stood next to Cady and rubbed her shoulders with his open hand. Cady poured herself a cup of coffee and drank, absently fiddling with her ring. Blue focused forward. He would not look at the pair next to him.

"Can you think of anyone who might want to hurt Rosalind?" Blue said to Ron as he stirred his coffee, not drinking it.

Eric shot Blue a look. Blue nodded, answering the silent question and confirming that Rosalind's death was no accident. Ron sipped his coffee and stared at the lines in the marble of the island counter top.

"Everybody loved her." Ron looked at Eric. "Everybody." Eric looked down at his coffee and took a sip.

"We all did, Ron," Eric said. "But is there anyone who might have had a beef with her lately?"

Blue shot Eric a look this time, admonishing him for interfering with his official investigation. There were too many cooks in Blue's kitchen.

"You all don't know," Ron said as the tears welled up again. "You don't know how special Rosalind was. You do, of course, but you don't. She would do anything for anybody. She taught those kids like they were her own. Some of them hated her because she was demanding." Ron stopped and stared at his coffee. He shook his head. "That's how we came to know Cady." He looked back at Cady. "Victor was in her first class at Waterloo. She got to know his parents that year, but it wasn't until Victor took over the winery that we got to know him as a peer. Add Sara into the mix and you couldn't have a better group of friends," he added as an aside to Cady. She nodded and turned her mouth into an encouraging smile. "She was strict, yes, but none of them really hated her, you know? Right?" He looked at Eric.

He stared back down at his coffee cup and told them what he loved about Rosalind. She was fierce and opinionated. She only argued when she was right. He had learned long ago not to argue with her. If she were arguing it was because she had already verified that she was right. If she didn't know or if she wasn't sure, she was gracious and always allowed that she didn't know. But if she were arguing, she would argue a person into submission.

Politically she didn't seem to have the winning hand, though. Her convictions were often too liberal and too loud for the small conservative town they lived in. She was on the Waterloo Town Board and her recent no-growth stance was often at odds with the free-market push toward commercialism. She wanted to keep Waterloo the small, quaint Village that it had always been. She did not want the town around the Village to expand into super big box stores and shopping plazas. In the last few years, several such proposals had come before the Board for the Town of Waterloo. She voted no on every expansion proposal that didn't involve some individual trying to start up a business to add to the community. Mulligan, who also sat on the Board, had tried to reason with her. Ron assured Blue that Mulligan was no threat, but he explained that their last argument at the Town Board meeting was explosive. Mulligan had tried to tell her that the Village inside the town borders was always going to be preserved. There was no place in the Village for giant superstores to land even they wanted to. But the town acreage surrounding the Village was dilapidated and could be revitalized by allowing high commerce to settle in. She countered that the hardware store, the beauty parlor, and the green grocer, at least, would all be bankrupt within a year. He conceded that that may come to be but it wasn't guaranteed. And the high commerce would employ scores of people currently struggling and out of work, not just the ten or so she was talking about. They always came to the same impasse and the Board always overruled her and the superstores had started coming.

When Rosalind found out that Mulligan and his team had been subcontracted to help build the first big superstore, she threatened, on the record at a Board meeting, to sue him for breach of fiduciary duty and fraud. Neither cause of action would stick, she knew, but she was so angry that he was profiting from his yes vote on the Board that she wanted to ruin him. He explained that he had never been contacted about a job before his vote but that being able to employ his whole crew through the winter was exactly the type of opportunity he had always argued that this town needed. But Rosalind was stubborn and had made her mind up. The rift became a cavern and she never lost the opportunity to point out what she believed was his duplicity. Even so, Ron was sure it was all political and that Mulligan would never do his wife physical harm.

As Cady listened, she added that she had tried but couldn't talk Rosalind out of her hatred of Mulligan. Cady could see both sides and she adored both people, and she knew Mulligan wasn't a schemer. The last time she'd seen Mulligan before her birthday party, he'd asked her to talk to Rosalind for him. He told Cady that he was going to be forced to deal with Rosalind if she wasn't able to talk some sense into her. Rosalind's slander was getting out of control and he said he couldn't take it anymore. But Cady knew Mulligan. He was not Blue's man.

Ron went on as though Mulligan's name had never been brought up. Rosalind organized the Seneca Falls Women's Rights Convention Days festival every year. She felt the residents of Seneca Falls were more interested in preservation and keeping the quaint, familiar atmosphere it had always had than the residents of Waterloo were. If Rosalind had lived in Seneca Falls and been a member of their Board, she may have been more popular at the meetings. Ron said they both knew she probably would not be re-elected to the Town Board in Waterloo. Since the last election, the Board had approved two superstores. The town residents seemed happy.

She was ready to step out of political office. She needed a rest. One of her favorite getaways was a quick trip to the casino a little over an hour away. Ron nodded at Cady as he told Blue about the Skana spa at the casino. He invited her to join him in telling them about their trips there. He and Rosalind used to go with Victor and Cady. Now he and Rosalind went alone. Cady silently declined to add to his story and let Ron tell it himself. They spent a few weekends a year at Turning Stone. He would play poker or bingo. She would indulge in the luxury spa. They would meet for dinner. It was relaxing for both of them. He mentioned that Rosalind had designed a casino cabinet in the wine cellar. Everything for and from the casino in one place, she always used to say. Ron told them that they were just there last weekend. He nodded at Eric. It was uncharacteristic of them to go before a big event. Normally, they would have booked the weekend to recover from the festival, but Rosalind was particularly stressed this year and was having trouble dialing down at the end of the day. Ron took her so she could get a massage and a four-star meal. It had worked. She came back glowing. He came back $200 in the hole.

He planned the trips because she held on to stress with a clenched fist. And stress made her angry. Stress made him tired, he noted, but she got short-tempered. She put so much effort into her job, it took her the summer to recoup her stamina. If she could manage her stress, she was the best teacher anyone could hope for. She was one of the most difficult teachers, to be sure, but when the students came back to pay a visit to the high school after moving on to college, it was Ms. M'Clintock they came to see. It was she who had prepared them for the rigors of college. It was she who had challenged their minds. It was she who they recommended to their younger siblings as the best teacher at Waterloo High School. She was never the easy A, but she created learners more than any other teacher at the school. There were a number of teachers like her in that regard, but her pedagogy along with her subject matter brought out a special flame of emotion in the students she taught.

"She had a student once who wrote a paper on *The House of Mirth*," Ron said. "The paper analyzed how life was *not* that different for women today. She taught students to think. So many students would have argued all the ways in which women have more choices now and how untrapped women are today. Easy. Not Rosalind's students. I even read the paper. It was high-end work. I questioned whether the student may have bought the paper but she was convinced she hadn't because of all the discussions the student had initiated during 5th period about the book and what she was writing. They worked hard to impress her." He said he knew how hard it was to get students to want to impress a teacher. She did it every year.

She allowed for genuine argument. They spoke in her class and were held accountable for their thoughts and views. She would argue with her students and make them stand up for themselves. She would discuss their grades with them and make them defend their positions with rhetorical analysis if they ever questioned a grade she gave them. It was not a method of shutting down discussion, though, so they came. They discussed. They argued. And, with her students, sometimes they won. She was a chore, but they loved her by the time they left her.

Ron wondered out loud how they were going to do without her. No one had any idea how to respond. Blue asked a few more questions. Finally, he let out a heavy sigh full of exhaustion and geared up for the real reason he'd had to visit Ron.

"Where were you last night? Did you come to the festival at all yesterday?" Blue asked.

"I was home reading. I was tired." Ron looked up from his coffee. "Wait." Realization dawned on him slowly. "You think I killed her?" He had settled into the conversation about his wife, blankly remembering what he hadn't even had time yet to digest. His startled eyes at Blue's question shook Cady out of her trance as well.

"No." She reached for his hand. "He has to ask everyone where they were when Rosalind . . . last night. He asked me and I know he's asked Eric, too. We all have to account for our whereabouts. It's just procedure. It has to go in the report." She looked at Blue.

Ron looked from Cady to Eric to Blue. "I was home reading last night. You want to know what I read? I was reading *Day After Night*. Rosalind bought it for me for my last birthday. Historical fiction. You want to know which part I read? Which chapter? Which scene?"

"No," said Blue. "I'll note that you were home alone reading. Is there any particular reason you didn't go to the birthday party?"

"I was feeling under the weather. My asthma was acting up. I'd been at all the opening events the night before and the heat was just making it hard for me to breathe. I told Rosalind to give my regrets," Ron said.

Blue noted what Ron had said. Ron looked ill but with the wash of grief, it was impossible to tell if he were actually sick.

"I'm tired," Ron said. "Is there anything else?"

Cady looked at Blue, pleading with him with her eyes to let the man rest.

"That's all for now." Blue stood up. "I'll follow up with Mulligan." All eyes turned to him. "To clear his alibi." He didn't want everyone in the room coming to Mulligan's defense. He felt no need to apologize for doing his job but he needed to quell the team effort that seemed to be building.

"I know him to talk to him and I know where he lives. You call me if you think of anything else? Anything you heard Rosalind say or do recently that might help us figure this out." He handed Ron his card and wrote his cell number on the back. "I know you have my number but take this so it's somewhere close. You call anytime if you need anything."

As Ron led them back into the foyer and to the front door, they passed a stack of wine bottle boxes, waist high, two deep. Blue laid his hand on the top box.

"New shipment?" he asked. Everyone who knew the M'Clintocks knew they were wine connoisseurs and had an extensive wine collection in a custom made wine cellar in their basement. Blue had first gotten a personal glimpse of his teacher and her husband when he was in high school working for Victor at his family winery after school and on weekends. Blue worked with Clint, Victor's brother and the vineyard manager, with the grape vines during the growing season and then with the general maintenance and janitorial staff during the dormant season. Rosalind and Ron used to walk among the rows of trellises in the spring and summer. They would inspect the grapes. They held hands and would talk and talk. They would eat lunch in the winery cafe and sometimes dinner, always accompanied by a glass of wine. They were favored customers. To Victor, they had grown to be more like family over the years. Rosalind had taught all three of the

Nicholas children but Victor, the oldest, only nine years younger than her, had always been her favorite. Rosalind and Ron had both liked Blue because in addition to being one of her brightest students, they saw him as a hard worker, not afraid to get his hands dirty. They would always stop and chat with him if he were in the field when they would walk through. They started out like typical adult-teenager conversations. How are your classes coming? What are your plans for college? It wasn't until Blue returned from Fishkill that he became more like friends with them.

"Yes," said Ron looking at the boxes. He sighed. "We got this shipment in last Wednesday and Rosalind has been so busy with the festival that we hadn't gotten around to putting it away downstairs. That's why it's so blasted cold in here. Not that I mind," he said absently laying a hand on his chest. "I hate the heat. Especially heat like we're having. Wet air. Hard for me to breathe."

"Let me take these downstairs for you," Eric said. "I haven't seen the wine cellar since it was finished."

"Of course," Blue said. Blue took off his jacket.

"I got this," Eric said. "You go ahead. I know you've got more to do than hours in the day to do it."

"Just grab the door," Blue said. "It won't even take five minutes if we both do it."

"You don't have to," Ron said.

"Don't be silly," Cady said. "Let these guys do something for you. You and me, we can just watch them work." Cady smiled at Ron. "Better yet, why don't you go on upstairs and I'll wash up the coffee cups. We'll be out of your hair in no time."

"You're always the funny one," Ron said smoothing down the ring of short hair that male pattern baldness had left him. "But I am suddenly very sleepy. Thank you, Cady." He labored up the stairs. Cady washed the cups and set up another pot of coffee to be brewed at the touch of the on button. She left a note next to the coffee pot to let Ron know it was ready to go. Blue and Eric moved the six boxes of wine to the cellar and laid them out in single rows so Ron would not have to lift them again. Just open them and file the bottles away in the appropriate holes.

Cady did not go to the cellar. She did not want to see all the bottles of wine lined up in their individual mahogany cubed slots with such care and love. She hadn't seen those cubes in years. She didn't want to participate in a tasting around the tall bar table or stand on the high-polished wood floors. She had learned a great deal about wine when she was dating and then married to Victor. She loved good wine but after Victor disappeared, she never went wine tasting and she never accompanied Rosalind down to her wine cellar. She hadn't stepped foot onto the Nicholas Winery and Vineyards since she moved from her home there five years ago. Although the trauma and sting of his disappearance had faded over time, being in his world was still too painful. He had been gone six years, almost to the day, but there were still some activities that she relegated to her memory life, like some songs she always turned off if they came on the radio.

She never again went to the Turning Stone Casino either. Cady had never been a gambler but she did attend shows there with Victor and Rosalind and Ron. It was one of the things they did as couples. They'd go on Friday, have a gourmet meal and long, lively conversation. They'd take in a show. On Saturday Rosalind and Cady would have a spa day. They would start with a gentle yoga class and then a 90-minute massage after the healing waters. The spa specialized in the healing waters ritual. The guest would take a short sweat in the sauna. Then a brief, cool shower. Then, a few minutes in the steam room to open all the pores followed by another cool shower. Then a leisurely soak in the hot tub. Men and women had their own quarters for the healing waters. The final step was the communal mineral pool housed in a large room with high ceilings and huge high windows that bathed the room in soft, diffused light. Cady and Rosalind always started with the mineral pool since that was the only place bathing suits were required. It was cooler than the other activities as well and the first time they followed standard procedure, Cady ended up chilled at the end. They turned the ritual around from that point on. Donning their Turkish terry cloth robes, they would wait in the women's lounge, on long chairs bathed in gas-powered but surprisingly warm firelight, to be collected for their massages. Rosalind always got the hot stone massage and Cady went for the Swedish massage. By the time they met again in the lounge an hour and a half later, they were both dozy with relaxation.

They would eat lunch at the Wild Flowers restaurant and then go back to the spa for a facial and spend the rest of the afternoon napping in their own room or reading in the mineral pool room on the deeply cushioned lounge chairs listening to the trickle of the mineral fountain in the middle of the pool. Victor and Ron would play poker all day. They would sometimes join their wives for lunch. Sometimes not. Rosalind and Cady would always order room service on Saturday evening and hang out in one of their suites watching movies in their comfiest clothes. Ron and Victor would play poker well into the evening. Sometimes Ron would break off to go play bingo in the giant bingo hall. A weekend at Turning Stone would end on Sunday morning when they would all eat in the casino's diner and then drive home.

Cady thought of the wine cellar and the slim cabinet Rosalind had designed to hold all of their bingo daubers and their diamond casino card that kept track of their frequent player points. Sometimes Rosalind played the slots, but like Cady, she never had a stomach for playing with her money. Rosalind had a place for everything. Cady strived for that order with her emotions but she wasn't so particular about her physical surroundings. Rosalind was a feverish scrapbooker and had an entire room set aside with a large square table in the center and shelving on every wall for all of the toys that go with that hobby. The room was always impeccable unlike Cady's art studio, which was always this side of tussled.

Rosalind had made a scrapbook for Cady and for Sara commemorating their camping weekend last summer at Cranberry Lake in the Adirondacks. They had one page of camping pictures and the rest were resort pictures from when they gave up because of the black flies and rented a hotel with a pool at the base of the mountain. Rosalind was crabby when they woke the first morning and the black flies had descended. Sara had picked the weekend and she'd thought they'd planned it late enough in the season but a late frost had extended the season for the biting nuisances. When Rosalind got cranky and set her jaw, Sara and Cady tended to get quiet. She could be caustic but they both knew it would pass quickly. Cady and Sara had talked many times about how Rosalind's emotions flailed. Sometimes you got hit but that was true with the positive emotions as well.

At the campground, Rosalind had taken a picture of a chipmunk on a stump, which was teeny in the picture surrounded by woods all around. She should have zoomed in but photography was not her strong suit, despite her love of scrapbooking. By the mid-afternoon that first day when they were lounging by the pool with cocktails, they were all cheery again and Cady and Sara, who were no better with a camera than Rosalind was, teased her about the screenshot of their outdoor adventure the rest of the weekend. The scrapbook's cover featured the microscopic chipmunk on the stump and was ironically labeled "Summer Camp."

When the wine boxes were stacked, and they walked back out into the early Sunday afternoon sun, the heat physically slowed them down. No one was out on Virginia Street. Eric had pulled his Mustang convertible in behind Blue's Crown Victoria in Ron's wide driveway.

"What next?" Eric said as they made their way down the stairs.

"I'm going to head to the station," Blue said.

"What can I do to help?"

"What do you need?" Cady and Eric both spoke at the same time.

"This isn't the Mod Squad," Blue laughed. "I have work to do at the station. Cady, I'll take you home."

"Okay," Eric said smiling too. "You guys need anything over there, give me a call. I'm not on duty again until tomorrow morning." He turned to Cady. "I can take you home."

"Thanks both of you. But I'm going to walk."

"In this heat?" Eric said.

"Yeah." She looked up. The sky was darkening and a breeze had started up just since they had walked out of the house. On normal summer days in the Finger Lakes region, the weather was ever-changing. It would start out cool and cloudy. The haze would burn off by 7:00 a.m. and the sun would shine brilliantly on the deep greens of the trees and grasses and the bright colors of the flowers that sprouted from every yard. It was a time that was both lazy and alive. The sunshine would often give way to a drop in temperatures of 20 degrees or more in the afternoon followed by a thunder storm that would pelt the foliage into submission and drench the landscape. As often as not, the sun would come back out and dry the earth within the hour. On days like today, there was no haze and no cool morning, but the skies often pulled in dark either way.

"It looks like the storm is coming through after all," she said. "I don't mind the heat. It's only a half a dozen blocks to the library. All the coffee has made me restless. I might even take the long way home to clear my head."

They said their good-byes and went off in their three separate directions, leaving Ron to mourn his first day on this earth alone in almost three decades.

CHAPTER 9

CADY MADE IT HOME before the first rain drops fell on the hot sidewalks and rooftops. As she slipped off her shoes and dropped her keys and the Sunday newspaper she had bought on the way home onto the pedestal table just inside her front sliding glass door, she heard the plops of the fat rain that preceded the deluge of the typical Central New York summer afternoon thunderstorm. She switched on the ceiling fans and left the door open with the screen shut. The angled roof partially covered the deck and protected the doors and Hero's window from getting wet. She had known the storm was coming. Sara had told them it was in the forecast and was threatening the Sunday activities at the festival. They would be able to put on the play under the covered pavilion at People's Park but they would play to no audience if the grass were wet. They were sure to have to cancel the Ladies Vintage Baseball Game if it were raining, which would have been the worst of all the events to cancel. Two teams of local women in full costume of long black skirts, white long-sleeved blouses and low heeled boots came out to play a real baseball game around padded bases and with no gloves. It was always a fun way to cap off the well-designed annual community event.

"Quit yer bitchin'," Rosalind had faux scolded Sara. "If you quote me one more online forecast from that damn phone of yours, I'm banning it. Those predictions are never right. I say there will be no rain. There. It is done." She turned from them and waved a pretend wand in the air. "And if it does rain, this blazing July sun will dry everything within minutes." She turned back. "I hope so anyway."

She would have nearly gotten her wish. It was just after 1:00 when the storm clouds opened up. The baseball game was scheduled to start at 2:00. It was the final event for the festival. They would have made it through the Ice Cream Social and Picnic and Womenspeak, the reader's theatre presentation at People's Park. They would have made it mostly through the Freedom Singers scheduled in the pavilion after the reader's theatre. In truth, people would have started for their cars when they saw the rain clouds moving in. The baseball game would have been postponed until after the storm, and depending how long it rained, it would have been simply cancelled and the festival put to bed for the year.

Cady knew that People's Park was quiet today. She drew a glass of water from the door of the fridge and settled into her love seat that looked out onto the deck. She saw Hero as he galloped up the stairs and hopped onto the window ledge. He pushed his paw and then his face through the cat door mounted into the window and pulled his fluffy body all the way through. He leapt down from the inside window ledge and sauntered over to Cady, wiping the outside air onto her pant legs. He marked her whenever he came home. It was like he was sharing his adventures with her.

"C'mere, you fluffy ferdle," she said patting the cushion next to her. He jumped up and immediately started cleaning his paws. His fur was dry. His fur was always dry. He'd come trudging home in the middle of the night in a snow storm. His feet would be wet, but his fur was dry. It was like he moved too fast to get wet.

The sky clapped with a fury that startled both Cady and Hero. As they gazed out the opened sliding glass door, the rain fell in a sheet. She left the windows open to smell the rain freshen the world outside. The sound of the rain is what she liked best. It was deafening when a storm like this one came through. Thunder and lightning and pounding rain where minutes before she was wilting in the summer muggy heat. Mesmerized, Cady folded her feet under her and watched the storm pass. As it eased to a dappling rain and the thunder echoed miles away, she reached for the paper and a sip of cool water. Hero had settled in for a nap in a circle next to her with his head tucked under his feet and his fluffy tail covering his eyes.

She had glanced through the front page story of Rosalind's death when she bought the paper on Main Street. Now she read it more carefully. Delaney had filed the story on time and it was the story above the fold in the Sunday edition of the *Finger Lakes Times*. Delaney hinted that Rosalind may have been murdered but nothing had been confirmed at the time the paper went to press. At this point, it was labeled an unattended death. Delaney's story focused on Rosalind's life. The fact that she died at the festival she organized every year. The fact that she was wearing an authentic mid-19th century vintage costume down to the collar and shoes, as she was known to do every year. She noted that anyone with information about Rosalind's death should contact the New York State Troopers and gave the address and phone number of the Waterloo Trooper's Station on Waterloo-Geneva Road. She did not mention Blue. Articles never mentioned police officers by name. It was customary to note that the entity was conducting the investigation. The Troopers or the Seneca Falls or Waterloo Police Department. If someone had information, they were to contact the entity and the information would be shuffled to the correct officer. Which officer may be assigned to any one criminal investigation was not publicly advertised.

Delaney noted that Rosalind was a teacher at Waterloo High School, that she was survived by her husband who was a professor at Hobart and William Smith Colleges in Geneva where he had taught history for over thirty years. Rosalind was on the Waterloo Town Board. She organized

the Seneca Falls Women's Rights Convention Days festival every year and was chiefly responsible for its
resurgence as a legitimate community event. The story
appeared with a photo of Rosalind from last year's festival
that Delaney must have found in the newspaper's morgue.
She noted that details of the funeral arrangements would
be forthcoming.

She got all the facts right. But there was nothing there
of her friend. The dimensions of her life and her personality. Delaney hadn't interviewed Cady for the story. If she
had, she would have known that Rosalind was in the book
club that met once a month at Cady's house along with
Sara and the double A's: Alice and Amanda. That Rosalind
always brought the wine even when it wasn't her turn to
bring snacks. That she had the kind of insight into litera-
ture, whether modern, classics, American, British, that
attested to having read thousands of books.

Rosalind eagerly brought difficult books to the book
club's attention. They'd be on Rosalind's list for months or
years before her pitch for their worth would finally bring
them onto the agenda. The book club's tastes ran more
toward Jodi Picoult or Sara Gruen. Thoughtful books with
interesting characters and themes to discuss. That night,
the women were gathered in Cady's apartment. Conversation about the book Rosalind had chosen was slow to get
started. Sara put on one of Cady's Caribbean cds, low and
slow in the background. The women were seated in Cady's
conversation pit. Spring hadn't let go of its chill yet and
they were inside, bundled against a late season snow-

storm. Rosalind poured them all a glass of Malbec, which she had paired with a sausage and cheese tart Amanda had brought from Wegmans.

"I can never get over how adorable this apartment is," Amanda said. She leaned back in her chair and stared up at the high-beamed ceiling.

"I am lucky," Cady said. "This whole area up here was originally a cavernous meeting room with these high ceilings. It was converted into a small theatre with raised seating over there," she pointed to her bedroom, "and a stage and what amounted to a closet for the back stage over there." She pointed to her kitchen. "Long before me, it went through its final transformation when the library director then had it converted to a two-bedroom apartment for him and his family. He had some of the ornate stained glass windows replaced with ones that would open and installed a sliding glass door as a front door. That one stained glass above the door is the only original one left." They all looked above the sliding glass door. "He had the original forest green and brick red painted this soft cream color but the original routing on the high carved beams was left intact." She looked up. "It could use a fresh coat of paint."

"Well, I love it," Amanda said. "Perfect for one person. And who can beat the commute?" They all laughed.

"Okay," Rosalind said as though calling the class to attention. "Enough chit chat. It wasn't an easy book but we loved it, didn't we?" The group looked down at their wine glasses. "Okay, we hated it! I know. But can we at least talk about why it was so brilliant before we disparage it like troglodytes?" They went on to talk for hours about *Cloud Atlas*. It was exactly the type of book that Rosalind would pick when it was her turn—intelligent, postmodern, interminable.

Cady had read twenty books the first year she moved from the vineyards, her second year without Victor. Rosalind read every one right alongside her. Rosalind's friendship had helped calm her then. She and Rosalind became close friends that year. How could any of that go in the newspaper?

Cady folded the front page and laid it on the coffee table. She scooted down into the love seat and pulled the soft nap blanket that Sara had given her after seeing it advertised on TV from the back of the love seat and covered herself. She left Hero uncovered, snuggled and snoring softly into the crook of her legs. She lay on her side watching the rain wash the streets clean. The temperature had dropped 20 degrees since the storm broke. The breeze allowed her to sink under the blanket and envelop herself in softness.

CHAPTER 10

WHEN CADY WOKE UP the sun was bright on the horizon and her deck was shaded with late summer afternoon gray light. In her sleep, she had kicked the blanket off of her and Hero was now asleep on the club chair. He was laid out flat on his back with his hind legs splayed out and his front paws stretched out to the left of his head. She had slept for four and a half hours. She felt groggy and it was hot again. She stood up to stretch the sleep out of her body. As soon as she did, she realized she was famished. She hadn't eaten since her party the night before. The adrenaline and coffee had fed her until now. She padded barefoot to her kitchen and opened the refrigerator.

Blessedly, Sara had been by to drop off the leftovers from the party. She must have scored them from Lauralei. Cady hadn't noticed anyone had been in the apartment until she opened the fridge and saw the piece of bright yellow construction paper with red and blue writing on it saying, "Eat me! Love, Sara." There was one piece of the lemon cake left. The party goers had seconds of every-thing. But that one piece of cake was like manna from heaven. She ate the whole piece without a second thought. When she was done and washing her plate, she knew that wouldn't be enough to quell her hunger.

Instead of heating up the party leftovers, she filled her stockpot with hot water and turned her burner on high. She pulled a bag of spinach capellini out of the cupboard and grabbed two tomatoes out of the ceramic bowl on her counter. She chopped the tomatoes and tossed them into a small pan she set to heating with olive oil in it. She shook in a little garlic powder, minced onion, and Italian seasoning. While she waited for the water to boil and the tomatoes to cook down, she grabbed a nectarine out of the fruit bowl in her fridge. The cool, sweet-tart flesh of the nectarine made the back of her jaw tingle. She walked to the screen door and stood looking out at the dry, hot neighborhood that opened out in front of her view. It was closer to high seventies, low eighties now and the heat was drier. The air was higher in the sky rather than feeling so low you could reach out and touch a piece of it. She ate down to the pit, threw it in the garbage can next to the stove, and checked the pasta water. When it boiled, she added a small handful of kosher salt and the pasta. Twelve minutes later she was eating a bowl of pasta pomodoro and drinking a glass of Cabernet. Fruit and dessert before dinner.

She sat at the dining room table facing the sliding glass door. She used one of the beautiful pasta bowls her mother had given her when she moved into the flat above the library. She used real silver and washed it by hand. She drank out of deep delicate wine glasses and always used cloth napkins. It was one of the concessions she refused to make to living alone. She didn't always cook full meals just for herself, but whenever she ate anything more than a sandwich or a piece of fruit, she ate sitting down with a crystal glass of ice water, and if it was dinner, she would often have a glass of good wine. In the morning, it was a cup of the rich, dark coffee with real cream in a fine bone China cup.

Hero had awakened to the sound of the fridge opening and he had had a full conversation with her about what he would like to eat and how he would like it served. One packet of Wellness grain-free tuna flavor with a side of Solid Gold Indigo Moon dry food to clean the teeth. Always fresh, cool water. If she were eating fish, she would share. Pasta, even the healthy kind, was not Hero's favorite, so he stuck with the daily special. When he was done, he proceeded to groom himself to the fluffy perfection that he was before and after every meal and every nap. Cady never had to comb or brush him. A flea treatment once a month and all the petting he could stand was all he needed to be the cleanest, most beautiful cat in the neighborhood. And he smelled like heaven. At least once a day, she would stick her face into his belly and rub into his fur. She would kiss him a million times a day.

After dinner, Cady felt restless. She had four messages on her answering machine. She'd long since eliminated voicemail from her cell phone. She'd answered a couple of texts letting people know she was okay. She'd talked to her mother late the night before. With the time difference between New York and California, it was early enough to call her mom even though she was bone weary when she got home from Rosalind's crime scene. She had needed to talk to her mother before she could settle down enough to sleep. Even so, she wasn't able to sleep well. Enid was shocked and concerned. She'd told Cady that she would be on the first plane in the morning to come be with her. That would have helped a great deal. Cady loved her mother. More than that, she liked her and valued her company and her perspective on life. But Cady knew her mother was deep into writing and needed to finish the draft of the manuscript she was working on before the new semester started at the university where her mother taught. Cady had Sara. She assured her mother that she'd be all right and that she would check in every day. She also promised that she would lean on Sara as much as she could, not a trait of Cady's that came naturally. Cady promised she would try. She knew that Sara would need to focus her attention on Natalie and she didn't want to interfere with their already difficult relationship.

To keep her promise, though, and to calm her restlessness, she called Sara, who was grateful to hear from her. Natalie had gone to Chris's house, so before a half hour had passed, Sara was at her sliding glass door with a bottle of Cabernet. Cady hugged her deeply and held up her own glass, half full. She opened Sara's bottle and poured her a glass.

As they settled into the chairs on the deck, Cady said, "I'd offer you a piece of cake, but you know I inhaled it as soon as I found it. Thank you for that, by the way." She smiled. Hero flattened into the chair next to Cady and immediately fell asleep again.

"I just ate dinner," Sara laughed, "but don't feel bad. Natalie and I shared a big piece last night when we got home. Lauralei dropped everything off in our garage fridge. God bless her. We both were needing a carb binge to settle our nerves," Sara said. "It actually helped to eat a little bit together. I'm glad you called, though, because we both needed a break, I think. And I really needed to be with just us, so your timing is perfect."

Sara was as close to being Cady's people as Cady had in her adult years. Sara and Rosalind, although Rosalind had one percent more of a mom vibe than did Sara, even though Sara actually was a mom and Rosalind was not. Rosalind was born parenting people around her. Sara was more like a petulant sister. Both of them thought like she did. They laughed like she did. Sara was the librarian at the local high school. Sara took Cady under her wing the minute she was installed as the librarian at the Waterloo Library. They became immediate best friends forever.

Cady had just gotten married to Victor the month before she started as the full-time librarian. She had been the part-time library assistant before that, while she was getting her MLS degree. Sara showed up at the library to introduce herself. She had heard that Cady would be the new librarian and she wanted to welcome her to the neighborhood. Instead of the old standby of "let me know if you need anything," Sara showed up to give Cady tips on ordering and to discuss databases Cady might be interested in and conferences they might attend together. Cady was so grateful that she took her up on every offer and they spent the majority of that summer together, after her honeymoon, getting Cady established. Sara had summers off and only did intermittent drive-bys to the school library to catch up on things she'd let slide in the busyness of the school year and to do her monthly ordering.

Cady and Victor had become friends with the Crosses and the M'Clintocks in that same summer. Cady met Rosalind and Ron through Victor. For the first time, Cady felt like she fit in somewhere and could make this her home. Victor was busy with the vineyards and she was busy in her new career, but because they did not have children yet, after work meant their time was their own and they took advantage of that time and the bounty of the Finger Lakes. She was settling into her community.

"I think I just carbo loaded for the week," Cady said. "But I actually do feel better. Less jangly. I'm glad the same worked for you two last night."

They talked as the sky darkened and the twinkle lights on Cady's deck came on. They talked about Rosalind and Natalie and how Natalie was coping with the trauma of finding Rosalind's body and what the new order would look and feel like without Rosalind.

After a lull, Cady said, "Blue was here this morning." Hero stretched big and jumped into Cady's lap.

"The detective?" Sara asked, pouring more wine into both of their glasses.

"Yes." Cady was feeling the wine and relaxing into the ease of the evening with her friend.

"What for?" Sara asked as she slid off her Crocs and curled her feet under her in the chair. Sara was the queen of comfort. She wore her favorite Bermuda shorts and a short-sleeved T-shirt. Her glossy brown hair was cut in layers that flowed and curled around her face. She resituated her headband to keep her bangs from flopping in her eyes. "Is there news?"

"He wanted me to do some basic research for him. We went to see Ron."

"How is he? I should have gone over today. We both thought about it all day. We talked about going. We talked ourselves out of going. We should have gone."

Cady laughed, "He was in no shape for company. You guys made the right decision. Blue had to go on official business and I asked to come along to help Ron cope with that official business."

"Must have been awful," Sara said. "I just feel sick about this. Will he need help with the funeral arrangements? Of course he will. Let's think what we can do to help."

"I'm sure he will. Their world was pretty insular so I don't know if he has anyone who can help him. Besides us."

"I'll go over tomorrow and take him to see Jeff, if he doesn't already have plans," Sara said. "Jeff was there to pick up her body. He probably already has plans. I'll go over anyway. Just to see."

"Good call," Cady said. "I can help after work." They were quiet for a long minute.

"What?" Sara said looking at Cady.

Cady crooked a smile and looked away.

"Cady."

"What, what? You're plying me with alcohol!"

"I'm plying you with nothing. Spill." Sara laughed gently. "Did Eric come by today?"

"No," Cady said quickly. "I did see him. He stopped by Ron's house when we were there. Small town. Everybody's everywhere. But I'm thinking he may not be right for me."

"Don't be ridiculous! He's perfect for you."

Cady gave Sara a knowing smirk.

"Okay, he's not perfect. He doesn't have his own place. He may be in need of gambler's anonymous. But he's so prettyyy," she whined.

"That he is," Cady agreed.

"You're a match for his scorching good looks," Sara said.

Cady laughed that off as she did any comments about her beauty. She actively warded off the frump-a-dump that could easily set in for her lack of caring, but she did not see her lithe frame or natural symmetry as anything but functional. In Victor's eyes, she had felt beautiful, sexy. Since, she felt creative and interesting on her best days. Blank on her worst.

"Is it because he uses hair gel at work?" Sara said.

"No!" Cady protested. They were both laughing now and feeling warm, a welcome respite.

"Then what is it?" Sara asked.

"I just don't think I have it for anyone." Cady got serious. "I don't think I'll ever have it for anyone. I don't know if moving on with Eric is a mistake or if not moving on sooner was a mistake. I feel paralyzed by the unknowns. When I think about Ron and Rosalind and how perfect their marriage was and how it's now all gone. Ron will now be . . ." She couldn't finish the thought let alone the sentence.

"Cade," Sara stilled. "Mistakes? We're all in that club. And we've suffered tremendous loss. But Rosalind and Ron? All relationships have troubled spots. And an ending is never easy. You know that better than most. I do too. But we're better now. We don't have to live in abject fear and settle because it's better than being alone. We can heal."

"I don't know if that's true. I think I made a mistake not accepting it all sooner and just forcing myself to move on. I don't know if I can now."

"You can. You don't actually know how bad it was for me when Marshall left. We were friends but not like we are now. I hid the worst of it from everyone. Except Natalie. The mistakes I made with Natalie will be with me for the rest of my life. Ever since Marshall walked out on us, I've had less of a hold on her every year. I try to comfort myself that it would have been the case with a teenage girl anyway, even if her father were there to help with the parenting. I'll never know.

"Natalie is one of the most accomplished girls in her grade. She is smart and beautiful and as grown up and independent as any of us at times. But she latched on to Chris at the beginning of her sophomore year and the two of them have been like an old married couple ever since—an old married couple as sexually active as their teenage hormones demand they be. I knew this but could never bring myself to talk to Natalie about it."

Cady was uncomfortable hearing about her friend and employee in such intimate terms but she let Sara continue. It would have made sense for her and Sara to bond over their lost husbands but instead they spent a year not engaging with each other. Their common trauma was too much to look at in another person. When they drifted back together, because of Rosalind, it was understood that they didn't need to talk about their lost year with each other. But Cady had always known that at some point they'd face it. She felt as if her skin were itching and her head were two sizes too big, but she needed to sit still and let Sara talk without interruption.

"When Marshall left, I went into a deep depression that left me virtually nonfunctioning for the better part of that year. I got up and went to work. I showered most days. I managed to get groceries a couple times a month. Other than that, I spent every waking, and sleeping, hour in bed.

"I had no idea how the break up was impacting Natalie. It wasn't that I didn't care. I simply couldn't rise out of the fog that was covering my every thought.

"I rarely ate. At some point, Natalie started to cook. I don't even remember when. She lived on TV dinners and canned raviolis for a while and then started to make simple dishes like spaghetti with sauce from a jar and baked chicken with Campbell's cream of chicken soup on it.

"I had her so young. I wanted to have had more kids but the years got away from us. Marshall was always gone for work, and extra-curriculars, I later found out. When he got tapped to join the CNE Search Team, it was all but over."

Cady knew well of Marshall's turn with the Civilian Nuclear Emergency Search Team. He wasn't in the military, but for the hold the job had on his life, he might as well have been.

"I functioned as a single mother for most of Natalie's life," Sara went on, "and when Marshall was home, I had to tell him what to do as though he were a guest with a few responsibilities. When he was home, we would have the same fights over and over. I barked. He obeyed. He was home less and less until he wasn't home anymore. I worked hard and involved myself in Natalie's life to the point of forgetting I had a life at all. The extra 50 pounds I was carrying when you and I met was not the norm, as you can see. Living that life left me soft and slow. My life as Sara had faded away piece by piece. If it weren't for you and I sharing the same job, I'm sure we would never have connected either. I wasn't connectable at that time. And if we hadn't attached before our respective husbands disappeared, we probably never would have.

"During the year after he left, I didn't gain any energy, but I did shed all those pounds, and more, because I couldn't bring myself to eat. It was like having the flu for a year. I lay in bed alternating between sleeping, watching TV, and doing word search puzzles. My mind wasn't sharp enough for crosswords but sometimes I needed a rest from the nothingness of television. I could not concentrate, but I could damn well circle words when I found them hiding in those endless squares of disembodied letters.

"Natalie would come into my room after school and try to share the day's events. She would ask how I was feeling. I would put on a strong face, but the bed I had taken up residence in belied any optimism I tried to portray. She took to changing my sheets when I was at work. I used all my sick days and all my vacation days. I rarely worked a full week during that whole year. I would shower on weekends with the intention of getting up and doing something productive. The burst of enthusiasm would disappear before my shower was done and I always ended up right back in bed, letting my hair air dry on the pillow.

"After a while, Natalie simply learned to function on her own. She made her own lunches and dinners and ate

Pop Tarts, bought in bulk, for breakfast. She washed her own clothes and got herself to and from school. She did her homework and didn't cause me any trouble. She eventually stopped popping her head into my bedroom when she got home from school and went about life in her home like she was the woman of the house. The whole house would have fallen down around us if Natalie hadn't stepped up. I had friends, all of them acquaintances except for Rosalind and you, who tried to help at the beginning, but I was so ashamed of my situation that I downplayed it at every opportunity. I never offered to help you as much as I wanted to either." Sara hesitated. Cady knew this time was like a blur to them both. Rosalind was Cady's anchor. She could not have survived without her. While Cady gravitated to activity and to Rosalind, Sara gravitated to the isolation.

"I knew Rosalind was there for you," Sara continued. "She tried to be there for me, too, but I wouldn't let her. No one ever knew I was falling apart. Everyone told me I never looked better as I was dropping weight. That the color had faded from my skin and my eyes were dead did not register with anyone enough for them to come to the rescue. Natalie was my savior. If Natalie had started acting out or getting into trouble, I would never have been able to hide that in such a small town. We had a tacit agreement that we were in this alone. A family secret. My friends and coworkers knew I was getting divorced and knew I was turning down social invitations but after several attempts, they all moved on to live their own lives.

"From that point on, Natalie and I functioned more like roommates than mother and daughter. I slowly pulled out of my funk. I got out of bed one Saturday morning, took a shower and got dressed instead of crawling back into bed. Natalie wasn't home and I remembered vaguely that she had a swim meet. Natalie swam for the local Y and was in the final days of the season. I hadn't been to a meet all year. I hadn't been to a parent-teacher conference or an open house or a chorus concert or a cross-country meet. Nothing. But this was the morning that I got up and stayed up. I checked the calendar to see where the meet was and decided to go. When I showed up, Natalie waved at me from across the pool, but didn't come over to me to say hello. I felt like a drug addict who was just released from rehab and everyone was looking at me like I had leprosy. It was more likely that no one noticed me at all, but my prolonged absence felt conspicuous. I apologized to Natalie when we got home that evening. Natalie hugged me and said she was glad I was feeling better. She went off to do her homework and didn't linger. I had imagined that I would be able to talk to Natalie about how Natalie was coping, but that moment seemed to have long since passed.

"By then, Natalie had all but grown up. She was in eighth grade and never again required the kind of mothering she did when we were all a family. We both lost our entire family, not just a husband and father. The happy family had turned into a broken shell of a home that left the two of us to battle between ourselves because Marshall Cross had all but dropped out of our lives, not just mine, hers too. We fought sometimes, but mostly we just lived side by side. I worked and took care of the house. I cooked again and took the pressure off of Natalie to be the homemaker, but I've never again had any say over Natalie.

"In the years since Marshall left, the thing I miss the most is no longer my husband himself. It was no longer even being married, although I have found married life in a small town was easier to navigate than being a single mother in her late 30s. No. The thing I miss the most is being a mother. I'm not interested in having a teenager as a roommate. I want to kiss boo boos and tell bedtime stories and make popcorn and watch movies on Friday nights. I want to tell Natalie that she absolutely cannot have sex with Chris and have control over where she goes and with whom she spends her time. I realize these are probably illusory dreams for mothers of teenagers anyway, but I know I would have had a better chance at a parental role with my daughter if I had been able to hold it together when my marriage broke apart. My heart was broken and I failed. I failed my marriage and my daughter and now I just have to endure until Natalie is old enough to leave home. Maybe we'll have a better shot as mutual adults.

"I see Natalie repeating my patterns already. This Chris Temple is big and dumb and able to be led around by Natalie. Although Marshall isn't dumb, I will say that. I see Natalie as the one who makes all the decisions and takes charge. Chris follows along like a happy puppy. I know he's happy to have a beautiful, competent girl like Natalie on his arm. I don't see him as caring much beyond that. Natalie could do worse but I know all too well the trajectory of a forceful woman coupled with a man willing to be told what to do. At some point, he wakes up and realizes his masculinity has been stripped. He's not living the easy life he thought he was. His starlet of a wife looks at him with disdain because he's a follower and not a leader. He takes no initiative. She no longer finds him sexy and his chief reason for hanging on to her has long since dried up. She is bored and intolerant of him, but it is always the man who makes a change. It is the man who finds the next starlet who will look at him with gleaming eyes and find his cuteness charming and his accommodating nature alluring. It is the man who leaves the relationship. I know all too well. And Natalie is repeating my exact same pattern. And I don't know how to fix any of it."

They were both quiet for a long time.

"I had no idea," Cady said finally. She put her hand on Sara's. "I'm sorry you had to go through all of that alone. I would have done anything for you. I should have known."

"You can't know what people go to such great lengths to hide," Sara said.

"I never knew what happened with you and Natalie. She's such a great kid. You did better than you give yourself credit for."

"Natalie is great. She had a good foundation. Her blossoming has happened despite her parents, though, I'm afraid."

"Does Marshall know any of this?"

Sara blew out between her lips. "He wouldn't care even if he did. He's got a whole new life." She turned to face Cady. "My point in sharing all this darkness right now is not to dredge it up but to promise you that healing is available. Whether we make a monumental mistake we can't take back or whether we have to live with a hole of unknown the size of Texas in our hearts, we can still heal."

Sara leaned in. "You are the most beautiful woman I know. You're smart and sassy and, dammit, people like you." She smiled. "Rosalind's death is not Victor's. It exists all on its own. You don't have to think about dating anyone right now. This is awful what's happened. But it does not mean that every love will end in tragedy. It does not mean that."

Cady adjusted in her chair. "But Sara, he drives a Mustang." Cady attempted to lighten the mood.

"Eric? He's a nice guy. He'll relax eventually and let you see that."

"I can see that," Cady said. "But that's just it. He's a guy. Victor was a man. His body, his voice, his hands, his life. Maybe I'm just too old to go back to the guy thing again. I just don't feel, let's say, amorous, when he's around. But he's hot so maybe it's me. Maybe I won't ever feel that again. All my friends are married. Or have kids already. It's like I'm the only one left in the world in this in-between place."

"I thought you might have a little fun with Eric. There haven't even been any viable candidates in a long time. He's not the one. Let's just go with that. And have some more wine," Sara said.

They drank the rest of the bottle and had a friendly buzz on when Sara walked the few blocks home in the still summer night. Cady sat out on her deck with Hero in her lap and drank in the deep night air. She had tried to lay down her relationship with Victor. She'd been trying for six years. Sara had laid it down. She had healed. She had reached acceptance. Maybe her extended collapse had allowed her the space to move on. Sara had paid a heavy price. Maybe Cady needed to allow herself to collapse. To be vulnerable enough to lose. Maybe she could gain only by being willing to lose.

She had extended periods of time where she felt like she was healed and had let it go, but she knew whatever stage of grief allows a person to genuinely move on had been interrupted by the abrupt nature of his departure and the complete lack of any sign as to what happened to him. For years now, her healing had revolved around accepting the mystery. Just when she would get close, a lead would pop up. She'd find a notice of a John Doe in a morgue or a tip would register on the website Cady had set up—someone claiming they saw someone matching the description. One woman wrote in last year to say she was sure her new husband was Victor. They always led nowhere but she could never resist following them.

She thought about their meeting at the *It's a Wonderful Life* celebration. She spent more time with him in the cold than she ever had in the hot summer months. When she thought of him, she often pictured him in his overcoat and gray flannel scarf, even though he had disappeared in July. The twinkle lights she strung on her porch were like a beacon in the dark for him to find her if he ever came back. Like the thousands of lights that covered Bailey Bridge the night they met.

Rosalind's death had cut her so deeply that she felt her old wound closing up. It was no easier finding the body than it was never finding the body. She had entertained a version of the story where he left of his own accord. But all versions led her to the same loss. Loss of Victor and loss of her life for the last six years. Perhaps she could look forward now instead of always looking back. She stared out at the darkness for a long time before she gave in to sleep and went inside.

CHAPTER 11

"BLUE. I'M GLAD you made it home. What's up?" Eric said as Blue got out of his car in the driveway. Eric was unloading two bags of groceries from his own car. "I got a few things for you here. I thought this might be a tough week so I just doubled what I got and you can put it in your fridge. I got you your near beer." Eric indicated the two six packs of Coors Light that were still in his opened trunk.

"Ah, the stuff that helps me keep my girlish figure," Blue said. He looked at Eric. "Beer is beer. Now, a good wine? That's another matter. And thanks. You didn't have to." Blue gripped his briefcase in his armpit and grabbed the beer.

"How you let that discerning palate loose on Coors Light is a mystery. But whatever. I needed groceries anyway. Let me take this stuff in and I'll bring in your stuff in a minute. Stick the beer into your fridge. I don't want it polluting mine." Eric took both bags into his garage apartment. He unloaded the English muffins, bananas, apples, single servings of blue cheese stuffed flank steak in metal tins, deli sliced ham, a frozen dinner, crackers, cheese, and sliced pepperoni. He had gotten the identical menu for Blue. When Eric came through Blue's back door with his bag of groceries and both steaks, Blue had already showered and changed into loose-fit jeans and an old twisted cotton short-sleeved Henley. He'd turned on the oven on his way through. He popped the caps off two beers.

"What a day," Blue sighed out as he toasted Eric to thank him for the beer and groceries. "You eat yet?"

"No, but I got us both steaks. They'll be done in less than twenty minutes. Won't even heat up the house." Eric tossed Blue the box of crackers. "Open up the crackers and cheese and we've got ourselves a gourmet dinner." He pronounced gourmet with an emphasis on the ending "t." Blue liked Eric's easy humor. There was nothing pretentious about Eric. Around Blue. Blue was aware of how Eric sometimes tried too hard around others. While that could make Blue uneasy at times, Eric was always comfortable when it was just the two of them. It was easier to be around Eric than even his own brothers.

"Deal," Blue said. Eric placed both of the steaks in the oven. Blue ripped open the crackers and Eric sliced off half a dozen pieces of the sharp white cheddar cheese and pulled a few slices of the pepperoni. They ate and drank until the steaks were done and then ate them like they had just come in from a hunt. They did not say a word until they were done eating. After they ate, they put their plates and silverware in the dishwasher and went out to Blue's front porch where Eric lit up a cigar. He offered Blue a cigar, as he always did, but Blue declined, as he always did, unless he were several beers into a long night of beer drinking. Blue hadn't had a cigar in a long, long time.

They sat on Blue's front porch as the sun was setting behind his house. His house on Center Street was in the heart of the Village of Waterloo. His street was quiet but during the school year there was a lot of traffic when school was starting in the morning and when school was letting out in the afternoon. The entrance to Waterloo Middle School, which was attached to Waterloo High School, was on Center Street. It was down several blocks from Blue's house, but he still noticed the traffic—cars with one parent at the wheel, kids in the back seat. School was not due to start for another month and a half, and Center Street felt like a ghost town after the storm had washed through. The sun was setting. The weekend was coming to a close.

"So. How goes it on the murder squad?" Eric asked after he had lit his cigar and put the one he had brought for Blue on the table between them.

Blue let the low humor pass without comment. "I don't know, man. Rosalind. I still can't believe it. I've worked cases of people I've known before. But Ms. M'Clintock?" Blue set his second beer down and rubbed his eyes. "It feels like everything has changed. Not just her life, but everything."

"You're drunk," Eric said, trying to lighten the mood. "Nothing has changed in the world. It's a tragedy. Anyone's life lost is a tragedy. I was crazy for her. Remember that?"

"Y-uh," Blue said. "I think everyone remembers that. If for that alone, I should be looking to you as a suspect."

"Don't be funny," Eric said. "She was so hot then. If she hadn't failed me, I'm sure I would have stolen her away."

"She didn't fail you." He looked at Eric as though they'd had that particular conversation before, then let it go, as he always had before. "I've been doing this a long time and I've never had it hit so close to home." Blue rocked rhythmically in his Adirondack rocker, dragging deeply on his beer.

Eric leaned forward, elbows on his knees, feet planted firmly on the ground. "We're going to find who did this. She deserves that. She deserves that and so much more."

"I need a bigger team. I need more resources. I feel like a fucking Sheriff Andy Taylor trying to solve a murder when all we know how to do is arrest thieves and wife beaters."

"Blue." Eric crooked his head to look at him.

"I know. Shit. I'm tired. I need to sleep." Blue's loyalty to the New York State Police ran deep and his commitment to keeping the people in his town safe was unending but when he felt threatened, like he'd failed to provide law and order and saw no clear way to adjust the balance of power so the good guys had the upper hand again, he had a tendency to blame his outfit for not giving him everything he needed lightning fast. It happened during every difficult case.

"They can't expect us to fight crime without our capes," he said to the night air. "You working tomorrow?" The feeling of blame also passed as soon as he said it out loud. He could only complain like that to his best friend.

"Yep," said Eric, "I got the morning shift at the mall. Got to protect and serve those who buy and sell."

"Okay." Blue ignored his self-deprecating humor. "When you get off, call me. I want to take your statement, too. I'm too tired right now to see straight, but I do want to dot all the i's and cross all the t's. You know?" Blue dragged the last of his beer. "I'm heading in. Feel free to sit out here and finish. If I don't go up to bed, you'll have to drag me up like the drunken sailor I was when we were in high school."

"Whatever you need, partner. I'm always here for you." Eric saluted, sat back in his chair and took a long drag on his cigar. Blue went inside, closed the front door and locked it. He climbed the stairs of his creaking old house, stripped to his boxer briefs and fell into bed. He slept within seconds and he never so much as twitched a muscle as the night wore off his exhaustion.

CHAPTER 12

ON MONDAY MORNING at 8:45, Cady headed down the stairs of her flat to open the library by 9:00. Hero padded silently down the stairs next to her. As she opened the doors to the library corridor, Hero slipped passed her and found his morning spot on the book shelf extension across from the circulation desk. He sat there every morning as the library buzzed to life around him. Today his ears were perked at full-alert. He eyed the room like a watch dog.

Alice Jones was already there preparing for the Toddler Time Summer Reading Hour held every Monday, Wednesday, and Friday at the library. The books and crafts that Alice chose were designed for children who had not yet started school. On any given day, between three and a dozen children attended with their parent. Alice was promoted to part-time Director of Children's Programming before Cady came to the library, and the two of them worked harmoniously together. She had raised eight children of her own and she always joked that eight was, in fact, not enough, and she wanted to work with kids forever. She had come in early because she knew Cady would need the extra help. They had texted a few times on Sunday and Cady had assured her, against Alice's protests, that she'd be there to open, that the order and routine would be comforting.

As Cady came through the double doors leading from her apartment to the main corridor of the library and locked them again behind her, Alice said, "How are you feeling?"

"About how you'd expect." The two women hugged. "How about you?"

Holding on to Cady's shoulders, Alice shook her head. "I'm sorry this happened on your birthday. I wanted to tell you that specifically. You know I'm sorry it happened at all, but I want you to know I'm thinking about you here, too."

Cady patted her arms and pulled away. "Thank you. I think I'm done with them. Birthdays." She eked out a smile and started toward her desk.

Natalie was also there. She had opened the cash register and was starting up the computers at the circulation desk. She had already turned on the public computers. As soon as Cady came through the alcove to the circulation room, she saw Natalie. Hero was already watching her.

"What are you doing here? You don't have to be here," Cady said as she walked directly to the circulation desk.

"I know. Thank you," Natalie said. "I couldn't stay home another minute. My mom was treating me like a head case. She's freaking me out way more than I already am. And I'm freaking out plenty. I had to do something other than sit around thinking about Ms. M'Clintock. I can't get her image out of my head and it's making me crazy."

Natalie had been Cady's permanent assistant for the last year. She was about to be a senior in high school and Cady would gladly give her a full-time job after she graduated. They had talked about Natalie's plans after high school. She was undecided. She was proceeding like she was going to apply for college, but Cady could tell she wasn't fully committed. When she found out Chris wasn't going to bother with college, she began to understand Natalie's hesitancy. For now, Cady was grateful to have both Natalie and Alice as trusted colleagues. There were a few other employees who came in for various shifts to help sort and stack books but Alice and Natalie made up the core of her staff.

"But what about your friends? Chris?" Cady asked. "Wouldn't you be better off taking some time to be with them?"

"I was at Chris's house yesterday. Plus, they all have to work or do something else today. I just need to be here doing something normal. I thought maybe you would be taking today off." She looked at Cady. "I'll stay with Mrs. Jones if you want to do that. You know there won't be hardly anyone in here today anyway."

"You're an angel, but no," Cady said as she wound around the counter to the staff side. "I'm feeling like you. If I don't keep busy, I might spontaneously combust. I'll tell you what I do need, though."

"Anything," Natalie said.

"We definitely don't need to have a book club meeting today. Would you text everyone and cancel it for this month? Tell them we'll hold *Ten Cents a Dance* over till our August date. Fletcher wouldn't mind under the circumstances." Cady knew Natalie didn't feel obligated to be at work. She could have taken the day or the week or as much time as she needed off. She'd told Sara to be sure Natalie knew that. But Natalie didn't operate that way. Natalie liked to keep busy. She liked her job and Cady noticed.

"But tell them if they want to come in and talk, they're more than welcome. Every one of you has had Rosalind as a teacher. With school not in session, it will take some time before they're able to set up formal grief counseling for you guys."

"Will that help *you* today?" Natalie asked.

Cady tilted her head. Natalie often surprised her with her maturity. So many kids were self-involved. Not even oppressively so, just factually so. Natalie had skipped that stage and moved right into empathetic young woman. Cady now had some more insight into why.

"I think it will." Cady smiled.

"Okay then. But while I do that, you may want to take a look at this." Natalie handed Cady the Monday edition of the *Finger Lakes Times*. The library had a subscription to several regional and national newspapers. During the summer months, there were no deliveries on the weekends because the library was closed on weekends from Memorial Day through Labor Day. It used to be open seven days a week, but the schedule had fallen prey to budget cuts like most every other community service.

Rosalind's death was again the headline story. "Murder in the Finger Lakes," read the headline. Oh God, Cady thought. That it was murder was now public knowledge. As she read the story, it was clear Delaney was not focusing on Rosalind's life, or even Rosalind's death. Delaney noted that the police were confirming that she had been murdered. She stated again what Rosalind's job was and who her husband was. But this story focused on the Convention Days festival as though the police had determined there was a nefarious connection between the site of the murder and the motive for the murder. Maybe Blue had discovered something since she last saw him. Delaney reported the names of the other organizers and a list of the details for which Rosalind was officially responsible. She had interviewed several people for the story.

Delaney gave the usual historical background for the convention, as did the feature article that ran every year but this one: The first Women's Rights Convention was held in Seneca Falls in 1848. Organized by Elizabeth Cady Stanton and her friends, it marked the since-recognized beginning of the movement that would lead to the passing of the 19th amendment to the Constitution giving women the right to vote seventy-two years later in 1920, as well as modern feminism in the United States. The women had come together at a social gathering one afternoon in mid-July in Waterloo. Their conversation turned to politics and the New York Married Woman's Property Rights Act, which had passed three months earlier. Lucretia Mott and Stanton had been discussing women's rights privately for years. Their enthusiasm built to such a pitch that afternoon that the women decided to hold a convention to discuss the conditions and rights of women. Five days later, the women gathered with some 300 others, including 40 men, in the neighboring town of Seneca Falls, where Stanton lived. Stanton had spent the five intervening days drafting the Declaration of Sentiments that would serve as the agenda for the convention. She followed the format of the Declaration of Independence and created 18 charges against men. To the 18 charges, Stanton drafted 11 resolutions that would make women equal in all areas. The ninth resolution boldly asserted that it was time women took up the responsibility of gaining for themselves the right to vote. Women's suffrage was the only resolution that met resistance at the convention. Stanton believed it to be critical because without the power to make laws, all other rights would be at the mercy of those who could. It was ultimately Frederick Douglass, a former slave and the then editor of the *Rochester North Star*, an anti-slavery weekly newspaper, published some 50 miles west of Seneca Falls, who persuaded the convention participants to accept the resolution.

As a monument to that original Convention, a refurbished Wesleyan Methodist Church, where the Convention was held, still stands in Seneca Falls across the street from People's Park. Built in 1843, it was a grand building at the time of the Convention in 1848. Today, it has been preserved as a tribute to the site where a profound change in American life was set in motion.

Cady got frustrated with the history lesson, as though this were a feature about the festival, and skimmed to the one quote that was made by a source who declined to be identified: "She fought with everyone who came in her wake the week before the festival." Cady knew from experience not to cross Rosalind during the week or so before the festival. Her nerves were always on edge and her temper flared. She got so stressed every year by the festival that every year she swore she would have nothing to do with it beyond attending the closing baseball game in future years. She cared so much about women's rights and honoring those women who organized and fought for their equality, and her own, right in Rosalind's own backyard more than 150 years ago, though. Every year, she got sucked back in and loved every minute of it, except for the several days leading up to the festival weekend. But this year was different. Ron was right when he said Rosalind was relaxed and having fun at the festival. She had even mentioned to Cady that she intended to take a spa retreat the weekend before the festival every year.

*　　*　　*

Cady couldn't believe this was the sole quote about Rosalind. From what details the article did give, as the one the day before, this one gave an incomplete picture of a passionate woman, dedicated to a cause. It painted her as a megalomaniac who ordered everyone around and was begging for a fight like the one she lost so violently on Saturday night. Someone fought with her, though. Someone had given that quote.

When she was finished reading the story for the second time, Cady looked up. "You cannot be serious. Delaney knew Rosalind, didn't she? Who is this person I'm reading in the paper about? I hope Ron is not reading these stories. I'm sure he will eventually, but I don't know if he could handle it right now."

"I know," Natalie said. "Makes her look like a real bitch. Sorry." She looked at Cady who was still scanning the paper. "I didn't know she was killed, though," Natalie continued. "This is the first I heard of that." Natalie shut her eyes as if to block out the picture forming in her mind.

The kids and their parents, all mothers, had begun arriving while Cady was still reading the paper. By the time she looked up, the children's room across the corridor from the circulation desk was filling up and sounded like a playground full of outside voices. "Let me go see if Mrs. Jones needs anything," Natalie said. She could not think about her teacher being murdered for one more second. She needed to keep moving.

As the morning wore on, Cady was not able to get any work done. She read all the stories in the papers covering

Rosalind's murder. They were all sounding about the same as if the reporters were all at the same press conference that told Rosalind's story in one way and one way only. There was something missing in each of the stories, although none of them lacked quite as much heart as Delaney's. In each story, the focus on the festival was bordering on a hatchet job. The festival had taken a lot of bad press over the years. A decade ago, the festival had been reduced to no more than some speakers, some walking tours, and an excuse for a drunken party on the streets of Seneca Falls for an entire weekend. Rosalind and her committee had changed all that. But once the benefit of the doubt is gone, it's a long road, if not an impossible climb, to gain it back. The newspapers reported the brawls from the past and although the festival had been a safe and family-friendly event for years, Rosalind's murder reduced it to its least hospitable moments.

At noon, Cady was about to go upstairs quickly and call Blue to see if there was anything else she could do to help with his investigation. She was stacking up the returned books on the rolling cart when Chris, Kiery, and Taylor came through the corridor and into the main room to the circulation desk. Jonathan slipped into the corridor a minute later, followed by the pizza delivery guy. Everyone in the book club had shown up.

"I'm glad you guys made it." Cady felt fragile at the sight of them.

"Natalie texted," Taylor said. "We all wanted to come."

"Here, I got the pizza," Chris said as he took it from the delivery guy while Cady paid. "Can we set up in back?" He started toward the fiction room without waiting for an answer.

"Alice, are you okay watching the desk during book club time?" Cady asked.

"No problem," Alice said. "You go on back. Take your time. I'm fine out here."

Natalie followed Chris and the pizza back to the fiction room and laid it on the T-shaped table where they usually gathered to talk about the book they had read. Hero ambled after them and resumed his place on the chair at the head of the table closest to the front door. He sat with all his paws gathered together as if he were invited for dinner.

"I'll get napkins and plates," Kiery said quietly and headed to the supply cupboard.

"I brought these cannolis for after," Taylor said. "I figured we needed something extra sweet and creamy today. Ms. Colette gets a chocolate one," she said to everyone. If Natalie was the adult of the group, Taylor was the gourmet. She was also obsessed with chocolate. She said it's what gave her her silky chocolate skin. Taylor was always making jokes about her skin color. She was from one of the few African-American families in Waterloo. Cady always sensed that Taylor was trying to get the upper hand. If she drew attention to herself first, no one else would need to.

They served themselves and settled into their usual spots around the table. "You guys are too much," Cady said. "I'm glad you came," Cady said again as she took the napkins from Kiery. She noticed Kiery's hands were shaking. Jonathan hovered, not offering to help, not making small talk.

They all fell silent as they filled their plates and found a chair. They ate and drifted into their own thoughts about the death of their friend and teacher. Jonathan was in her class in 12th grade. The rest had had her in 10th grade and were on their way either in the next month or the next two years to having her as a teacher in their senior year.

"Ms. M'Clintock was a great teacher," Natalie said, naturally taking charge. "I remember in 10th grade when she took us to see *Macbeth* at the Smith Opera House in Geneva. She got us backstage to talk to the actors after. Shakespeare was like a Rubik's Cube to me before that, but that play was so cool. She was so cool."

"Yeah," Chris said, "I remember when she let me read *The Hunger Games* for my end of the semester book project. I was afraid to ask her because I thought she would think I was trying to cheat the system. Nat had just read all three books and was begging me to read them. Now, me. I'm not a reader. You know I'm in the book club for the ladies." He laughed and Natalie rolled her eyes. "I thought I'd kill two birds, you know." He stopped and looked around awkwardly. "Ms. M'Clintock said to me," he continued, "that if there was a book that would hold my interest of the appropriate reading level—she meant not a picture book, in my case—that I thought I could write ten pages of analysis on, she was all for it. Nat said I could write a book on that book. Whatever, but I didn't have any trouble filling ten pages, I'll tell you that."

"I remember when we read *Beloved* and she cried." Taylor turned to Cady. "It wasn't like she fell to pieces or anything, but when she was talking about the story one day, her voice cracked. She felt things on a level that most grown-ups I know don't seem to. I could tell that about her."

"We won't get to have her for our senior year," Kiery said, her own voice cracking. Hero had nestled into Kiery's lap after she was done with her lunch and had promptly begun to snore. She rested her hand on his belly. "I just realized that. It's like there's this big hole, like something bigger than her is missing all of a sudden." Kiery looked at Cady.

Cady had been listening to the memories of her dear friend, twirling her ring. Suddenly, she felt her face flush. They all looked at her and then in the same split second looked away. She had never talked about Victor with any of them. It was not a secret, but all of these kids would have been actual kids when he disappeared. There was silence as they all stumbled for something to say next.

"Ms. West fought with her on Friday night," Jonathan said. Everyone turned to him in unison. He hadn't said anything beyond hello since he had arrived. He'd sat there dull and quiet and although Cady was no grief counselor, she knew enough not to force any of them to speak if they didn't want to. She had always been comfortable with silences, although Jonathan's silences had a tendency to be unnerving.

"What do you mean Delaney . . . Ms. West fought with Rosalind?" Cady said.

"I saw them," Jonathan said. He leaned forward in his chair, both hands splayed out on the table in front of him. "They didn't see me, I don't think. But they were spitting mad. I couldn't hear everything they were saying, but they were fighting about the story Ms. West was writing about Convention Days." He leaned back. Pulled his right foot up to cross over his left knee. "It didn't mean anything to me at the time, but I went back and checked on Sunday, when I found out she was dead, and the story that appeared on Saturday, the day Ms. M'Clintock was killed, was only a little story. Nothing specific about this year. They must not have settled whatever their fight was."

Cady blinked at him. She'd never heard him speak so many words at one time. It had never occurred to her to check the newspaper for the write up of the start of the festival on Friday. "Did you tell the police this?" Cady asked.

"No. They haven't asked me anything," Jonathan said.

"Well, make sure you do. I'm sure it means nothing, but all the information should be out on the table. Let Detective Emerson sort it out."

CHAPTER 13

LIKE ON CUE in a blockbuster movie, Blue came through the front door of the library. He turned into the main circulation room and seconds later, came back through the corridor to where the book club sat finishing their cannolis. Hero bolted off of Kiery's lap and cantered over toward Blue.

"Detective," Cady said as she stood up. "We were just talking about you. How are things on the case?" She walked around the table to meet him at the alcove that marked the entrance to the fiction room. She did not expect he would fill her in, especially in front of the book club kids, but she was more than a little glad to see him. He had texted her to see if she was holding her book club today, but she thought that meant he'd find her later, when she was free.

"I'm sorry, Cady, but I'm here to take Kiery Fuller in for questioning."

It felt like the air sucked out of the room. Kiery looked up. She had begun to clean up the pizza detritus when Hero jumped off her lap, but when she heard her name, she stopped.

"What are you talking about?" Cady said slowly, lowering her voice.

"Kiery?" He put his hand on Cady's shoulder and led her gently back to the center of the fiction room where the kids were sitting at the table. Kiery stood frozen holding a pizza box. "I need you to come with me. I need to ask you a few questions."

"Blue," Cady said. "She's not going anywhere with you. What's this all about?"

"I need to ask Kiery a few questions," he repeated.

The kids erupted when he spoke. Taylor stepped in front of Kiery. Natalie took the box out of Kiery's hand. Chris moved toward Blue as they were all speaking at once.

"About what?" Cady's voice was getting louder. She moved over to where Kiery stood.

"That's between me and Kiery." Blue was starting to bristle. He had known this would be a difficult moment but he was not interested in fighting with Cady about doing his job.

"She's a child. She's not going anywhere. Kiery," she said, keeping her eyes on Blue, "call your parents."

"Her parents are on their way to the station already. Mr. Peterman is picking them up. We're meeting them at the station."

"Eric? What's going on here? Can I talk to you? Privately?" Cady's jaw was set and she started to walk toward the front entrance of the library. Blue followed her. There was only one way out of the library unless you set off the emergency alarm by using the back door. He wasn't worried about Kiery bolting.

When they stepped out into the sunshine, so bright it made Cady squint and Blue put on his sunglasses, Cady said in a low voice with rising anger, "What is happening here? You come in here like the SWAT team and try to take one of my students out of here like a common criminal? Is that why you texted me? To see if your fugitive was with me?"

"This is not your business," he said.

"The hell it isn't. These kids are with me. What happens to them is absolutely my business. You can't use me to get to them."

"A: there was no SWAT team," he said. "And B: Kiery is a suspect and I need to question her to determine if an arrest needs to be made."

"You couldn't have called me first so I could get her alone or bring her myself?" Cady was nearly yelling. "You couldn't have brought her parents here with you. She's sixteen years old for God's sake."

"Cady," he said taking off his glasses and looking her in the eyes, "she is a murder suspect. I don't need your permission to pick her up anywhere and question her. I asked Deuce to pick up her parents as a courtesy. That's not standard operating procedure but I thought given her age, it might make things go smoother. At sixteen I can question her with no one present. She's an adult in the eyes of the law."

"I can't believe you'd come here with that load of crap," she said. "You came to me for help yesterday and today you come and ambush me. There is no reason you couldn't have called me."

"Cady." Blue let out a long sigh. "Maybe I should have called. I'm so fucking exhausted right now I can hardly see straight. Pardon me for my bad manners in not keeping you informed."

She did not bite.

"Look," Blue continued, "I met with Sara this morning. I asked her about the records from the festival that you and I found were missing."

She raised her eyebrows at the insinuation that he had anything to do with finding the records. He went on.

"She showed me everything you had found. She also showed me the paper notes from the weekend's worth of activity that she hadn't had a chance to enter yet. What I found there means I have to bring Kiery in for questioning."

Cady was torn between asking about Mulligan to get the pressure off of Kiery and wanting to protect him as well.

"Have you followed up on *all* your other leads?" she hedged.

"Cady, how I conduct this investigation is not up for discussion."

"You're not taking her anywhere without me." She walked past him into the library. "Stay here," Cady snapped as she flung open the door and went inside. Blue obliged not because she'd ordered him to, but because he could see this all going smoother with Cady's help.

Five minutes later, Cady and Kiery came out of the front door with the whole book club in tow. Cady had her arm around Kiery. Taylor was holding Kiery's hand. Cady had arranged with Alice to take care of things at the library until it closed at 5:00. Cady didn't carry a purse. She had her keys in the pocket of her cargo pants so she was perpetually mobile.

"I'll follow you down and wait until her parents arrive." Cady was visibly calmer, although Blue suspected that was a front for Kiery's benefit.

"What did I do?" Kiery asked Blue. She was frail, a slip of a thing. She was the same height as Cady, but where Cady was thin and muscular, Kiery was just thin. She was pale. She had dark brown shoulder-length hair with bangs cut across her forehead. She was a quiet, artistic girl. She was sometimes mistaken for emo because the look in her eyes suggested a darkness that never quite surfaced.

She and Taylor had been best friends since kindergarten. Taylor had blossomed into a voluptuous outgoing girl. She was the group's fashionista. She wore the T. J. Maxx version of haute couture. She was always put together. Her hair was clipped short to her head and she always wore large dangling earrings. She was all curves where Kiery was lithe and sinewy like a runway model.

Taylor was gregarious to Kiery's quiet spark. Taylor was friends with everyone at school while Kiery's friends only extended to the book club and the adults in her painting workshop with Cady.

"I just need you to answer a few questions," Blue said.

"Don't worry," Cady said. "Your parents are meeting us at the station. You don't have to say anything until they get there."

Blue sighed. "I'll handle it from here, Ms. Colette."

Cady let Blue take Kiery to his car. She told the kids not to worry and that everything would be all right. She asked them to go back in and clean up the fiction room. She asked them to stay calm.

The trooper station was a five-minute drive from the Waterloo Library. Cady got in her compact Honda CR-V, rolled down all the windows against the July midday heat, and followed them to the station's parking lot. As she drove, she fought with her phone. She could not drive holding it so she tapped it into speaker mode and speed dialed Sara. She could not imagine why Sara had pointed the finger at Kiery for anything having to do with what happened to Rosalind. Cady was starting to panic when Sara's phone went straight to voicemail. "Dammit!" she yelled at the air. She flipped on her air conditioning even though she was only minutes from the station. Her temperature was rising well beyond the pot boiler of the day. She figured Sara was at Ron's talking over funeral arrangements and would have turned off her phone out of respect.

When she pulled into the trooper station parking lot, Eric was there already and Kiery's parents were filing out of their car, parked next to his Mustang. They both stood by Blue's car as he parked, and when Kiery got out, they took her in their arms.

"Mom, what's happening?" Kiery said as the tears finally started to flow.

"They just want to talk to you, Sweetie," her mom said into her ear as she continued to hold her. "Don't be afraid. We're both here." She then turned to Blue, "What do you think you're doing? Bringing in a kid without any proof? She's got rights too." She had left Kiery and deigned to confront Blue like she was ready for a cat fight.

"Mrs. Fuller," Blue started. Eric stepped up to where Blue was standing.

"This is bullshit," Kiery's father shouted. "We want a lawyer."

Blue took a deep breath. He had expected Eric would calm them down. Maybe there was no calming them down.

"Would you like to talk about this inside?" Blue said. "It's awfully hot out here."

"Bre," Cady said. "Let's go inside. You don't want to do this out here."

"We're not going anywhere until you bring us a lawyer," her father said to Blue.

"Okay," Blue said. "We can do that. I can hold Kiery while you go hire a lawyer. I don't provide lawyers. If you need a court-appointed lawyer, paid for by the state of

New York, then you can file the paperwork and give your financials to the judge and he will make a determination as to your eligibility. Kiery and I will wait if that's what you want to do. Or, we can go inside where it's cool and Kiery and I can have a little talk. It's actually up to Kiery." He looked at Kiery. "Would you like a lawyer?"

"Am I under arrest?" Kiery said.

"No. I just need to talk to you. It's that simple."

"I don't need a lawyer," Kiery said.

"Kiery!" her mother yelled.

"Mom, it's okay."

"Fine. But we want to be in the room when you talk to her."

"Mom. Really, I'll be okay," Kiery said.

Her parents relented. Their body language had not caught up with their agreement, but Blue proceeded anyway.

When Blue got Kiery settled in an interview room, Cady and Jay and Breandra paced in the waiting room, which was more like an ICU waiting room than an inviting place for people to wait. Stark and white with cushionless plastic chairs.

Eric had gotten off the early shift and was still in his uniform. He had offered to pick up Kiery's parents when Blue mentioned he was going to track down Kiery at the library. Having Kiery's parents there was not necessary so Blue hadn't asked a fellow trooper to do it. He told Eric to make it clear that they were being asked to come as a courtesy only. Eric sat in the waiting room with the pacers.

"Did you know Rosalind M'Clintock?" Blue asked Kiery.

"Yeah." Kiery sat on the edge of her chair and slipped her hands under her thighs.

"How did you know her?" he asked.

"She was my English teacher last year. I had her during second block every other day. We're also in the same painting workshop that Ms. Colette teaches on Fridays."

"How did you do in Ms. M'Clintock's class?"

"Okay." Kiery shrugged.

"What grade did you get?" Blue asked

"I got pretty much B's most of the year."

"What was your final grade?" Blue asked as he wrote on his yellow pad.

"I got a C. Minus," Kiery said.

"Why did you get a C minus if you'd been getting B's all year long?"

Kiery shifted in her chair. "Cause I didn't do so good on the final project."

"Why not?" Blue asked.

"Cause it was hard," Kiery said.

Blue raised his eyes from his yellow pad. He paused and looked her in the eye, inviting her to fill the silence with the rest of her answer.

"Cause I didn't turn it in," Kiery said.

"What was the project?"

"It was a 10-page paper on a book. I read the book but I'm not much of a writer." For the seniors, Blue knew the project was the same except the paper was a 20-page minimum and the quality was expected to be college-level analysis. He remembered his paper for Ms. M'Clintock. He hadn't had her for 10th grade English, but she was his English teacher his senior year. He'd read *The Sun Also Rises* and his paper analyzing the novel in the context of World War I was some of the most sophisticated writing he had ever done, even through his four years of college.

"What book did you read?" He needed to throw her some softballs to get her to relax a little.

"*White Oleander*."

"Did you like it?"

"Yeah. I could relate," she said.

"Then why didn't you do the final project?" he asked.

"It just got away from me. I started it. I turned in all the stuff leading up to it. I'm glad I didn't fail."

Blue tried another line of questioning. "How well did you know Ms. M'Clintock through the painting class?"

"Not much. I mean, we painted. I'm the only kid in the class. All the rest are adults. They talked some but not too much to me." Kiery sat up straighter. "I go there to paint. Ms. Colette gives us the paint and the brushes and the canvases. She sometimes lets me into her studio during the week. I love to paint." When she was done, she crossed her arms and hunched her shoulders.

"You cold?" Blue asked.

"A little. I'm always cold." Blue looked over his shoulder at the two-way mirror. A minute later, a trooper tapped on the door and entered a foot in. He handed Blue Kiery's mom's sweater and stepped back out into the hall, shutting the interrogation room door behind him.

Blue resumed after Kiery had pulled the sweater on over her head. She had worn a white tank top and skinny black jeans to the library. She checked groceries at Wegmans during the summer and she had worked the early morning shift. She requested the time of her book club off. She tried to get Friday evenings off for the painting workshop but that wasn't always workable. Most teenagers got scheduled for the evening and weekend shifts. She had started the job when school let out in June. She was hoping to keep working there during the school year, but she hadn't yet asked her manager whether that would be possible. Wegmans had been on the top 100 places to work in *Fortune* magazine for years. Kiery liked her job and knew that her only chance to go to college was to get one of the generous scholarships Wegmans gave to their graduating seniors every year. The C- she had earned in English last year had ended her chances of getting an academic scholarship. She had never been top of her class anyway, but such a low grade in a core course put her out of the running for good.

He tried a different tactic, the one he'd had in mind since talking with Sara.

"Did you paint a painting called," he looked down at his notes, "*Poppy Fields*?"

"Yes," she said without elaboration.

"Do you have the painting in your possession now?"

"No," she said.

"Where is it now?" Blue asked. He'd thrown her the softballs, now it was time she told him what he'd brought her there for.

"I don't know," she said.

"Kiery. Is that true? You don't know where the painting is?"

"It's true. Someone bought it but I don't know who," she said.

"Did you get paid for the painting?" he asked.

"Not yet."

That wasn't the right answer. Not yet? He tried to remain calm. "So you will be paid for the painting?"

"Yes. Well, I don't know how now."

He looked at her waiting for her to explain. She was hiding something and he was getting tired of pecking it out of her.

"Ms. M'Clintock was supposed to pay me," she volunteered. "I don't know how it will happen now, but I'm not worried about it."

"So you knew that Ms. M'Clintock put your painting in the silent auction?" Blue asked, watching his lead fold up and scurry out of the room.

"Yes."

"Why wasn't it listed under your name? Because you're a minor?"

"No," Kiery said. She looked over his shoulder at the two-way window again. "I didn't want anyone to know I had painted it." She looked up again. "I didn't want my parents to know who painted it. They don't understand. They would tell me to learn a skill. Do something useful."

"How did you know the painting had sold?" Blue asked.

"Ms. M'Clintock sent me a Facebook message telling me it had gotten the highest price at the auction. She was excited. I was too, when I found out. She was so nice. We never talked much outside of class. But she liked the painting. When I told her I wouldn't sell it and why, she said she would cover for me and no one would ever have to know. I owe her my first semester at college. Community college, but still."

Knowing Kiery was not the hottest suspect anymore, but to dot his i's, Blue asked, "Were you invited to Ms. Colette's birthday party last Saturday night?"

"Yeah," Kiery said.

"Did you go?"

She shook her head.

"Why not?" Blue looked up from his yellow pad.

She bit her lip. She looked just beyond his shoulder to the two-way mirror. He saw where she looked and turned around to look over his shoulder.

"There's no one there but the guy running the recording," Blue said as he turned back to her.

Kiery started picking at the skin around her thumbnail. "We just didn't go," she said.

"Your parents were invited, too, right?"

"Yeah," she said. "We were gonna go, but we didn't. I felt bad. I knew Ms. Colette would have had a nice party."

"Where were you on Saturday night?" Blue asked.

"Stayed home." Kiery shrugged. She looked like she was ten rather than a nearly grown woman. The more Blue questioned her, the more she shrank into herself. The smaller she became.

"Were your parents home with you?" he asked.

"Yeah."

"Were you together all night? Can they confirm you were home all night?"

A tear ran down Kiery's cheek. "No."

"Kiery, why not?" Blue leaned forward and put his elbows on the table. His instincts told him the confession he was about to hear was not that Kiery had killed Rosalind on Saturday night.

She looked away. "Because they were drunk and fighting even before we were supposed to leave." She had all but evaporated from the room. She scanned the floor to her right. She chewed her lip. Her eyes were glassy where they were vulnerable a second before.

"Did they hurt you?" Blue said. He wanted to reach out and hold her hand. This frail girl who had nearly broken through a minute ago. She was steely and taut now.

"No."

"They're not going to hear the tape we're making, Kiery," Blue assured her.

"They didn't," she said softly. "They hurt each other. They always hurt each other. Well, my dad always hurts my mom. If you think I could hurt Ms. M'Clintock because she gave me a bad grade, or even if she *had* stole my painting," she took a deep stuttering breath, "I couldn't. I couldn't hurt anyone. You look at my mom. She won't let you but if she did, you'd see. I could never hurt anyone."

"But they can't confirm you were home," Blue sighed. He wished she could give him an alibi.

"No. They don't know anything about me. I could come and go any time of day or night. But I didn't that night. I was online. You can check if you want."

"Facebook? You were chatting with someone?" he asked.

"No. Not chatting. All my friends were at the party that night. I was on, though. I was logged on as my avatar. My other avatar. No one knows it's me but you can check."

"But you can log on from your cell phone," he said.

"I don't have a cell phone."

"I thought every teenager had a cell phone."

Kiery looked at the door where on the other side her parents paced in the hallway waiting for her to be finished. "My dog ate mine," she said.

CHAPTER 14

CADY, BLUE, AND ERIC sat in the waiting room at the Trooper barracks after the Fullers had taken their daughter home. Blue had decided he did not have enough to hold Kiery and that he knew where she'd be when and if he needed her. Her alibi was shaky but could be checked. He could ask Cady to check it but he was hoping to get on-the-ground computer support in the next day or two. Her motive, if he could even call it that, had crumbled. Blue was tired. This case wasn't wrapping itself up neatly and if he didn't find a promising lead in the first few days, he knew the chances of solving the case decreased exponentially as the clock ticked on. Blue wasn't inclined to discuss the details of his investigation with either of them, but Cady pushed.

"What could Sara have said to you to make you think that gentle girl had anything to do with Rosalind's death?"

Cady asked. She was more perplexed than angry after having waited through the long questioning session.

As Blue remembered what his conversation with Sara had been about, he used the long-standing police tactic of simply not answering. Sara had showed him the ledger for the silent auction. He'd seen in the brochure of events that was part of the crime scene paraphernalia that the silent auction closed just before the keynote speaker took the stage on Saturday night. There was an entry for $2,550.00 for a painting called *Poppy Fields*. The painting had been listed in the auction as having been painted by Anonymous. Sara and Blue were both struck by the entry in the ledger that said, "$2,550.00, Poppy Fields, Rosalind M'Clintock." Sara had told Blue that the painting was painted by Kiery in Cady's studio. She'd worked on it for several sessions. She'd been proud of it. Sara had not known why the painting was listed as anonymous, nor why the payment credit went to Rosalind directly. Sara told Blue that she was sure there was an explanation.

Twenty-five hundred and fifty dollars was not a sum worth committing murder over, but he'd seen murder committed for less. It's not the sum as much as the motive behind stealing the money. If Rosalind was trying to steal from Kiery, she could have gotten angry enough to have lashed out in a blind rage. Blue knew it was thin, but it was a lead. He had to follow the investigation where it led.

"Blue. Let us help," Cady said.

"It doesn't matter now," he said. "It looks like Kiery's in the clear. I was concerned about the painting that Kiery sold at the silent auction. It looked like Rosalind was trying to pocket the money. It didn't seem like murder money but to a kid like Kiery, it well could have been."

Cady almost laughed but refrained because she could tell Blue was in no mood. "I wish you would have told me what the lead was. I could have disabused you of that notion at the library. If Sara didn't know about the deal that Kiery and Rosalind had made then Rosalind was better at keeping secrets than Kiery was. She told me that night before she left my studio. She was a little starstruck that any piece of hers was getting any attention. She was sure it wouldn't sell at all. I hadn't realized it had."

Blue smiled. "I'll make sure to share all my leads with you from now on. That was the only thing untoward about the festival. That I can see anyway. There's some angle I'm missing." He looked at Cady. "Yes, there are other leads that I am working on." Cady cringed. She knew he meant Mulligan was up at the suspect board.

At this, Eric decided to join in. He'd been listening to the story about why Kiery was not a viable suspect any longer with interest.

"And Ron told you where he was when Rosalind was killed," Eric said.

"Yes, but Ron reads for a living," Blue said as he sat making random doodles in his notebook on the other side of the counter. "Just because he could tell me the plot of the book on his coffee table doesn't mean he was actually at home reading when he says he was."

"So, he effectively has no alibi?" Cady asked.

Blue did not respond but looked up from his notepad. He stood up. "It's not your coffee, but it's caffeinated. Want some?" Cady shook her head. "Deuce?"

"Sure," Eric said.

"I know Kiery," Cady said. "People must always say that, huh? But I know about Kiery. She's got a sadness about her. I see it in her art. I see it in her every move. But she's not got a violent bone in her body."

"Homicide isn't always intended," Blue said as he brought the coffee to Eric and set it on the counter. "Sometimes people do things accidentally. Sometimes people have a lapse in mental capacity. Sometimes emotional trauma drives them beyond rational thought. Sometimes just for an instant."

"But what would be her motive?" Eric said, taking the cup and sitting down again. "Her parents told us out here that Kiery didn't do well in Rosalind's class." Eric snorted a laugh out. "If that's a motive, sign me up. She made me fail a hundred years ago. Didn't make me want to kill her."

"She doesn't have an alibi," said Cady looking at Blue. Blue sat back in his chair and tapped his pen against the inside of his left ring finger. "She's no more a suspect than Ron is. Am I right?"

Blue tapped his pen.

Cady ignored that Blue was ignoring her. "Okay, you're not going to like this, but a thought occurred to us today."

"Us?" Blue said.

"My students and me," Cady said. "They came by not for the book club but just to talk about Rosalind and what had happened." She hesitated. "What about Delaney?"

Blue stopped mid-tap.

"What *about* Delaney?" he asked.

"She was overheard having a raging argument with Rosalind on Friday night," Cady said. "You can't ignore someone having a pissing match with someone one day and the next day one of them is found murdered."

"What on earth does Delaney have to do with this?" Blue stood up.

She stood up and came to the counter. "If Mulligan fighting with Rosalind makes him a suspect, the same has to go for Delaney."

"I'd say it isn't the same at all." Blue's neck was reddening.

"Calm down," Eric said to Blue as he put his coffee down. They were all standing now. "What was the fight about?" he asked Cady. "Who overheard it?"

"I'd rather not say who overheard it," Cady said, backing away from the counter and standing straight. "But it was about the story Delaney was writing about the festival. The story that didn't get printed. Apparently it was knock down, drag out. Wouldn't you think you at least have to ask her about it?"

"I am not questioning anybody on the say so of 'someone' who refuses to be named," Blue raised his voice. His body was still, his hands gripped the edge of the counter.

"Look," Cady said. "I know as well as anyone what it feels like to suspect that someone you love has done something wrong. Half the people who live in this town think Victor ran off. That he either ran off with another woman or ran from the law for something illegal. You think that idea hasn't occurred to me, too? He disappears on my birthday without a trace, and for six years I wonder every day what took him away from here. If I ever saw him again, you bet your ass I'd ask him. Right? Your ex-wife had a public screaming match with Rosalind and the next day Rosalind is murdered. You don't see it as your duty to at least question her? If she denies the argument, I'll give you the name of the person who witnessed it. Will that help?"

Blue and Cady stared at each other. Blue's jaw flexed. Eric was caught between them. "I know what it's like, Blue," Cady said. "You don't even want to contemplate someone you love has done something bad. But unless you entertain the thought and investigate like you're trained to do, that thought will haunt you."

"Back at you with Kiery and Ron. Maybe even Mulligan. They're all suspects and you can't bear that thought," Blue scored.

"That's why they pay you the big bucks, Trooper," Cady said. "To bear it." Silence filled the room.

"Okay," Eric broke into the tension. "What are the chances of this being some stranger to us all? We all have to get used to the idea that we most likely know the person who did this. Or know someone who knows who did it. I mean, what are there, like twenty people who live in this whole county?"

Blue broke away from Cady's stare. "Twenty-five, at last count," he said.

Eric laughed to lighten the mood. "Delaney, for all her amazing qualities," Eric said, "*is* a hothead. You of all people know that. There's no chance she's capable of killing anyone, but you said yourself, sometimes it's an accident. Sometimes people explode in the heat of the moment. Delaney is the hottest woman I know." Blue snapped his head toward Eric, his eyes flared.

"I'll question her," Blue said, his body alert. "But if it's going to be a valid tip, you have to give me a name," he said to Cady.

"Why can't it be anonymous?" Cady asked. "If someone called into your tip line and refused to leave their name, would you decline to follow up?"

"Cady. It's my ex-wife." His plea was genuine.

"Jonathan Peck," she said. "He never said I couldn't tell you. I told him to tell you himself so you'll probably hear from him soon. He's one of the students in my book club for high schoolers. Well, he just graduated. He didn't actually graduate. He failed Rosalind's English class as well."

"Does she pass anyone?" Eric spit out.

"Did," Cady said. "Did she pass anyone? And yes, she did. Does that make Jonathan a suspect because he failed her class?" she asked Blue.

"Let's just say I'll want to check his alibi," Blue said, knowing he'd already be on the list of possibly disgruntled students his team was checking out. "He was at your party in the park, right?"

"Actually, no," Cady said. "He wasn't there. Well, he stopped by before the party really got started. Just for a minute."

"Was he invited?" Eric asked. Blue looked at him.

"Yes," she said. "All the book club kids were invited. Their parents, too."

"Why didn't he stay?" Blue asked.

"I honestly don't know," Cady said. "He's not the sociable type. I'm surprised he came at all. It's not like there was a formal RSVP list. Just a picnic in the park with some cake. We didn't even want to invite him but when we decided to invite the club, we couldn't very well exclude him. We only invited the kids because of Natalie. I never asked him why he didn't stay. Didn't ask Kiery or Taylor why they weren't there at all. When I saw them today at the library, it didn't seem to matter."

"It may very well matter," Blue said. "I have no idea yet what matters."

It was getting late. Alice would have closed up the library.

"Why don't we head out and get something to eat?" Eric said. He took his keys from his duty belt and stood up, readying to go. "I just have to get out of this uniform first."

"Oh, that sounds good, but I'm going to pass," Cady said. "I need to be heading home." She stood up and stretched. She was exhausted and would have paid her retirement fund for a four-poster bed and a sleep mask to appear right then and there.

"Yeah, me too, but I'm not heading home yet," Blue said. "Everyone's out on the road, so I can get some work done here quietly. Shift change doesn't come for another two hours. I'll catch you there when I get home," he said to Eric. "Leave me some take-out."

"You got it." Eric and Cady started walking toward the door. "Why don't I take you home, Cady?"

"Thanks, Eric, but I drove. I'm all set."

Cady stopped. "I'm going to visit your little prisoner's room. Down the hall, to the right?" she asked Blue.

Eric stopped.

"Yes," Blue said.

"Thanks," she said. "Hey," she turned to Eric, "thanks for the offer. Both offers."

"Sure thing," he shifted awkwardly. "Sleep well when you get there." He bent down and kissed her on the cheek, brushing the crease of her lips.

"I will. You too." She stood there for a half a beat.

"I'll catch you later," Eric said to Blue as he put his hand up. He started out the door. Cady started down the hall. Blue stood at the counter, his whole body vibrating.

CHAPTER 15

WHEN CADY CAME out of the restroom, Blue was standing at the back counter, pouring another cup of coffee. "That stuff is going to make you sick," she said.

"I know. Sure I can't convince you to drink the Kool-Aid with me?"

"No thanks." She rubbed her stomach. "I'm already not feeling well."

"You okay? Why don't you sit down?"

"Thanks. I'm fine." She scrunched up her face. "This is surreal. It's doing a number on me."

He sat behind the desk in the reception area. She sat in the chair at the edge of the desk and shifted to face him.

He leaned forward. He didn't ask her to explain, but he indicated full interest if she were inclined to talk.

"It's like six years ago." She looked around. "You've given the place a facelift since Victor went missing, but the layout is the same. We sat here six years ago talking about what might have happened to him." She could never bring herself to say Victor was dead. She believed it in her heart, but she couldn't say the words. Only that he "went missing." It was the only truth she knew for sure.

"I couldn't solve that one," she said. "You couldn't solve that one. I need this one solved. This might be just another case to you, but I feel like my guts have been ripped out. I loved Rosalind. She was one of my dearest friends. She was a good and decent person. I loved Victor. We were supposed to grow old together. I can't live through another unknown."

"It's not just another case, Cady. None of them are just another case. I take my work very seriously."

She looked at him.

"I took Victor's case seriously."

"I know." She looked away.

"We're going to find out who did this," he said as he reached out and put his hand on hers.

"I wish I could believe that," she said pulling her hand away. "It's not that I don't believe you'll try." She looked at him quickly to reassure him. "I don't think I can live with two unsolved mysteries in my own back yard. I don't get close to many people. After Victor. I was so thrown by that. By his disappearance. I didn't think I would live through it. If he had died, I think it would have been easier. Closure. People need closure." She looked into his eyes. "I've had to find my own closure on Victor. I know he's dead," she paused. "I've never said that out loud. I've known for years. I've mourned him. I loved him and he's gone. When I think of Rosalind hanging in that water by the strap of her costume I can barely see straight. Do you know how close Ron came to being in my shoes? Never knowing what happened to her?"

"I know how awful this is for you," Blue said gently. "I can put your mind at ease in that small regard, though. If Rosalind's dress hadn't got caught on that hook, she would have sunk, yes. But she would have surfaced. At some point, unless she was weighted down, which she wasn't, she would have surfaced."

"Yeah, I suppose in a morbid way, that is a comfort," Cady said. "It's the not knowing that has been the burden all these years. No. That's not true. Yes. It is. It's both." She smiled. "It's just that if he had cheated on me and left me for another woman, I could have gotten mad and gotten over it. If he were murdered, I could have gotten mad and gotten over it. If he died accidentally, same. It's the not knowing."

She looked at him and leaned forward. "I have to know what happened to Rosalind. I'm sure Ron feels the same way, but I am only speaking for me. I feel like I may be able to move ahead if I can just know this one thing."

His onyx eyes held hers. "I will not give up until I find out. I will not let you down again." He paused. "Contrary to popular opinion, I am not in the habit of disappointing women." He crinkled a smile. "I've investigated a lot of homicides in my time. Even before the Violent Crime Task Force was created. There's not a lot of violent crime here," he paused again, meeting her gaze, "relatively speaking, but I've been a trooper in other parts of the state. The American underbelly is alive all over."

Cady sat back in her chair. "This isn't a case that sits well with you either."

"No, ma'am," he said as he eased back in his own chair and picked up his coffee cup. "Rosalind had become a friend since I moved back here."

"I meant about Delaney, too," Cady said rubbing her stomach. "I'm sure she had nothing to do with any of this."

"Whether she did or didn't, it's not going to be easy to talk to her about it. It's not easy to talk to her about anything."

It was Cady's turn to inquire without asking.

"It seems we both have a fractured past when it comes to love," he said.

"You guys did all right. That little girl of yours is worth the stars and the moon, isn't she?"

"Of course. She's my heart. But Delaney? We were good for a long time. Sometimes I think it all went bad because I brought her here."

"To Waterloo?" Cady asked. "She didn't want to say goodbye city life?"

"No. She did. Well sort of. She wanted to make me happy. We talked ourselves into believing it was the right thing. Or I talked her into believing it. It was the right thing for me to come back home. It was the right thing to raise Mollie in a beautiful place like this, but it was not the right thing for us as a couple."

"Seems like it would be hard to see it that simply," she said. "Was that the reason you guys broke up? I'm sorry. That's probably too personal."

"No. It's all right." She gave. He gave. He leaned side-ways onto the arm of his chair. "She needed her space." He crooked his head to the side to look at Cady. "Cliché, huh? Especially in a place where we have nothing but open space. Truth is we weren't connecting for a long time. Nothing in particular happened to set us off. She just up and decided one day. To me, it would have been easier to just stay living in the same house. Easier to raise Mollie."

"She's a sweet little thing. Where does she get her blond hair?"

"I was a towhead when I was a kid. Hard to believe now, I know." He raked his long fingers through his dark, cropped hair.

"Every time I see her she seems like she's grown a foot. She's a girly girl. I can tell because she's always got on a pretty little dress." Cady smiled. She liked children. Not all children, but the ones whose parents paid enough at-tention to them to raise them right but not so much attention that they thought the world revolved around them. Mollie was an adorable little girl. Cady never saw her with her parents, though. Only Aunt Jessica, who was "Aunt Jessica" to everyone who knew her. She brought Mollie to the library regularly to sit in the children's room and take as many books home as she could carry. Mollie was a fanatical reader, even though she could not yet technically read. She turned each page and scanned it as though she were a speed reader. When there were pictures, she would stop and study the pictures like an archaeologist, as if each one had a hidden and secret meaning. She and Aunt Jessica planned every time they came in that Mollie would be in her book club as soon as she started ninth grade.

"Which is funny because that girl thing is all her," Blue smiled. "Since she was old enough to pick out clothing, which she barely is even now, she would pick the dress and the shoes with the clicking heels. We'd dress her in a pair of jeans and she would take them off and put on a dress. Most parents have to teach their kids to get dressed. It's a whole phase. Not us. Mollie found her way into her own clothes. Now we don't even bother trying to put her in pants. We probably would never have found this out about her but my mother gave us a couple of fluffy dresses for her first birthday. She wasn't even walking yet. I still believe she started walking so she could get to those dresses."

Blue caught himself going on. He smiled and looked out the window over Cady's shoulder. Then he looked back at her. "Did you ever think about having kids?" he asked. "Now that's me probably getting too personal." He tilted his head, tucking his chin in.

"You give me five cents and I'll give you five cents. Then we'll be even." She breathed out a soft laugh. "I was supposed to have a bunch by now."

"A bunch?" he smiled. "How many would a bunch be?"

"Two. Four. I wanted two. Victor wanted a dozen. He used to joke that he needed pickers in the fields."

Blue laughed. "What? I wasn't good enough labor for him?"

"You grew up. That was your only problem. He figured we'd have as many as my body could tolerate. I am an only child, so two seemed like enough to me. But now, it's a moot point. Rosalind and I used to talk about not having kids. They always wanted children and it just didn't happen for them. We both see, saw, see, oh I don't know. The kids we work with often seem like family. Except they grow up and go away." She paused. "And they don't support you in your old age," she smiled.

Dean Kennedy came through the front door. "Hey, Blue." He waved and went through the swinging half door toward the locker room. Cady and Blue stood. Time to brief the commander on the status of the case.

"Hey, one more question?" Cady asked. Blue looked up. "Why do they call you Blue?"

He smirked, half embarrassed. "That's the easiest one all night. I'm at a party in high school, drinking with my friends out on Turtle Island on the canal. I was lit. My friends were teasing me about being all snobby because I worked at the winery. I had said something snarky about good wine and they went for the jugular. To defend myself, I stood up on the pulpit rock out there, the one that's big and flat. I lifted my beer and made some speech about being blue collar to the bone and damn proud of it. From that point on, the only people who ever called me *Dan* were my parents, my teachers until they knew me, and my zone sergeant, who's never gotten to know me." He bowed with a small flourish as if he'd just delivered a Shakespearean soliloquy. "Plus, my middle name is Blumenthal. There's no escaping it."

Cady whistled. "Daniel Blumenthal Emerson? Your parents must have loved you."

"What about you? Cady? Any relation?" he asked.

"No. I was named after the great Elizabeth Cady Stanton, but no relation. My mother is, let's say, a fan of the women's rights movement. You'll have to buy me a glass of that good wine if you want the story on my last name," she said as she walked backward to the door and turned around and left the building.

By the time Cady made it home, the heat had broken and the sun was warm and inviting instead of punishing. She climbed up the back stairs to her apartment. Inside, she opened all the windows, closed all the curtains and shed all her clothes in her bedroom. She went to the kitchen, filled a glass with water from the fridge door, and cooled her bare feet on the tile and drank the water down. She went into the bathroom and turned on the shower. She stood in the hot shower and let the day drain off of her. She re-shampooed her hair and soaped her body twice with her citrus body wash. She stood under the hot water for a long time and let the spray pelt her body. After she finished, she turned the water cool and stood under it for a minute. She dabbed herself off with a towel, rung her hair so it was not dripping and moved to her bed to lie down on top of the towel while she air dried. As she stared at the ceiling, fan spinning around, no lights on, drapes drawn, it was not Rosalind she was thinking about. It was not Eric or Kiery. The musky smell and dark eyes. The way he had enveloped her in her kitchen. She fell asleep thinking about Blue.

Blue sat down in the guest chair in Dean Kennedy's office. He had gone over the case from the beginning with Dean. The entire station was focused on lending whatever support to the investigation that they could. He had been relying on Dean's lifetime of experience to help him sort through the shifting details and assign whatever work would be done by a road trooper so Blue did not have to slog through all the administrative duties.

"Status?" Dean said. Dean Kennedy fell into the generation between Blue and his father, somewhere between old school and new. He ran a tight station and as a result, the group of troopers who were assigned there were like family. At 50, Dean was fit and could take a man half his age with one blow. He always finished in the top three in his age group in the local Musselman Triathlon. He trained twelve months a year and skied every weekend during the winter. He and his perpetual girlfriend, Joy, were the kind of encouraging competitors that drew their friends into their athletic adventures. They made staying fit look sexy, possible.

"The high schooler is a no go, I'm thinking. I'll need some computer help to verify her alibi. She was floating around online, she says." He rubbed his eyes.

"You look like a bag of assholes," Sam Baldwin said as he walked in and got a look at Blue. He pulled out the chair next to Blue and sat down. Blue smirked and rubbed his eyes again.

"What do we know?" Sam said.

"We're just getting up to speed," Dean said. "Blue?"

Sam was the assistant DA who would be prosecuting this case when an arrest was made. Any time there was an ongoing investigation he'd be prosecuting, he got involved earlier rather than later. He and Dean had been partners on the road and when the funding came through to create the Violent Crime Task Force, nicknamed the Victor Frank, although that was never something Blue shared with Cady, Dean and Sam were assigned to run it. Sam retired at his 20-year mark since he'd gone to law school part-time as his retirement plan.

Dean had moved up the chain of command after bringing Blue in as Sam's replacement. There hadn't been enough violent crime in the area to warrant two officers assigned full-time to the task force. Blue was on his own, with Dean as his back up. Sam was the senior assistant district attorney and as such he prosecuted any felony-level offenders, including murderers.

"The financial angle from the festival seems cold," Blue said, leaning back in his chair, every muscle in his body was aching. "The interviews with the other high school students are proceeding. All the initial reports are that the students who didn't do well in her class and who would have had a burn on about her were actually the ones who liked her the most. Weird but seems true at this point. Her husband doesn't have an alibi." He hesitated. "So there's that." Murderer Hunting 101 says to look to the husband as the chief suspect. Blue's instincts told him Ron could never have anything to do with hurting Rosalind. But he wasn't so sure he should trust his instincts now that the suspect pool just deepened by one.

"He'll follow up on the husband," Dean said to Sam. "Mulligan?" Dean asked.

"How does Mulligan factor into this?" Sam asked.

"Seems he and Rosalind had a very public rivalry," Blue said. "We have an interview set up for tomorrow morning. He was in Buffalo with family on Sunday and stopped off in Rochester on his way back today to bid on a city project."

"Rochester?" Sam said. "Since when does his crew work out of town?"

"And since when do we wait for murder suspects to come to us?" Dean said.

"He's not a flight risk." Blue bristled. "Any more than Kiery Fuller was. Nobody looks good for this right now. I'm following up everywhere and it's leading me nowhere."

Sam leaned forward. "When we caught a break in the Amaligo case, it was because two statements in a thousand pages of interviews didn't set right with Half-lobe over here." He pointed to Dean. "We had all but given up. Months of investigation. We were looking at a cold case."

"It was the nephew and the wife," Dean cut in. "It didn't even seem like they knew each other. Hardly at all. But I saw them together one day at the ice cream stand. I just felt like all of a sudden they knew each other in a way that was different from how they were portraying it. Nothing I could have testified to but I saw it."

"So he goes back through hours of interviews from both of them. Pages and pages of transcripts."

"It was right there the whole time," Dean said. "So subtle. He said his uncle took long walks in the evening. She said her husband took long walks in the evening. He was killed on the trail in the morning so those statements, taken days apart, never meant anything out of context."

"It was that they knew his schedule," Sam said. "They both knew. It was the crack in the veneer we used to get a confession out of the nephew. We weren't even originally going to interview him. You just have to go where it goes, Blue. There's no rushing it."

"Mulligan will be here tomorrow. I haven't had a second free anyway."

"I'll take some of the interviews if you need," Dean said. "I've got Dave and Chunk interviewing the students. Whatever you need."

Blue took a deep breath and let it out slowly. "Look, there's one more name to add to the list of people we need to talk to."

All three men sat forward.

"Delaney," Blue offered while staring at his hands, palms together, elbows on his knees.

"Your ex-wife?" Sam said.

Blue said nothing.

"How does she factor in?" Dean said, unfazed.

Blue explained the argument that had been overheard between Delaney and Rosalind. And both agreed she needed to be interviewed.

"You just go where it goes, Blue," Dean said.

"How do we know?" Sam asked.

"A tip. Some other high schooler. I still need to talk to him about it."

"Be careful on this one," Sam said. "You know I don't care how you go about getting your information. Just make sure it comes to me clean. If she's a legitimate possibility here, maybe we should send in another officer for that interview."

"Is this tip legitimate?" Dean asked.

Blue looked away. "I think so."

"Okay," Dean said. "You need to follow up, you do. I'm going to take that interview, though. You're too close."

"No," Blue said. "I need to do it."

"I'm going to side with Dean on this one, Blue," Sam said. "I need to be able to use whatever evidence you're gathering. If you end up with some miraculous confession from your ex, that's going to prove problematic at trial if she says you coerced it."

Blue looked at both of them. "I'll do it." There was nothing more to say.

CHAPTER 16

BLUE KNOCKED ON Delaney's front door. After he'd
driven home, he had walked the few blocks to Delaney's
house in the early evening warmth. He wanted to clear his
head before talking with her. He was dreading the conversation, but he acknowledged that Cady had been right. He
at least needed to ask her about the fight with Rosalind.
Sam and Dean had agreed.

"Baby Blue," Aunt Jessica opened the door, beaming at
her nephew. She stepped aside so he could come in.
"What's wrong?" She instantly changed her tone when she
took in the full measure of Blue's tension.

"Nothing. Where's Delaney?" Blue asked.

"Or Mollie?" Aunt Jessica was hoping to divert the im-
pending crisis she felt by drawing his attention to his
daughter. Mollie and Delaney came into the living room
where Blue was standing.

"Daddy!" Mollie squealed and ran into Blue's arms.

"How's my talented little noodle?" He swooped her up in his arms and kissed her all over her face.

"What's up?" Delaney said from across the room. He hadn't been scheduled to come over and, although off-schedule visits weren't unheard of, she knew he was in the middle of a murder investigation and hadn't been expecting to see much of him for a while.

"I knew Mollie was about to be tucked into bed and I wanted to read her a bedtime story. Is that okay?"

"Yes! I've got a book, Daddy," Mollie said as he put her down. She ran over to the bookcase by the door and pulled out *One Kitten for Kim*. He had read that book to her every time he put her to bed when she was a baby. She always called it Daddy's kitty book.

"Can I put her to bed tonight? I need to talk to you when I'm done but I need to spend some time with Molls before this day is over."

"Of course," Delaney said. "Is anything wrong?" She looked at Aunt Jessica, who was staring at Blue.

"Let's go read, Heart of my Heart," Blue said, ignoring Delaney. He took Mollie, already in her pajamas, up the stairs and read her the book twice before she fell asleep. Blue sat in Mollie's bedroom for a while before coming downstairs. He wanted to soak in the innocence that was her room. Her bedroom at his house was as it always had been. Delaney had bought all new furniture and decorations when she moved out. It was never lost on Blue that Mollie had two complete worlds in which she functioned.

None of his brothers or sisters or he ever had such a nice room growing up. Mollie had two.

Blue came into the kitchen where Delaney and Aunt Jessica were sitting at the table.

"Want a cup of tea? The water is hot," Delaney asked Blue.

"Thanks. No."

"Sit down," Aunt Jessica said.

"I'll stand."

"What is it?" Delaney said. She stood up and tossed her tea bag in the garbage. "You're making me sweat. Has something cracked with the case?"

"That's why I'm here," Blue said. He shifted as he stood in the doorway.

"Let me get my notepad," Delaney said putting down her tea cup.

"It's not fit to print, Delaney," Blue said.

Delaney stopped and regarded him. She was going to make him be the one to speak next. Aunt Jessica stared at him from her seat at the table.

"I need to know where you were on Saturday night at 8:30."

Delaney blew out a laugh. "Jesus, you scared me." He did not waver. "You're not serious." He did not move. "Um, Blue, are you asking me for an alibi for Rosalind's murder?"

Aunt Jessica stood up. "She was with me. What is this all about?"

"Aunt Jessica, no." She gently patted Aunt Jessica's shoulder. "I want to know what's going on here. Blue?"

"I'm doing my job," Blue said.

"Veto," Delaney said. "Do better or get out."

"We could both get out to the station if that would make you more inclined to answer my question."

She glared at him. She always had the upper hand in arguments when they were married. Not because she was always right or because she was better at arguing, she was just more relentless than Blue. He was always drained by the drama and so gave in when it didn't matter. And it almost never mattered.

"Why don't we sit down," Blue said, letting the trooper face relax a bit.

"I'll stand," Delaney said.

"Come on." He sat. "I'll explain if you sit."

When all three of them were sitting, Blue said, "It has come to my attention, in the course of my investigation, that you had a heated argument with the victim the day before she died and that maybe the story you printed in the paper on Saturday was lean in retaliation for whatever the victim said that made you mad."

Delaney went pale as Blue explained why he was there.

"Sweetheart," Aunt Jessica said, "it's us you're talking to. Family. Let's just talk this out."

"Are you telling me," Delaney broke in, "that your organization sent *you* over here to question *me* as a suspect?

This is unfrickenbelievable. Isn't this some sort of ethics violation or something?"

"It's my job," he said, unflinching, his eyes penetrating. "I'm good at my job." Blue saw Delaney retreat. No one else would have picked up on her surrender. He saw it before she spoke.

"I was here. I was asleep at 8:30. Aunt Jessica was here, too."

"Okay. That's good," Blue said. "Talk me through the night."

"It's like she said," Aunt Jessica said, "we were all here. We had decided not to go down to the fireworks. Delaney thought they might scare Mollie and I've seen enough fireworks in my lifetime to blow up a city so I didn't mind. We were here watching *Finding Nemo*, yes, for the umpteenth time. Delaney and Mollie both fell asleep on the couch. I fell asleep in the chair. We all stayed like that until Delaney got the call to go to the park to cover the story. I stayed here with Mollie."

Blue looked at Delaney.

"It's just like she said!" Her upper hand had receded long into the distance. "Who told you about the argument?"

"What did you two argue about?" Blue asked.

"It was nothing," Delaney said. She was embarrassed now about the pettiness. Blue let her continue. "I felt like she was calling me a bad mother because I am a working mother. In retrospect, she probably wasn't talking about me at all but I took offense to her characterization of mothers who will do anything for their children and I sort of snapped."

"Snapped," Blue said it like he was contemplating the weight of the word.

"No. Not snapped," Delaney said. "I got mad. I didn't want to give her the benefit of my services so I walked away and didn't answer her calls. I ran a shell story from the details of last year. I know Saturday's story is supposed to be the big feature for the festival every year. Look. I'm not proud of myself but I didn't kill her!" Her tension was rising.

Blue put his elbows on the table and dug his thumbs into either side of the bridge his nose.

"Okay," he sighed. "Okay."

Aunt Jessica helped extract them out of the morass. "Why don't you walk me home." She put her hand on his arm. "If you're done here."

CHAPTER 17

AS BLUE AND HIS AUNT Jessica walked down Delaney's long driveway and out onto the sidewalk on Stark Street, Aunt Jessica slipped her arm into the crook of Blue's arm and they strolled into the darkening summer night.

"You're tired," Aunt Jessica said.

"AJ," Blue said as he patted her hand nestled in the crook of his arm, "you do not know the half of it."

"Why was it you who had to question Delaney? Wasn't there someone else who could have done that for you?"

"I didn't want anyone else to," Blue said. "When I spoke with Dean about it, he suggested he should go make the alibi check. I told him I wanted to do it. Sam even said it might not look good if I did it alone. I told him he need-ed to trust me and he said he'd allow it to stand for now. Everyone's working hard to find Rosalind's killer. I can't start passing off my responsibilities because they involve people I know. I might as well turn in my badge if that were the case."

"Maybe he was right. Isn't this one a little too close to home?" Aunt Jessica asked.

Blue stared into the distance as they walked down Wright Avenue. The sun was setting and a calm was descending on the little village. The air was still and clear and every house's garden threw off a sweet fragrance.

"Your Uncle Fred had to question his old college roommate once," Aunt Jessica said. "He did it but he told me he always regretted it. Things were never the same between them."

"What did he have to question him about?"

"It was a burglary," Aunt Jessica said. "Ancient history. Dale didn't do it but there was some evidence to suggest he might have been involved."

Aunt Jessica married Fred when she was 20 and he was 23. He had just become a state trooper. She met him through her brother, Blue's father, who was also a trooper at the time. They moved into the house next door to where Blue currently lived. Fred retired after a twenty-year career as a road trooper. He had started his second career even before his first one ended. He had started to buy rental properties a few years before he retired. They were landlords for two houses when he retired, and in the ten years after he retired and before he died, he had purchased another four. He had been gone for sixteen years now. Their five children had long since grown up and moved away from Waterloo.

Aunt Jessica never worked outside the home while Fred was alive. She didn't take over the business when he died. Rather, she hired a management company who sub-contracted with Mulligan and his crew for any repairs and upkeep the buildings needed. The management company took care of turning over the rentals and maintaining the yards in all seasons. They paid the taxes. All she was re-quired to do was have a monthly meeting with them where they reported to her in detail all that had happened in the month and allow her access to the financial records. Between Fred's pension and the income from the rental properties, Aunt Jessica was a wealthy woman. She al-ways said she did not have Kennedy money but that she never had to worry about taking care of herself or being a burden to her children.

"Things aren't the same between Delaney and me any-way," Blue said.

"You two do just fine by each other, from the way I see it anyway. I see both of you nearly every day. She strug-gles to maintain a career and be a full-time mother to Mollie. It's difficult, near impossible. And it's not the same for you."

"What are you talking about?" Blue said. "I have Mollie half the time."

"It's not the same for women. Today. If she's not with Mollie because she's working, she's judged. That's what she was so all fired up about when she fought with Rosalind."

Blue looked sideways at her as they walked. They turned onto Center Street.

"You don't think she feels the judgment?" Aunt Jessica continued. "This town is too small to hold Delaney. I could see that when she first arrived. This is the most wonderful place to live and I wouldn't want to live anywhere else, but Delaney is not the same as I am. I'm not entirely sure if Delaney would be happy anywhere. I think she knows that about herself. I'm sure that's at least part of the reason she stayed last year when you two divorced."

"Whether she feels judged or not, it looks bad," Blue said, "having such a fight with someone who dies the next day. Someone who is murdered."

"What would Rosalind M'Clintock know of what mothers will do for their children?"

Blue stopped, surprised by the sudden turn in Aunt Jessica's tone.

"No. That's not what I meant. Sometimes that woman just brought out the prickle in a person."

"What are you not telling me?" When she did not respond, he turned to face her on the sidewalk. "AJ?"

"Nothing." She composed herself. "It's just her position on the Town Board about restricting growth in the Town surrounding this Village. All my children had to leave because there is nowhere here for them to work. I had to watch every one of them pack up and sail off because there is no work here. Rosalind never had to suffer that. Her ideals about the quaintness of our little way of life here were all well and good, but they mean nothing if you're alone and living here without your children." Her pitch was rising as she spoke.

Blue took her in his arms. She breathed deeply. There was nothing for him to say. He had been to each of the bon voyage parties for all five of his cousins when one by one they grew up and got jobs elsewhere. He knew his aunt fared well most every day but there were times that the loss of her husband and the distance of her children came crashing in on her. She was his rock. His sounding board. For all she gave him, he gave her whatever comfort she needed whenever she needed it, even if that was almost never.

She patted him on the back by way of thanking him for the hug.

"I'll be fine. You know that. I just never did see eye to eye with that woman. It's a terrible thing that's happened to her and I vow this moment to let go of any ill will I ever had toward her."

He took her arm into his and they proceeded up her walkway toward her front porch.

"Someone was not able to make such a vow," Blue said.

"Yes, it seems that's probably true." She stood to face him at the base of her porch. "And I think things will be okay," she said. "With Delaney. She comes from cop stock. When she settles down, she'll realize it was better you came than anyone else."

"That's exactly the opposite of what you just said," Blue said. "Tell me what you really think."

"About you having to question the mother of your child about being a murderer?" Aunt Jessica said.

"It's my job to be able to believe anyone is capable of murder," he said.

She took both of his hands in hers. "Baby Blue, are you really asking if I think your ex-wife is a murderer? Because if you're asking that, I can give you an answer. I can tell you unequivocally no. That woman is hard-cut, like a diamond. She is tough and will always get her story. She doesn't give in freely and she has trouble turning all that off when she comes home but I know there isn't any malice in her. She doesn't like to be wrong and likes it less when you call her on it. It sounds like that's what Rosalind did. Call her on her *big city* attitude." Aunt Jessica emphasized "big city." "But she'll go lick her wounds, write a tirade on small town, provincial attitudes, stuff it in her journal and take a hot bath. She's predictable. She's tired. She's lost. But she is not a murderer. Not even in the heat of passion.

"And luckily neither of us has to ponder this question for another second because I can assure you she was with me and Mollie on Saturday night. After we decided not to go down to the fireworks, we watched *Finding Nemo* and Delaney, tired as she always is, fell asleep with Mollie cuddled in her lap on the couch until she got the call about getting the story on the trouble at the festival. Just like I said."

Blue thanked his aunt for the talk and kissed her goodnight. Instead of walking next door and crawling into bed, he decided to go check on Ron. He wanted to stay close to him and see how he was doing.

CHAPTER 18

CADY WOKE UP two and a half hours after her dreamy nap had begun to the familiar plunk plunk of Hero coming through the cat door and leaping onto the floor from the window sill. He immediately started to call for Cady. He found her in her room, on her bed. "Dinner time?" she asked in a whisper. He climbed to her head and kneaded her hair for a minute. Instead of settling down to sleep on her pillow, he got up and began to talk to her again. "Okay. I'm up." She scooped him up from the bed and cuddled him like a baby, curled in the crook of her arm. His fur was like an angora sweater against her bare skin. She set him down in the kitchen and opened a packet of food. He promptly showed his gratitude by digging in without complaint.

It was dark out. Cady peeked out her kitchen window shade. It was lowered to half-mast because the cat door took up the bottom half of the window. She had mounted a lockable cat flap window insert with two opaque side pieces that let in light, but that no one could see through. Although the sun was down, the sky was not yet black. She decided to take a walk to see how Ron was doing. He was well known as a night owl and he was often up reading or working into the middle of the night.

Hero slipped in and out of her legs as she tried to walk toward her bedroom.

"I'm gonna fall!" she squealed at him. He meowed back.

"C'mere." She scooped him up and poured him onto her bed. "Now stay, so I can get dressed." She laughed at herself for giving him commands like a dog. He jumped right down and followed her to her closet. He circled around her every move as she put on her clothes. He was talking with her like he had something urgent on his little kitty mind. "You'd think Timmy was in the well or some-thing. Calm yourself." She petted him smooth from his head to his tail. "Everything's all right. I know I'm going to be an old cat lady, but with you, who can complain? You are my Hero." She picked him up again and put him on the bed.

She put on fresh underwear and a matching Victoria's Secret bra. One of the habits she picked up when she was with Victor was wearing expensive underwear. Cady had always been thin, but when she met Victor, she lost the jiggle around her middle that had always made her self-conscious of wearing bikinis and sexy lingerie. She instead went for the tankini and Jockey underwear. She didn't work out any more with Victor or eat any less, but the French paradox grabbed hold of her and drinking wine and eating real meals with fine cheeses and fresh gourmet ingredients slimmed her down without effort. She ate less well these days and didn't drink as much wine but she had never regained the tummy she had in her teens and twenties. And where Victor bought her underwear of the rich and famous, she was happy now with Victoria's Secret. It was like she was still keeping Victor's secret. When she wanted to be casual, she ordered from the Athleta catalog. Or Title Nine. Other than a dress here or there for some fancy function she couldn't beg off of, she shopped out of these three catalogues for virtually everything she owned.

She held up her silky summer weight skort and asked Hero his opinion. Hero had settled on the bed and was not talking to her anymore. The skirt had thin shorts that hugged her legs under a flippy, sporty skirt. She slipped on a short-sleeved T-shirt and her crisscross Jambu sandals. She unhooked her door key from the key chain and slipped it inside the hidden pocket at her waistband. She swirled her hair into a high pony tail and splashed water on her face. She rarely wore make up.

When she came out of the bathroom, Hero was curled up on her bed, bathing after an afternoon's adventures and an evening meal. He was all talked out. She picked up the towel off the bed and hung it back up on the hook in the bathroom. She realized she had fed Hero but hadn't eaten herself. She opened the jar of peanut butter from her fridge and dipped a spoon into it. She checked the fridge with the spoon of peanut butter in her mouth. She grabbed an apple and sliced off a hunk of extra-sharp cheddar cheese from Sauders, the local Mennonite store. She ate the cheese and thought about settling down on her deck with a glass of pinot noir to enjoy the perfect summer night. Instead she polished the apple as she tapped down the stairs. The white fairy lights glowed on her deck. She left the curtains closed and the windows open when she locked up.

The night was warm and dry. The soggy humidity had been washed away with the storm the day before. It was crystal clear and the first quarter moon was waxing. As she stepped up on to Ron's porch, she finished the last bite of her apple. The porch light wasn't on. She rang the doorbell with her right hand and held the apple core in her left. She went around to the edge of the porch and saw that Ron's car was parked in the long driveway. She went back and knocked on the door softly. If he were asleep, she did not want to wake him. Rest would not come easily for him for a long time. As she knocked, the door swung open a crack. It was a heavy wooden door that Ron treated yearly to prevent it from warping in their intemperate climate. She stepped in.

"Ron," she called. "It's Cady." She dropped her voice to a whisper. "You asleep?" She was about to turn around and go home when she caught sight of the cellar door ajar. She came in and shut the front door behind her. "Ron," she said in a normal voice as she passed by the cellar door. "It's Cady. I'm just going to throw my apple core away." She went into the kitchen and tossed her core into the compost jar and washed her hands. It wasn't as cold in the house as it had been the day before. With the wine safely in the cellar, Ron must have turned the air conditioner to a warmer setting.

"Ron?" she called at the top of the cellar steps. The lights weren't on in the cellar either. "You down here?" She flipped the cellar stairs light switch in the hallway but the light didn't come on. She started down the stairs and as she did, her eyes trying to adjust to the dark, she saw a foot at the bottom of the stairs. She took two more stairs and saw someone lying face down. "Ron!" she screamed. There was no light downstairs and when they installed the wine cellar, they had covered over the basement windows to regulate both light and temperature. She rushed to his side. She knelt down next to him into a pool of liquid. She felt a small disc embed in her wet knee. As she reached for Ron, she swiped under her knee to clear it away, her hand now dripping wet.

"Ron, can you hear me?" She put her fingers on his neck. She thought she felt a pulse, but she couldn't be sure. She was shaking. They had talked about replacing those old rickety stairs at the time they installed the wine cellar, but they hadn't. It was on their perpetual home-owner's list of things to do. She was about to call an ambulance when she was hoisted up by her armpits like a rag doll and thrown against a wine rack. Her head hit the cork end of a bottle square in her temple and she was dazed. She slumped against the rack and tried to focus but her attacker came at her in the dark. He was dressed all in black with a ski mask over his face. As he lunged at her, she thrust both her feet up in the air and caught him in the thighs. He jerked back. She reached behind her head and grabbed the neck of a wine bottle and flipped it out of its cubby hole at him. It landed in his rib cage with a thud and bounced as it hit the floor. She scrambled to her hands and knees and tried to escape. Her hands and bare knees were slippery. Wet. With Ron's blood. Or her own. She couldn't tell. The slick wood floor was not giving her any traction. As she lifted one leg to try to stand up, she saw the wine bottle come down. She felt her brain shake inside her skull. She saw a figure in black run toward the stairs and start up. She saw Ron lying at the bottom of the stairs. Then everything went black.

When Cady came to, she was being hoisted onto a gurney. There were people everywhere.

"She's waking up," the paramedic standing over her said.

Blue leaned over her. "Cady. Can you hear me?" He grabbed her hand.

She couldn't tell what was going on. "Ron," she squeezed out.

"He's on his way to the hospital right now," Blue said, walking with the gurney to the cellar stairs.

"We have to take her up," the paramedic said.

"Wait," she said. She grasped Blue's hand with the strength of a baby. "Ron. He's alive?"

"Yes," Blue said. He looked at the paramedic. Their eyes met. "He's going to be fine," he continued.

"Blue." She couldn't move her head. She had a brace around her head and she was immobilized from the waist up. "Blue," she said again.

He leaned over her so he would be in her line of sight.

"We have to go," the paramedic said, waiting at the bottom of the stairs to haul Cady up and into the ambulance.

"It wasn't a woman," she said. "It wasn't Kiery. It wasn't Delaney." As the room went black again, she felt herself tilt and she felt like she was flying.

With Cady and Ron safely in the ambulance and headed to the hospital, Blue's eyes set black in a near blind rage. He hadn't been there to protect them. Ron might die. Cady's eyes were pleading. She needed from him what he couldn't give. He had discharged Delaney as a suspect on the way to see Ron. Whatever flimsy case was still left against Kiery had just dissolved with Cady telling him it was a man who attacked her. It might not be the same person but that thought was not gaining purchase with Blue. It was time for Mulligan. He was scheduled for an interview first thing in the morning but Blue no longer wanted to wait. He would get that alibi or he would make an arrest. How long ago had Cady and Ron been attacked? It could have been hours ago. Where would their attacker be?

Blue went to the one place he knew Mulligan to hang out in the evenings. The Pit Stop bar on Main Street. If he weren't there right now, he would hunt him down and close his case. If he were there, he would crack him and he'd have no choice but to offer his confession.

"Mulligan," Blue almost whispered, deep in his throat.

Mulligan was just turning from the bar with a fresh beer in his hand. "Hey, Blue. Beer?" He held up his beer and pointed to the bar offering to buy a round.

"When did you get here?" Blue held his stance.

"Just in," Mulligan offered. "What's up? We're just starting a new game of darts." He started to walk toward the dart board where his crew had spent the evening.

Blue stepped in Mulligan's path.

Mulligan stopped. Took a step back. "Something wrong, Officer?"

"Just have to clear a few things up." Blue was rooted to his spot. Everyone in the bar was staring at the two men facing off. The bar was a tiny one-room dive that was like Cheers to many regulars looking for a cheap beer and a low-key night. Mulligan's crew stood up. None of them were fighters, but their boss was clearly about to get into something. They became alert.

Mulligan wasn't a fighter either. He'd probably never thrown a punch in his life. He'd never had to. He was a hulk of a man. Cady called him Mr. Clean as an endearment because he was tall and built like a hunky cartoon character with a wide muscled chest and a tight, small waist. And he was bald with a shiny head like the commercial. He lifted heavy weights every day of his life and his strength was unmatched by anyone in the area. It was a fact. No one questioned it or required proof. His affable good nature also made him a friend to everyone who knew him. Except Rosalind. She had taken a burn to him so hot that nothing anyone said or did could cool her down. It was on this point that Blue was proceeding.

"Where were you before you showed up here?" Blue asked.

"Tonight? Why?"

Blue did not respond.

"I was working," Mulligan said. "I told the guys to come on down and I'd meet them here as soon as I got done. What's going on? Something else happen?"

"What was your beef with Rosalind M'Clintock?" Blue asked.

"Blue. Seriously. What the hell is going on? I'm not answering another question until you tell me. Are you here to arrest me for not liking Rosalind?"

"I'm here to find out where you were tonight. And where you were on Saturday night between 8:00 and 9:00."

"Saturday? Look, Rosalind and I didn't see eye to eye politically. She was a loud mouth and was causing trouble with my business. But I'd already contacted an attorney to see about suing her for slander. He said I had a good case and was working on filling out the paperwork for a restraint or the thing you get when the court tells you to shut the hell up. Rosalind fights with everyone the week before her precious women's party. No use singling me out."

"Something you felt the need to tell the papers?"

"Goddamn right."

Everyone in the bar had taken to ignoring the two men when it seemed like fists would not fly. Mulligan's team, Ben, Brighton, and Lewis, had moved in to surround Blue, more interested in the conversation than in threatening him.

"Has something else happened?" Ben asked.

Blue knew these men knew Cady well. He wasn't about to tip his hand as to why he needed a second alibi.

"You'll need to tell me where you were tonight, Mulligan, or I'm going to have to take you down to the station where you'll be less comfortable, but you *will* tell me."

"I told you," Mulligan was becoming exasperated. "I was working. We have this house on Black Brook Road." He nodded to Ben. "The guys will tell you. And the homeowner was complaining about her door hinge not swinging right for the thousandth time. I told the guys I would take care of it and meet them here. I had to take the entire door off and shave down the bottom and install new hinges. It was hot as hell in there and now all I want to do is drink this beer and relax."

"And Saturday night?" Blue said.

"Blue! Is Cady all right?" They all looked at the burst of light created by the front door opening to the bright street lights and saw Delia Moelle standing there. "I didn't know you'd be here. I was coming to tell Mulligan."

"What's wrong with Cady?" Mulligan slowly turned his gaze back to Blue.

"She's in the hospital. Ron M'Clintock, too!" Delia went on. "I just heard it on my police scanner. Two people were attacked in his home. I know the address so I went down. I saw them being taken out in ambulances." Delia was flushed, pleased with herself that she had this information to offer as a commodity.

"And you think I did that?" Mulligan put down his beer on the table next to him and lunged at Blue. "Cady is my friend, you asshole," Mulligan said as he struggled to his knees after falling to the ground with Blue under him. He punched Blue in the mouth. "Just because you can't do right by that woman, don't you think you can come around here and accuse me of hurting her."

Blue regained his equilibrium after being sucker punched and twisted Mulligan's arm behind his back, wrenching him onto his stomach. He dug his knee into Mulligan's kidney and cuffed him. The fight was over before any of the bystanders had time to react.

"I would do anything to protect Cady." Blue was locked down, his movements automatic reactions to his years of training but his mind and mouth getting away from him. "Including arresting you right now for murder and attempted murder in addition to assaulting a police officer if you don't tell me right fucking now where you were on Saturday night."

Mulligan was cursing. "I was with my wife! We had to leave the party early to Skype our son in Spain. He's there for the goddamned summer in the foreign exchange program. My wife records every conversation for her scrapbook. You can verify it."

"I will. You can count on it," Blue said.

After he'd brought Mulligan back to the station and checked his alibis, he let him go without arresting him for assaulting a police officer. His pride might take more time to heal than his busted lip where Mulligan cold cocked him, but Mulligan was apologetic after the fact that, and against all his police training, he just let it go. He was exhausted and frustrated and frankly didn't need the extra paperwork. He was at square one. He knew he was running out of time.

When Cady woke again, she was in the hospital. She was no longer strapped into a neck brace. Before she opened her eyes, she could feel the dull throb of her head. She felt a hand on hers. Soft. When she slit her eyes open, she saw Sara sitting in the chair next to her bed with her head leaning on the bed railing. She was holding Cady's hand and rubbing her knuckles absently with her thumb.

"Sara," Eric whispered from the other side of the bed. "She's awake. I'll get the nurse." He stepped into the hallway.

Sara smiled at her and stood up.

"Am I okay?" Cady said.

Sara's eyes spilled tears out and she nodded her head. "You're fine. You've got the hardest head in the county. How do you feel?"

"Like I was attacked by a murderer," Cady said trying to sit up.

"You stay right where you are," Eric said as he came back into her room with the nurse behind him.

"Glad to see you awake," the nurse said. "I'm Ruby. I'll be here with you all night. How does your head feel?" Ruby placed both of her hands on the raised railing of Cady's bed. Her deep blue eyes focused on Cady. Cady noticed that Ruby was not fiddling with anything while she waited for an answer. She gave her attention like it was a priceless gift.

Cady raised her hand up to her temple. "Seems I've got a headache tonight." The clock read 11:50 but she had no idea if that was a.m. or p.m., or even what day it was.

"You took a hell of a beating," Eric said.

Cady focused on Eric and smiled. Then her smile turned to fear. "Ron. Where is Ron?" She looked from Sara to Eric to Ruby.

"Shh," Ruby said. "Mr. M'Clintock is stable. He is in a coma but he's stable. He's been through a trauma. He may need to sleep a little longer," she said and patted Cady's arm. She moved to adjust the vital signs monitor in back of Cady's hospital bed.

Cady started to cry. "Cade," Sara said. "He's going to be all right. And so are you." She tried to soothe Cady but her words didn't feel convincing. "The doctor said that you're going to be released tomorrow. They just want to keep you here tonight for observation."

"We should let her rest," Eric said.

"Yes, you should," Ruby said, her hands on her rounded hips. "Five minutes. No more," she said as she left the room.

"Hey," Eric said as he leaned in and stroked a piece of hair off her forehead. "You're going to be okay. So is Ron. Blue has security posted outside to watch over the both of you."

Cady smiled through her tears. With her cheeks still wet, she slipped into a deep sleep.

CHAPTER 19

WHEN SHE WOKE, she was alone in the hospital room. Again, she had no idea if it was day or night. The clock said 7:00 but the shadowy light outside her hospital room window provided no clue as to whether it was morning or evening. She had a bit of a headache, but she felt rested. Her room was full of cards and flowers. She had no sense of how long she'd been in the hospital. She sat up in bed slowly, testing her reflexes and gauging how she felt. She got up to read the cards and use the bathroom and when she came out, Blue was sitting in the guest chair by the door. He stood up as she opened the bathroom door.

"Aren't you a sight for sore eyes," he said.

She snuffled out her nose. "I'm having a bad hair day. Can't say the same for your lip?"

"You come sit down. Get back into bed." He stepped toward her.

"No way. I'm ready to get out of here. Is it day or night? Where are my clothes?"

"It's night," Blue said. "You've slept for nearly a whole day. And you're not going anywhere until the doctor releases you. Sara fixed everything at the library. She also brought in some clothes for you. They're over there. She stopped by to feed Hero and pick up something for you to wear home. I'm afraid your clothes from last night aren't wearable anymore."

"I was covered in blood, wasn't I?" she asked.

"Yes," he said. "They sterilized you from head to toe while you were out." He smiled, then stopped smiling. "Cady. I'm sorry. I wasn't there to protect you." His gaze was so piercing she had to look away.

"How could you have known? Really, it's not your fault." She met his gaze. "It's not. Can we talk about your face now?"

He looked at the floor. "Do you remember anything else? Besides the blood?"

"I do." She absently got back into the hospital bed and pulled the blanket up over her lap. Blue sat back down in the chair next to the door. He scooted it closer to the bed so he could hear her better. "I remember going to see how Ron was doing and his front door was open. Unlatched. I went in and found him in the wine cellar. He was lying face down. It was total darkness down there, but I could tell he was hurt. I thought he fell down the stairs."

Blue began taking notes on her description of the night's events.

"I knelt down next to him and it was like I was kneeling in a puddle of water. Blood," she continued as she pulled the blanket up higher. "At first I thought it was wine, like maybe he fell down the stairs with a bottle of wine in his hands and it shattered. But it was sticky. No. It was slippery. Slick. Thicker than wine. I was about to call for help when someone picked me up and threw me across the room." She turned to him and sat up straighter in the bed. "That's how I know it wasn't a woman who killed Rosalind. Did I tell you that last night?"

"Yes, you did. When I found you in the cellar," he said, "I was coming to check on Ron before heading home and I found the same scene you did, with the addition of you, of course. If Ron's door hadn't been open, I'm sure I would have just knocked and went on home. That air conditioning was just pouring out onto the porch."

"Thank God you did," Cady said. "I mean, thank you that you did." She met his eyes. "I shut the door when I came in. It has to be the same person, right?"

"We don't know that for sure. It'd be a hell of a coincidence if it were two random acts of violence in the same week on the same family, though."

"I'm not all that heavy, but the person who attacked me last night was male. No doubt about it. He had shoulders. Like you," she buffed herself up. "Boy shoulders. I didn't see anything else about who it was. It was totally dark down there. He was dressed all in black. Head to toe, even a ski mask."

"All in black?" He wrote in his notebook. He knew the ski mask was no coincidence. It was evidence of premeditation.

"I know. It was warm last night. That can't mean anything good. And they were man hands that grabbed me underneath my armpits and hurled me across the room. Little Kiery? You can file that one as a no way. And no way it was Delaney either."

"I know," he said. He looked down at the worn linoleum tiles on the floor. "I talked to her last night and she's got an airtight alibi. You can check Mulligan off your to worry about list, too. And just about everyone else on my list. I've been running down alibis and conducting interviews with students and faculty all day."

A tear slipped down Cady's face. "Gawd, what is the matter with me?" She wiped her face with the back of her hand. "It's like I'm watching a Lifetime marathon. I can't stop crying." She looked at him. "I am so not a crier."

"Y-uh, I can see that." He moved the box of tissues from the little plastic dresser top to the rolling table next to her bed.

She ignored him. She took a tissue. "This is just a lot, you know? Rosalind and then Kiery and now Ron. What's his condition?"

"He's still in a coma. They don't know much more at this point," Blue said.

"This lunatic has wiped an entire family off the face of the earth," she said.

"Let's stay where we are, huh?" Blue said as he reached for her hand. "Ron could come to in the next hour."

"You're right." She patted his hand and pulled hers away, grabbing another tissue. "Okay. I have to get to Kiery. Tell her we know it wasn't her."

"Cady. You don't have to get to anyone. We don't know it wasn't her. And when we do, I'll be doing the telling."

"But it wasn't her. You do know that, right? Aren't you at all relieved to know it wasn't Delaney?" Their eyes locked. Blue broke the gaze. "I am, about Kiery."

"I can't officially close the investigation on them yet, but with an alibi and what happened to you last night, I would be wise to focus on someone with male parts and man hands, no?"

Cady let out a sigh from her toes.

"What can you tell me about Jonathan?" Blue asked.

Cady blinked hard. "No."

"No, what?" he asked.

"It wasn't him," she said. She got out of bed and took her clothes into the bathroom. She took a quick but thorough shower. She left the door ajar while she slipped into the sun dress with twist back straps and a shelf bra that Sara had brought. With that and a clean pair of underwear, she took no time at all getting ready to leave, even though she was moving slowly.

When she was done in the shower and changing, Blue asked, "How do you know?"

"I don't. I just can't face thinking someone else I know might be a murderer. Might have tried to kill Ron. Me."

"I know this is tough. You want to take a rest?" Blue said.

"Tough?" Cady came out of the bathroom shaking her wet hair in waves around her face. "How do you do this for a living?" He looked at her. "I'm being serious. You've got to know everyone in this town by now. How do you investigate such brutality every day, especially with people you know?"

"Detachment." He shrugged. "I suppose it's like an ER doc or a lawyer. My sister represents children in family court. Custody battles and neglect and abuse cases. She's the reason I kept Delaney and me out of court. She tells me some cases have no real end. It's just one appearance after another until the kid ages out. At least with police work, there's an arrest. An end. I can do this, but that's a job I couldn't do. Everyone's got their limits, I guess. It's particularly hard when it's someone I know, though, yes. And, no, I don't know all 30,000 people in Seneca County." He smiled at her.

"Well, I bet you know half of them at least as well as you know me," she said.

"And it's particularly hard when it's a multiple," he said, absently.

"A multiple?" she asked.

"I ultimately have no reason to think the attack on you and Ron last night wasn't committed by the same person who killed Rosalind. There's someone loose in my town who is hurting people. I take that very personally."

"I'd say you sounded like John McClane right there if that hadn't seemed so damn sincere," she said.

He blushed at her seriousness. "So, what can you tell me about Jonathan? No stone unturned."

"Okay. I'm with you. Anything about anybody. Jonathan," she said.

As Cady was about to sit on the edge of the bed, Ruby and Cady's attending doctor came in and began the procedure for examining and then releasing her. Blue gathered up her cards from the book club kids who'd stopped by earlier in the day and the flowers from half the town. He noticed there was a card from Delaney asking her to be in touch when she felt up to it so Delaney could interview her about her experience. Blue put that card in his jacket pocket and stepped out to bring the car around to drive Cady home.

CHAPTER 20

"ANYTHING ABOUT ANYBODY," Blue repeated when they were finally settled in his car and driving toward Cady's apartment. The sun was blinding as it reached for the horizon but setting behind them as he drove.

"I would not peg Jonathan as a murderer, of course," Cady picked up the conversation they had started in the hospital room, "but he's one kid who I'll be glad to graduate out of the book club."

Blue nodded. He kept his eyes on the road.

"He's just odd," she continued. "I think of him as my own personal creep show. He's not a bad kid. He seems incompatible with the other book club kids. He doesn't strike me as the kind of person who would join anything let alone an extra-curricular book club. He's been in since tenth grade. He just graduated, sort of. He's taking summer school because he flunked Rosalind's class."

"It does seem like she was an especially hard grader, doesn't it?" Blue said.

"Is it possible that a failed grade could be motive for murder?"

"I've never seen it before, but that's not saying much," Blue said. "Sometimes it only takes a mustard seed to create a big hate that grows and grows. Did he ever say or do anything specifically that struck you as odd?"

"All the time," she spurted out.

"Such as?"

She thought for a minute. "Like the time right after school let out last month and he came to the June book club meeting. We were all talking about the end of school. That's when we found out that Rosalind had flunked him. That he had failed her class. That's how she would have put it. We were all expressing our sympathies and feeling bad for him because he had to attend summer school and he said, God, I hadn't thought of this until right now." Cady had turned to him, animated. "When he and I were alone at the supply closet, he dismissed it and said, 'It's nothing. She's pretty much dead already.'

"I just stared at him. Dumbfounded. It was such an odd thing to say." She nodded her head at him. Blue said nothing so she went on. "I asked him what he could possibly mean by that. He stumbled all over himself then and said he meant that she was dead to him already because school was out and he'd never have to take her class again. He apologized for sounding disrespectful. He knew she and I were friends. See what I mean? Odd. But in light of what's happened, maybe way more than odd."

"And he wasn't at your party?" Blue finally said. "You told me that."

"No. He wasn't there. Sara and I talked about it. I was glad he didn't stay. It would have been fine if he had. He's unobtrusive, at least. I can't say I dislike the kid, but I can't say I actively like him either."

"Why wasn't he there?"

"I don't know," Cady said. "Like I said, he came early and stayed only a few minutes, before it even started. And like Kiery, when we met yesterday at the library, we were thinking about other things. My birthday party was not on our minds at all."

"So, he wasn't at the party," Blue said. "He suggested Delaney as a suspect." He paused. "He might have another alibi. Maybe he was working."

"Maybe it's his black eyes that make him seem so sinister," Cady said.

"Hey, I've got black eyes," Blue smiled in spite of himself. "No cheap detective work, Deputy Colette."

"Yeah," she said. "You'd think they'd be blue." She leaned over to examine his irises from the passenger's seat.

"Save the baby blues for your boyfriend," he said.

She snapped into focus. "Boyfriend? What are you? In tenth grade? I don't have a boyfriend."

"Deuce would like to think otherwise," he said as he made the final turn down Cady's street.

"I hate when you call him 'Deuce'," she said. "No one else does."

"No one else knows him like I do," he said. "Good side step, though. If I weren't trained in the art of psy ops, I would have been thrown off by that dodge." He pulled into the parking spot next to Cady's car under her upstairs deck that she used for private off-street parking.

"I didn't dodge," she said. "Eric and I have gone out on a few dates. We've never even kissed, really. Not that it's any of your business."

"You're right. It's not my business. Jonathan is my business. Finding who killed Rosalind and who attacked you and put Ron in a coma. That's my business. Stop getting me off track." He opened the door and got out of the car.

She blew out a laugh. Heaving herself out of the car, she said, "Pardon the civilian mucking up your investigation," she teased. Then seriously, "It really could have been him. His hands were man hands. Jonathan is one of those students who is a full-grown man. Some kids grow into their twenties. Fill out, you know? He's a farmer, lumber jack, mountain of a man already. His baby face belies his full-grown physique."

"Tell me again, how tall? How wide?" Blue said as he came around to her side of the car.

"It's hard to say. I couldn't see anything. But his shape," she put her hands on the rounds of his shoulders. He tensed almost imperceptibly. "He was about this wide. And about your height. That was hardest to tell because I was on the floor the whole time. But Jonathan is about your size, right? I'm really bad at estimating."

"Did he speak at all? Did he grunt? Did you see his eyes? The color?" Blue asked stepping out of her measuring embrace.

"Like I said before, not a word. There are no windows in that cellar. There was no light. If there had been more time, my eyes would have adjusted more, but I could barely tell it was Ron on the floor. A body. His shoes. Then I was attacked." Cady's eyes glazed over.

"I'll have a talk with this Jonathan," Blue said. "Let me help you get settled in," Blue said as he turned away from her and toward her stairs.

"No, you go on ahead," she said. "I'm fine. I just need a Hero cuddle."

"Look," he turned back to her, "I've relented on a security detail because it seems clear there is no way this guy can believe you could identify him, but I need to at least make sure your apartment is secure," he said as he cupped her elbow and started again toward the stairs.

Blue went into the apartment first after Cady unlocked the sliding glass door. Hero was waiting on the deck and threaded in and out of Cady's feet as she walked from the top of the stairs to the door.

"Hero will protect me," she said as she bent down and picked him up with a grunt. "Ugh. I'm feeling it today," she said nose to nose with Hero. She stepped into the apartment as Blue was coming out of the bathroom.

"All clear."

"Roger. Over," she said. She put Hero down and walked toward the kitchen to feed him and change his water.

"Did you just say 'ugh'?"

Cady shrugged. "When you're feeling it . . ."

Blue heard someone come bounding up the stairs. He crossed to the open door to see who it was. Eric stood in front of the sliding glass door screen. "You made it home," he said to Cady behind Blue's shoulder. "I brought Chinese." He held up a brown paper sack full of takeout cartons. "Lily's."

"Yes," Cady said as she turned toward Eric at the door. "Just in time to sleep again." She set Hero down and walked into the kitchen area.

"Hey. Thanks, man," Blue said opening the screen door and grabbing the bag from him. "I'm starved." He set the bag on the table.

"What the hell happened to you?" Eric asked Blue.

"Trouble at the office."

"I am hungry, too. I can't even remember the last time I ate. You guys want some water? Or lemonade? I don't have soda, but I do have beer," Cady asked over her shoulder to Eric and Blue. She hadn't heard Eric ask Blue about his cut lip. They both accepted the water and she drew clear, cool water from the fridge door for the three Y chromosomes in her apartment. Hero drank like it was a hundred degrees outside. He never took his eyes off of the company in his presence.

The sun was setting a brilliant salmon on the horizon and then morphed into a deep cherry that filled half the sky and faded into a high, soft pink. The pink was streaked with thin indigo purple clouds. The air was still and warm. She asked Eric to flip on the ceiling fans and open the windows throughout the apartment. Sara had locked the place up tight when she had come that morning to feed Hero and get Cady a change of clothes. Cady set out three white plates and three apple green cloth napkins. She held up chopsticks and forks and they each chose chopsticks.

"Let's sit on the deck." She indicated that Eric should take the dishes to the table outside. Cady had purchased a small, slate patio table set when she had the deck built. She'd had to pay the store to deliver it because she could not lift it into her compact SUV let alone carry it up the stairs. She bought four of the end chairs with the arms and the tilting base. Her apartment was small compared to her home with Victor, but everything in it she bought with comfort and beauty in mind. During the summer when she hosted the book club, they often met on the deck and even with a chair or two from inside, the table fit perfectly on the deck with room to spare.

Blue grabbed his water glass and Eric's. He came back for Cady's, but they met in the doorway as they were both trying to come through. They danced around each other and their eyes met before he stood aside to let her get through the door. He brought the bag out and they all filled their plates with skewered chicken, steamed dumplings, sticky white rice, cashew chicken, cold noodles, and pork bao.

Eric knew skewered chicken was Cady's favorite because he took her to Lily's on their first date. They had walked from Cady's apartment the one block over to Main Street on an early summer's evening to the little Chinese restaurant on the corner of Virginia and Main Streets. It formed one quarter of the Village quadrant known as The Four Corners. Every small town had one. It was also the main stoplight in Waterloo—a four-way stoplight that was flanked by the Post Office, a bank, a store that was currently an antique store, but changed owners about once a year, and Lily's. The owners had immigrated from China by way of New York City almost two decades ago. Cady liked the restaurant not only for its proximity to her apartment but also because their marinated chicken was her favorite. She had gotten to know the youngest daughter, who was only a few years younger than Cady, because she came into the library regularly.

On the night of their first date, Lily's was having its grand reopening. They had moved to the corner from one storefront down and had built a full-service restaurant. To their already perfected Chinese menu, they added Japanese food and had imported a sushi chef from New York City. Cady had bonded with Sam Baldwin that night over being sushi virgins. Eric said he had picked the place for their first date because he loved sushi and was grateful such a restaurant had finally come to his small corner of the world. Sam was there with his friend, Clarke, and her son, Walter. Clarke and Eric were sushi aficionados and were trying to lure their respective dates into the fold. Cady liked the salmon nigiri but stuck with Chinese food for her main course. As they were leaving, Sam and Cady joked that they'd been hoodwinked. They both liked it, though, and Cady now had even more reason to visit the little restaurant.

As she was emptying Hero's dinner into his bowl, the phone rang. "Hey guys," she said as she picked up the phone and leaned out the door, "it's my mom. Why don't you go ahead and get those beers. I'll only be a second. None for me. I'm still pretty medicated." She pressed the talk button on her home phone and said, "Mamala," the smile on her face evident in her voice. Eric got up to get two beers from the fridge. He bent down to pet Hero who had followed him inside, but Hero dodged Eric's hand and slipped past him into Cady's bedroom where she was headed.

Enid, on the other end of the phone three thousand miles away, said, "Cadyla, how are you? I talked to the doctor last night and he told me you'd be fine, but I have to know from you." The worry in her voice was visceral.

"Not to worry," Cady said. "I'm home now and I feel fine. Really sore but that's all. It's really been a disaster of a week, though, huh?"

"Please let me come there. Or better yet, you come here. Get out of that murder trap town and come here for some peace and quiet." At 5' 1" Enid was all body. She wanted to be with Cady when she needed her. Physical presence was deeply important to her and moving across the country had been a painful decision. They'd made it together. Cady was newly married and had moved away from where her mother lived. When Enid got the opportunity to move to the more temperate climate of San Francisco, she reluctantly forged ahead and started a new life. When she moved she was too young for the transitional step, but at 64 now, she had recently been considering retirement so she could focus more on her writing as well as visit Cady more often. They'd talked about her moving back to the east coast when Victor disappeared, but for the first year it seemed like Cady was almost about to find him and then everything would be okay. By the time they both accepted that finding him wasn't likely to happen, they talked about Cady moving out west, but she could never bring herself to leave the area. They were, for the time being, separated by 3,000 miles.

"You are so sweet," Cady said, sitting on the edge of her bed. She rubbed her neck and then laid her hand on her knee and winced. A round bruise already deep purple was blooming on the front of her knee. One of many, she supposed. "I may take you up on that. But not right now. I need to be on the ground here. I'm being well taken care of." Cady stood up and looked out the bedroom sliding glass door at the two men on her deck, settled in like a force against the world for anyone who would dream of hurting her.

"Don't be a hero, Cady. Promise?"

"Oh, you have nothing to worry about on that score. I'd miss you too much to get myself in trouble here. Let's definitely plan a trip for me to come out there at the end of the summer. I could really use a Mamala hug."

"It's done. I'll get you some dates that would be good for me and we'll pick one that matches you. I can come there, too, if you don't feel up to traveling."

"No. You're right. I'd like to see the sunny California shores. Even if the sun never shines in the one California town you happened to gravitate to. Hey, I do have company right now, though. We were just about to sit down to dinner. Can I call you in the morning? Well, your morning?"

"Sure. Please rest well. Smooge Hero for me, okay?"

"Okay. I love you," Cady said.

"I love you, too," Enid said and they both clicked off.

When they were settled with food and drink, they talked easily as they ate on the deck with the sun setting. They were all tense and tired but they needed a break. They talked about things other than the case. They tacitly agreed between the three of them that they needed a few hours off of talking about and thinking about Rosalind and Ron and the events since Saturday. They granted each other a time out. Hero inched through the cat door and joined them on the deck. He sat on the chair next to Cady. He laid on his side with his arms out straight, like a lounging Sphinx. His ears twitched, peaked high, alert to the night sounds. He was licking his chops from his dinner, but he did not proceed to his comfortable grooming as he normally would after eating.

Eric asked about Cady's mother and whether she'd be coming back east for a visit. Cady said no but that she would like to fly out there soon.

"You might not be up for the wine, but I'm up for the story about your last name. Since we're talking about your kin," Blue said.

Cady smiled. "Oh, it's not even worth a good glass of wine." She leaned back in her chair. "My mother is one of the original feminists. Extraordinary woman. She's a professor and writer in San Francisco now." They both nodded. "She's also a lesbian. She and her best friend, also gay, 'created me' some thirty plus years ago." She used air quotes and knew neither of them would ask "how." No one ever did. "He and his partner were my fathers," she said and paused to think of them both for a minute. They let her have the moment. "He died of AIDS. Both of them did."

"Whoa, that is not normal," said Eric slowly. "I mean, you don't find that kind of homegrown story around here. How long ago did he die?"

Cady sighed. "That's a much longer story and for a day when we all have a little more energy." She paused. "But, my name. The little bit of back story helps with the name story. Just so you know what kind of woman my mother is. Even before I was born, she had changed her name to Colette. Have you ever read her?" They both shook their heads. "She's a delicious French writer. My mother has a bit of a love affair going on with France. No, I do not have a drop of French blood in me," she said before they asked.

"Do you speak French?" Blue asked.

"Not more than a few phrases, although I've always wanted to learn. Any language for that matter. My mother is fairly fluent." She started to feel self-conscious about giving so much personal information away. She wrapped up her rap on how she came to be. "Anyway, she wanted to start publishing. This was early in her career, before she even finished her dissertation. She decided to publish under a pen name so that if she ever got married she wouldn't have to worry about her publishing persona. This was when she still thought getting married and changing her name might be in her cards. She was confused for a long time. Times were different then. Not like they are today."

"I'm guessing it's not all that different today," Eric said.

"I don't know. There have been a lot of changes that make it easier for young people to come out. Not enough. You're probably very right about that." She paused. "Well, when she started to try pen names on for size, the name Colette stuck with her. She's always said it felt like who she was born to be. She had it changed legally in time to publish her dissertation and a family of Colette women was born, so to speak."

"We both have chosen names, so to speak," said Blue. "I didn't exactly choose mine, but it was chosen for me. Not passed down. Yours is sort of like that, too."

"Yes, I do feel chosen in the way I've come to be. I'd never be able to change it. That's why I'm not Cady Nicholas. Men never have to leave their heritage behind. For women, it's just expected."

"I thought you went back to Colette," Eric said. "I didn't know you'd never changed."

"Yeah, steady Freddy. That's me." She got up to get them another beer so as to end the conversation string. When she was seated again, she asked about them living together and Blue and Eric explained in turns that Eric lived in Blue's garage. They joked that he was the Alan Harper of Center Street instead of Malibu, California. Cady laughed. Blue said his ex-wife would never have gotten that joke. They talked about Eric working at the Outlet Mall for the security company. He was bored and felt unchallenged. He had mentioned as much before, on their first date. But now with Blue, he was passionate about it. Then, as he often did, he moved on to the funny story of the Outlet Mall week. He told the story of the week before when he caught a shoplifter trying to steal from the Wilson's Leather store.

"I'm doing a routine patrol. I come around the corner and I see this guy with his arms so full of leather coats," Eric held his arms out wide, "that he couldn't even see where he was going. They were piled too high. The idiot turns to his left and smacks right into me. I say to him,

'You going to wear all those?' I get the call about the robbery at that exact second on my radio." Blue and Cady laughed. "No," he continued, "I swear. You cannot make this stuff up." He started to laugh. "It's the most ridiculous job known to man. Blue does all the hard work," Eric teased, "but at least I get to have better hair."

Blue put his hand on his head and rubbed his short hair. "Just because they let you run around like a hair bag doesn't mean it's better."

"I was going to be a trooper," Eric said to Cady.

"Really?" she said.

"Yeah. I never made it to college, though."

"You could have," Blue said seriously.

"Is it too late?" Cady asked.

"For college or for the troopers?" Eric said.

"Either, I suppose," she said.

"Both," Eric said.

"Bull," Blue said. "It may be too late for the troopers, but it's not too late for anything else you want to do with your life."

Eric sniffed and brushed his hand across his nose. He waved them both off. "It's too late for all of it. I got a good gig right where I am. No regrets," he said.

"Why didn't you go?" Cady asked. She hoped he would reveal something of the gambling problem that she had heard rumors about.

"Our dearly departed," he raised his glass in a toast.

"Rosalind? What do you mean?" Cady asked.

"She flunked me in high school and I had to spend the summer after my senior year in summer school. Lost my mojo."

"Deuce," Blue said, leaning his head back on to the deck chair and staring at the stars.

"What?" Eric asked.

"She did not flunk you. You flunked an entirely different class." Blue turned to Cady. "This guy will have you crying a sob story for him. I love him like a brother, but don't listen to this garbage. No one has ever stopped him from doing anything."

Eric shifted in his seat. "I spent so many days in that damn 'optional' period after school in her classroom working on my homework. I read more that year than any year before or since. And my final grade in her class after all that effort? C. Not an A for effort or even a B for been there every day, but a C. She had always asked too much. And because I'd spent so much time on her class, I actually did fail History. Had to go to summer school. I was so mad when I found out I was going to walk across that stage as a fake. People I'd gone to school with since Kindergarten."

A heady silence fell. Cady never knew what to do with a story like this. Rosalind was a tough teacher. Demanding. She'd heard it before, tales of her unfairness. It was not the Rosalind she knew but she didn't doubt the facts of these stories. She never felt comfortable defending Rosalind but she also felt a little prick of betrayal any time she didn't.

"And what about you?" Eric said, sitting forward.

"Not that we're talking about me," Blue said, "but what about me?"

"You got dreams. You got a garage full of pieces of wood that were rotting away long before I ever got in your way. And isn't Rosalind the one who was never satisfied? She had you remake that damned chair three times. Don't tell me that didn't chap your ass."

"She wanted two small adjustments. It wasn't a big deal. And building furniture isn't a dream of mine," Blue said, dismissing his statement. "It's a hobby. I do it when I want. When I get busy, I don't do it as much. Simple as that. In case you hadn't noticed, I've been a little busy the last few years. Divorce takes up a lot of time."

They were all quiet. The sounds of the night spoke instead of them. The crickets and the cicadas sang in concert. The white lights on her deck glowed softly.

Cady yawned and stretched. "I'm fading fast," she said. They all stood up and started gathering the dinner dishes and take-out containers.

"It's time for you to get some rest," Eric said to Cady as they all made their way into the apartment. "Let me stay here tonight and bunk on your couch. I'm not working tomorrow and I'm not comfortable with you being alone."

"That's not necessary," Cady said.

"I couldn't ask you to do that, Deuce," Blue said. Both Eric and Cady looked at Blue. "I didn't hear you ask," Eric said with a smile. "If the State Police can't provide protection for an assault victim, it's the least I can do to stay here tonight and make sure she's okay." He looked around. "This isn't the securest apartment, with all these windows," he said. "I don't need a paying job to protect and serve Cady," he said as he stood next to her and put his arm around her shoulders, his firm hand giving her a squeeze.

Blue focused on Cady, "It wouldn't hurt to have someone here tonight."

"You know, I'm all Miss Independent and everything," she said, "but I think I would sleep better if I weren't sleeping alone." Hero was rubbing her legs with the length of his body. "I mean, not alone in the apartment." She moved away from Eric's embrace and her cheeks burned. "I'm still feeling a little groggy from the pain medication and I'm not sure I'd be as alert as I'd need to be if someone were lurking around outside. If you wouldn't mind, Eric, I have world class bedding I could set you up on the couch with." She started scraping the dishes and rinsing them in the sink.

"All I need is a sheet," Eric said. "I think we should lock the windows and doors, though. We need to lock up tight."

"We can leave them open a crack," Cady said. "I've got security locks. I think we'd suffocate without a bit of a breeze. The fans are great, but it can get hot up here."

Blue stood by the door awkwardly. "If you're sure about this," he said to Cady. "Thanks," he said to Eric. Eric smirked at him with his "stop being the big brother" look. Even though Eric was older than Blue by four months, Blue always played the big brother to Eric's younger sibling persona. Here, Eric wanted Blue to be sure he knew Blue was not running this show. He wasn't working for Blue. He was offering to protect Cady because he was dating her. Not because Blue had set up a protection detail.

After Blue left and Cady pulled out a sheet from the closet in her bedroom, Eric settled on the couch facing the kitchen. They said their good nights. She thanked him for staying. Cady changed into her light summer pajama bottoms and a spaghetti strapped undershirt. When she thought of Eric on the other side of her bedroom door, she put on a thin T-shirt over her undershirt and crawled into bed. She left her bedroom door open a crack so that Hero could come and go in the night. He curled up at her feet. Cady scratched his ears and thanked him for staying, too. She was sure he sensed the danger outside and wanted to protect her. He was her hero after all. Most nights he left her to her sleep and wandered the streets of Waterloo. Tonight he curled up tight next to her.

The room was warmer than normal because the windows and the door were three-quarters shut. She took off the extra T-shirt. She nuzzled her foot inside the crook of Hero's belly, the nearly enclosed circle he made with his body. The contact made her feel safe. She thought she might be restless but sleep took her over in minutes. The remnants of the drugs given to her at the hospital dropped her into a deep, dreamless sleep.

CHAPTER 21

CADY WOKE UP to a rapping on her living room sliding glass door. Hero was still snuggled against her. During the night, he had made his way to resting his chin on her shoulder and purring deeply into her ear. He started when he heard the knock. His ears perked up and he rose to alert. He slipped out of the bedroom through the crack in the door before Cady had her eyes fully open. When she made it to the living room, Eric was at the sliding glass door. He was wearing a sleeveless white T-shirt and the soft khaki cargo pants he'd arrived in the night before. He had the curtain pulled back to see who it was and was unlocking the latch.

"Who is it?" she asked from the doorway to her bedroom. When she saw him, she had a catch in her throat. She had known Eric was beautiful, but looking at his tanned, naked shoulders, cut like stone, she was aroused. She hadn't been awake long enough to come out of sleep completely and her mind rested for a second on what it would feel like to be in intimate proximity to his muscled body. Her body instinctively responded.

"Just Blue," he said, opening the door. As she had when she first met Eric, she noticed he looked like the lead actor does in a movie. Now she was picturing him as that lead actor when he first wakes up, rested and uncrumpled.

"Sorry to come so early. Again," Blue said to Cady as he entered, wearing a tan poplin suit, his tie already askew. He looked at the two of them in turn. Both Cady and Eric realized they were not as dressed as they would like to be. Eric reached for his short-sleeved T-shirt to pull on over his sleeveless T. And Cady dashed into her bedroom and put on her second layer.

When she was back in the living room, Cady said, "7:00. It's like we have a standing date." She normally would have been up and moving at this hour, but the attack, the stress of the murder, and the pain medication she'd been given at the hospital had made her bone weary.

"No problem," Eric said. "Come on in." Blue's nostrils flared as he looked at Eric. "You sleep well?" he asked Eric.

"Pretty good," Eric ignored Blue's mounting hostility. He turned to Cady, "How about you? How are you feeling?"

"I actually feel a bit restored." She bent down and scooped up Hero. She walked over to Eric who started to scritch Hero behind his ears. "My security force gave me a peaceful night's sleep." Hero wriggled and she put him down. "Everyone's hungry. As payment for services rendered, I will make breakfast." She smiled as she started toward the kitchen. Eric started to fold up the sheet on the couch.

"There's no time for that," Blue said sharply. Both Cady and Eric stopped moving and turned to him.

"What's happened?" Cady said. Her face went pale in anticipation of hearing of another violent outbreak.

"I need some more information." He had scared her. He could see it in her eyes. He relaxed his rigid stance and retracted his bark.

"Information can wait, Blue," Eric said calmly. "Cady needs to keep up her strength." He walked toward Cady.

"What information do you need?" Cady asked, standing squarely to face him.

Hero started to demand breakfast. He was clear that it was time to eat. They all three looked at him. He meowed at each of them in turn.

"Hero waits for no man," she said. "You talk," she said as she went for Hero's food. "I'll feed him and put on coffee." She stopped. "Do we have time for coffee?"

Blue hesitated. "You know you can't resist my coffee," she teased. He clenched his jaw, almost grinding his teeth.

"Let me do that," Eric stepped forward to open the cat food packet. Hero was talking more than any of them. "You make this famous coffee I keep hearing about. Blue, you talk."

Blue stood just inside the door watching the scene of harmonious domesticity. "You need to open the library," he said. He was looking at her. Cold. Demanding. Almost looking through her. "We need to get back on the computer."

"What are we looking for?" Cady asked as she filled the coffee pot with water and poured it into the coffee maker. Hero ate hungrily but faced the three of them instead of his usual position of facing the kitchen cabinets.

"I want to bring Jonathan in for questioning but I don't have any evidence to compel him to come in. If he's our guy, and I believe he's our guy, he won't come in voluntarily. My team has him on the list of students to interview but so far, he hasn't been available when they've tried to track him down. I checked his criminal history and he has none. Not even a juvenile record before he turned eighteen. But there's a psychiatric history that I can't get access to without a warrant." He stopped and Cady stopped. She was washing her hands and rinsing out coffee cups for them when she halted and looked down, waiting for him to not say what he was about to say next. He sensed her tense up on him. "Don't go soft on me now, Cady. It's not illegal if I don't use it to obtain the warrant." He looked at Eric. "Eric is good," he said to assure her he trusted Eric with her secret. "I just need to get in to find out if there is something there."

"You can't be suggesting that mental illness is the same as a propensity toward murder." She turned off the water.

"I don't think that," Blue said, walking to the bar between the dining room and kitchen areas, where they'd shared coffee a few days ago. "I need a basis for making him come in. You know there's something off about him. I need something concrete. I've been working on this all night and I'm coming up empty."

"Why can't your computer people do this?" She turned toward him. "I'm not your personal techie."

"I already told you why," he snapped. "I need this information now. There's a murderer on the loose."

"And the troopers don't care about that?" She raised her voice to match his. "They need some yahoo librarian to do their investigating for them?"

"Cady," Eric intervened. "Of course you don't have to do this." He looked at Blue. "And I'm sure the troopers are working on this night and day." He kept his gaze on Blue. "But if there's anything you know how to do that could help put this murdering bastard away sooner, I'm begging you to help." He held her bare arms gently and rubbed with his thumbs as he shifted his gaze to her.

"This *is* the mod squad," she said. Hero jumped on the chair next to Cady. He became agitated and began marking her. "All right. I need a minute to shower. I do have a job I need to do at some point." She turned to Hero on the chair. "Blue, you're making my cat neurotic. Why don't you guys get a cup of coffee and wait out on the deck."

Blue was unapologetic. He whipped open the screen and went out to stand on the deck. Eric poured two cups of coffee when it was ready, doctored them and joined

Blue in the early morning light on the deck. It was chilly for a July morning, breezy. Hero slipped out the door when Eric opened the screen. He hopped up onto one of the chairs and sat, alert in his Sphinx pose.

"She's in the shower," Eric said.

Eric put the coffee down in front of Blue on the deck railing. Blue ignored it. He ignored Eric.

"What?" Eric said leaning against the L of the railing.

"What, what?" Blue said.

"Cut the crap, Bro. Who shit in your corn flakes this morning?"

"There's a murder to be solved here. Bro," Blue said.

"We're all working to solve it," Eric said.

"You think *guarding a witness* is working to solve it?" Blue spat out, leaning on "guarding a witness."

"I think sleeping with Cady made her feel safe," Eric said without taking the bait.

Blue snapped his head around to look at Eric. "*Sleeping* with her?" he hissed.

"Yep. That's what I thought," Eric said.

Blue stared him down.

"When did you fall for her?" Eric said as he sipped his coffee.

Blue said nothing.

"You. Me. Now," Eric said. Blue did not respond. "No, I didn't sleep with her. I stayed with her in the same living space for one night. But if I had slept with her, I wouldn't have thought before this second that it would matter to you."

"You must be high," Blue said, picking up his coffee. "I couldn't care less where you laid your head last night. Or where she did."

"Y-uh," Eric snorted. "Look, if you're falling for her, you and I need to have a conversation about that."

"For fuck's sake, Eric," Blue said, "I am trying to catch a murderer here. Do you understand how little I care about you or Cady or whether the two of you make babies?"

"Okay," Eric said holding up a hand. "I'm sorry. I guess I got my signals crossed. Plus, you know she can't resist these pecs."

Blue screwed his mouth up and stared out off the deck. He drank his coffee.

Cady stepped out on to the deck. She was dressed for work. She had pulled on a muted, summer orange short-sleeved wrap dress that brushed her knees. The dress had a mid-cut V-neck. She looped a whisper-thin white scarf around her neck. She wore low wedge-heeled sandals and her hair was piled in a loose bun at her crown. She spent a lot of time on her feet during a day at the library so she always wore foot-friendly shoes. Her first year working there, she wore high heels often. Eventually she noticed that not a single woman in Waterloo wore high heels except for the attorneys she saw walking to and from the courthouse parking lot a few blocks from the library. She had dialed her wardrobe down after that to be more comfy casual, but still business professional. She'd found long ago that it was a hard balance for a woman to pull off business casual. The typical golf shirt and khakis a man could wear on dress down Friday didn't usually translate on a woman. She typically wore colorful wrap dresses or shaped cotton trousers with a fitted T-shirt.

She had upgraded her grad student look when she started working part-time at the library when she was first engaged to Victor. When she was at school, she wore jeans, turtlenecks. She had a pea coat that shielded her from even the most brittle wind. Her look was always simple and comfortable. The only two suits she had were the two suits she'd purchased to interview for the part-time assistant librarian's job. One was a sleek black suit, which she wore to her first interview with a royal blue sweater shell and black leather Mary Jane pumps. The other was a coffee colored sheath dress with a long suit jacket. The material was a delicate stretch corduroy. She wore her only other high heels at the time, a pair of chocolate brown leather pumps. She had never had footwear imagination. She still had only the two suits and she would wear them whenever she could get away with wearing the same thing without being noticed.

"Okay, Blue, you can come down through the library stairs," she said. "Let me get my coffee and we can go." She turned to walk back inside. They followed her. "You, Atlas, God of the chiseled pecs," she smiled at Eric, tilting her head to the side, "grab an apple," she said. "Or a nectarine." She picked up a nectarine and tossed it to Eric.

"The Colette B & B can't get the reputation of starving its guests. But don't eat the peanut butter. It's contaminated with girl germs." Blue smirked. "There's also a new toothbrush from the dentist in the medicine cabinet. If you want to wash up, I'll leave the door unlocked for you to join us when you're done." Eric nodded, set down the nectarine and his coffee and went into the bathroom.

She unlocked the double doors that led to the library. There was a set of double doors at the top of the stairs coming into her apartment and a set of oversized wooden double doors at the bottom of the stairs at the end of a foyer that led to the library's main corridor. The stairs had once led to the upper story of the house before it had been turned into the library, but when the library was created and the upper floor had been converted into a meeting space before the theater and finally the apartment, the door at the top of the stairs was installed. The staircase was wide and ornate. The stairs themselves were marble.

Many of the original features of the building had been replaced over the years as they wore out or needed repair. Cady had written a grant when she was new as the librarian for some restoration work to be completed. The major project she was able to complete was refinishing the floors. She had all the carpets replaced in the circulation room where the computers were housed and in the fiction room. The main corridor hallway, to which all the rooms of the library were connected, and the Children's Room had oak floors. She had them refinished over a weekend when the library was closed during the summer.

She had to coordinate the packing and reshelving of all the books that couldn't be hermetically sealed in their book shelves during the renovations. It took the better part of a summer to restore order to the small library. Part of the grant went to pay for lost revenue that would inevitably result from the chaos created by the renovations.

At the end of July, the library was decorated for summer. She worked with the local Boy Scout troop to help her decorate the library four times a year. She had taken down the 4th of July decorations but the generic summer décor was still up. She also decorated for the fall harvest and Halloween season, for the Christmas holidays, and for the spring solstice. For spring, she would force pots of bulbs to bloom in the window sills and change the Creative Live Wires in all the windows from dark stone and wood for the cooler months to shimmering pinks and iridescent blues and purples. In each window, she had hung a glittering silver thread strung with beads and dripping with charms. She had made each one at her beading table in her art studio and after so many years, she had one for each window. She had finally created enough of them to change them in the fall and the spring. She wrapped the ends of the thread around the tilt latches on all the windows. She called them Creative Live Wires because she felt like they were charged with creative electricity. It felt to Cady like they sent a current around the library that infused the entire building with warmth and frivolous beauty.

She unlocked the doors at the bottom of the stairs and Hero slipped through first. The patrons loved Hero and several people came to the library regularly just to visit him. She was fortunate that Hero was a non-shedding cat. Even with his long, silky cat hair, he never left it anywhere it wasn't supposed to be. And since he had hair and not fur, he had no allergic properties. Until Blue had told her a few days ago about the difference between cat hair and cat fur, she hadn't known why no one was allergic to Hero. Had he been a cat that shed and made the kids sneeze, she would have had to keep him out of the library. As it was, he spent the entire work day in the library with her and happily ascended the marble stairs for dinner and then out the cat door in her apartment for his night's adventures.

The library wouldn't be open until 9:00 and neither Alice nor Natalie would show up until 8:45. The library was easy to open. As long as a patron could check out a book or log on to a computer promptly at 9:00, everything else could unfold during the first hour. They also always made sure the cash register was open by 9:00. If patrons wanted to pay a late fine, Cady never wanted to make them wait.

Carrying her coffee cup, Cady stopped to turn on each of the six computers in the circulation room. By the third one, Blue was getting antsy and flipped the on switches on two of them while she got the final one. She turned on the computer at the circulation desk but left the cash register for Natalie when she got in.

"Come on." She started to move back toward her office behind the circulation desk. "We can use my computer in here again." Blue settled in at Cady's desk. She turned her computer on and as it booted up, she sat back and drank her coffee. Neither of them said anything as the old computer whirred to life.

"I am so going to get fired for this," Cady said as she finally started to pull up screen after screen, making her way to the medical records she had no business accessing. "This has to be illegal." Blue said nothing. Her palms started to sweat as she clicked through block after block and bypassed them with relative ease. "You've got the pull to rescue me if I get caught?" She was only half joking. She was getting irritated that Blue was letting her babble. "I'm breaking every HIPPA law there is." She kept on chattering away at the screen more than to Blue.

"Your skills have improved," he said finally as he leaned forward in his chair. He was referring to her rudimentary computer skills at the time she tried to help look for Victor. He had known she'd gotten better because she shared as much with him the previous winter. And he'd seen her do some basic hacking on Sunday.

It was her initial frustration in the search for Victor that sent Cady on a mission to learn computers from the ones and zeros up. She was entirely self-taught except for a few entry-level extension classes early on. She had been amazed at how much sense computers made once you understood even the most basic elements of code. Her understanding was so innate at this point that she no longer needed to study much. She needed to be active, on the net. The concepts were clear and the roadblocks surmountable. It was not an activity she told anyone about, not even Sara. She had come to Blue all those years ago with lead after lead that she'd found in local newspapers in the surrounding counties. None of them had panned out. Most of them were not even solid enough to warrant a follow up, but he always did. The lead she had shared with him last winter had felt to her like a solid breakthrough. A suspect was in custody in New Jersey. He was cutting a deal to reveal the names and burial sites of his twenty victims in New York. When it led nowhere and it was confirmed he'd never crossed paths with Victor, she started to spiral into a depression that was low-grade but constant, unlike the frenzy after his disappearance. Everything told her to stop looking, to let it go. She wished daily that she could.

"If any of these records were correctly protected," she said as she worked, "I wouldn't be able to touch them. I am not all that sophisticated but this stuff is small time. It's not like we're after Department of Defense secrets."

"Have you found anything else useful?" he asked.

She stopped clicking and looked down at the keyboard. She looked left at him. "Nothing worth coming to the police about." She knew he was talking about Victor and not their current search for Jonathan.

He nodded his head and she continued poking holes in what people thought was impenetrable security.

She had spent uncountable hours searching for any clue about Victor's disappearance. She scoured obituaries and John Doe morgue records. She had tapped into secure files all over the eastern seaboard. This was the first time since she'd developed any real computer skills at all that she was sharing her facility with anyone.

"I'm good at hiding my trail," she said, "but this seriously cannot get out. If you want to use any of this to prosecute, you have to make up some story about how you stumbled on it. Or give your own tech guys a hint and have them track this down."

"We're looking at getting some help out of Rochester or Syracuse. There's no telling when the lab will be recertified. Getting covert information out of my guys there would be worse than coming to you." He looked at her instead of the screen. "I won't let you get into trouble for this." His eyes were trusting. His trusting her made her trust him back.

Eric came in looking refreshed. "Any luck?" he said, rubbing his hands together as if he were cold.

"Still working," Cady said. Eric pulled up a seat behind and between Cady and Blue.

It took her less than fifteen minutes to hack into the personal computer of both of the juvenile psychologists in the county. Both of them had meticulous filing systems with their notes and reports in folders labeled by patient name. Her palms were sweating as she clicked on the folder labeled J Peck. She called their attention to the file as it was loading. When she was able to access Jonathan's psychological report, they all stared at the screen in disbelief.

CHAPTER 22

"THIS WILL PROVE Jonathan killed Rosalind," Eric said to the air, concentrating on the screen.

"It's not proof of anything," Blue said, also still reading the screen. "But, damn."

"Now I know why my creep show senses went off around Jonathan." She turned to Blue. "Is this a Columbine kid?" He did not answer.

What they were reading was a litany of diagnoses that characterized Jonathan as mentally unstable and a physical risk to himself and others. The starkest statement that capped the final paragraph in the long psychiatric report said, "Although the term cannot be applied to juveniles with medical accuracy, it is my opinion that Jonathan is a clinical sociopath. He shows no evidence of empathy toward others but does show a significant ability to act the part. He understands empathy; he does not embody it. His characterological disturbance is deeply entrenched and, without medication, and even possibly with medication, unlikely to respond to any form of treatment in the short term. Normal socialization is not likely achievable."

"Rosalind must have found out about this," Eric said. "She must have confronted him with it."

"I can't see her doing that," Cady said. "Even if she had gotten hold of this information. She'd told me a number of times over the years that she often wanted to get into students' health records. She suspected a lot of her students were imbalanced and they were medicated when their issues were nonmedical in nature. The principal would have access to this, maybe, but it would never end up in the hands of a teacher. I would hope."

"She's a psychiatrist now?" Eric said.

Cady didn't respond.

"This is what I need to bring him in," Blue said. "I don't even have to tell him I know this. Just hint that there is a psychiatric record that makes him a suspect. He'll bite. I know he will. Print this out for me. I'll head over to his parents' house now and catch him before he goes to work."

"Oh, no," Cady said. "There is not going to be a record of this little transaction. You want this information, you need to go through your super-secret cop-o-meter channels." She stood up. "That's it," she said grabbing each of them by a muscled bicep. "Both of you get out of here now. You got what you came for. I've got to get this place open. You do your job. I'll do mine." She ushered them out of her office and around to the customer's side of the circulation desk.

"And he won't be at his parents' house," she said. "He works on Al Thorpe's farm. I'll bet he'll have been there since before sun up."

"Damn. That's in East Buhwhatsit all the way at the south end," Blue said. "Fine. I'll head there. It's going to take me some time to get there."

"I'll go over to his parents' house. Just in case," Eric said.

"What about Cady?" Blue said.

"I'll be fine. You both go. Alice and Natalie will be here in a few minutes. I'll keep the place locked up tight until then. It's like a fortress in here."

Blue's gaze shifted between them. He grunted softly. "You see him at his parents' house," he turned to Eric, "just keep your eyes on him. Don't talk to him. Got it?"

"I don't want him to get away," Eric protested.

"I'll send a car over. You call me the second you lay eyes on him," Blue said. "I'll come there with backup. If I get him at the farm, I'll let you know so you don't have to stake out his folks' house."

Eric started to argue again. "Deuce," Blue said, "just do it. Or stay here with Cady. I can't have you spooking this kid. I never should have let you look at that report. I'm breaking protocol six ways from Sunday even talking to the two of you right now. I need to be in two places at once. It's leaving me a little desperate."

They confirmed that all the library doors were secure and then Blue and Eric walked out of the library together. Blue was on his phone making arrangements to get backup to all the appropriate places.

When they had left the library, Cady locked the front door behind them. She scooped Hero up and carried him back into the circulation room upright. He had been especially quiet while they were crowded around the computer. He laid a paw on either shoulder.

"We have some phone calls to make," she spoke into his ear as she rounded back behind the desk and into her office. She poured Hero out onto the chair Blue had been sitting in and sat down behind her desk. Jonathan's medical notes were still up on her screen. She shuddered with a moment of sympathy. She pictured the embodiment of all this psychiatric drama lifting her up off of the floor and flinging her across the room. The flicker of sympathy turned to anger. Her body ached from his attack. Her instincts had always told her there was something off about him. She thought about Sara's suggestion to take applications for the book club. She needed to protect her kids.

At that thought, she jerked herself to attention and picked up the phone. She tapped the names in her contacts. She started at the top of her list and called each one in turn. She did not come out and say that Jonathan was the one who murdered Rosalind, but she told each of them to be careful and to not be alone today. She wanted to protect her kids and give Blue time to catch up to Jonathan. She now knew him to be a sociopath but none of the book club kids would know that. Any of them would allow him to come in if he showed up on their doorstep. He could be looking for cover. They would be simply inviting in an awkward friend who had dropped by.

After she phoned the kids in the book club, she set about opening the library. The Toddler Time Summer Reading Hour was scheduled for this morning so Alice would be in to start preparing the Children's Room. Somebody closed the library last night. She hadn't even checked the cash register yet to see who signed off on the register tape.

CHAPTER 23

AFTER A QUIET DAY at the library, Cady locked up the front doors behind Alice and Natalie, after Sara had come in to pick her up. Sara had stayed for a few minutes to talk with Cady, to see if she needed anything. They talked in the air conditioned foyer of the old library building after Sara had arrived. They talked about Rosalind and Ron and how Cady was recovering, but Cady did not mention the possibility that Jonathan had killed Rosalind and attacked her and Ron. It seemed to fit his personality, although she would not have called him threatening or dangerous before this week. Cady wanted to protect Natalie and she wanted to make sure they all got to their cars safely, but she was sure Jonathan was in police custody now, so she was breathing a rounded sigh of relief.

Cady unlocked the double doors leading to her flat and let Hero go into the stairwell ahead of her. She adjusted the air temperature for the library so the air conditioner

wouldn't work overtime over night and followed Hero up
the stairs. When she unlocked the doors at the top of the
stairs, the heat felt oppressive. She immediately went to
open all the windows and sliding doors and turn on the
ceiling fans. She left the double doors to her stairwell
open to allow any residual cool air to infiltrate the steamy
upper-story flat. She filled a glass with cool water and
gave Hero a fresh bowl of water along with his dinner.

She kicked off her shoes and went into the bedroom to
change her clothes. She changed into a pair of worn boyfriend jeans rolled up above her ankles and a deep
burgundy fitted T-shirt. She kept on her T-shirt bra but
unlooped the scarf from around her neck and hung it and
her dress in her closet.

She walked out to the kitchen and tempered her bare
feet on the cool tile floor and contemplated dinner. The
thought of turning on the stove or heating up the oven
was intolerable. She checked the leftovers from her birthday BBQ. She made a face and tossed them all in the
garbage. She poured a glass of pinot noir and sliced off a
couple of hunks of cheddar cheese. She sliced up a Bartlett
pear and took it all out to the deck. Hero slipped through
the sliding door screen when she opened it and leapt up
onto the chair next to where Cady had placed her dinner.
He sat, licking his chops and scrubbing his face with his
paws while she went to the bathroom.

When she was in the bathroom, Hero came back into
the apartment through his door and started to tell her all
about the adventures he'd had the night before. He

seemed insistent that she come and listen so she hurried herself. When she came out of the bathroom, hands and face wet to allow them to air dry and cool her off, Jonathan was standing in her living room.

"Ms. Colette," he said. His long, dark hair was shapeless and parted to the side nearly covering one eye. He had his hands stuffed in the pockets of his dirt-crusted jeans. He was shifting and looking over her right shoulder.

"What are you doing here?" Cady said steadily. Hero had come to her feet and stood at attention.

"I needed to see you," he said. Neither of them moved from their spot. Cady's dinner sat out on the deck. "I needed to tell you."

"Tell me what?" she asked.

"What needs telling," he said.

"Why aren't you telling whatever it is you need to tell to the State Police?" She was trying to sound calm but her fear was rising.

"I can't let them find me," he said.

"How did you even know they were looking for you?"

"My mom called me. She told me Mr. Peterman was over to the house. He didn't say what he wanted, but he asked all kinds of questions about Mr. and Ms. M'Clintock. He demanded to know where I was. She put two and two together and called me. She told me to light out of there and never come back. This was my chance. I was out in the barn so when she called, I just skipped."

Cady started to inch her way to the kitchen. She was
hoping if she could get between him and the door that she
could make a break for it and be down the outside stairs
before he could catch her. The library door at the bottom
of the stairs was locked as it always was for the night.
Hero started pacing back and forth between Cady and
Jonathan. Jonathan paid no attention.

"Where have you been all day?" she asked.

"Trying to decide what to do," he said. "Trying to decide if I should come here."

By her third or fourth inch, Jonathan looked at her
squarely. "Where you going?" he said.

"Water. Just to get some water. It's hot in here," she
said as she started to move toward the fridge with pur-
pose.

"Please don't move," he said.

"Jonathan," she said dismissively. She was trying to act
like him being in her apartment happened all the time
and now she just needed to be a good host. "You must be
thirsty, too."

When she reached for the fridge door, he lunged at her.
At the same time he pulled out the buck knife he had been
worrying in his front pocket and flicked it open with the
thumb break. She screamed. He pushed her up against
the fridge with the knife close to her face.

"You don't need to be afraid of me, Cady," he said with
his face close to hers. He was holding her right wrist in his
left hand and gripping the knife with his right. He stood
nearly on top of her. This was a strength she had felt be-

fore. She knew she had to calm him or face another violent attack.

"What is there to be afraid of?" she said, shifting her eyes up to the knife by her temple.

He followed her eyes and jumped back softly. "I'm not going to hurt you. I just need you to listen to me."

"Okay," she said, letting a small breath escape. "You've got my attention." She stayed by the fridge. He moved over to the side of the dining room table by the sliding glass door.

"I didn't hurt nobody," he said.

"Of course you didn't," she said in her academy award winning sympathy voice. "Who says you hurt anyone?"

"I didn't hurt you."

"Jonathan. I know you didn't hurt anyone. Who says you did?"

"My mom says they're looking for me cause they think I killed my teacher. You know me. I wouldn't hurt nobody." He was pacing back and forth in front of the door.

"Why would they think you did?" she said, stepping toward the library stairs. "Have you ever hurt anyone before?"

He stopped. He looked at her. "What do you mean?"

"Nothing. I just wondered why anyone would think you had anything to do with what's going on." She was babbling.

He looked at her, eyes searching. "I hurt someone."

"Was it Ms. M'Clintock?" Cady asked, holding her breath.

"I am in my mind now," he said. "I wasn't in my mind then." He was talking more to the table than to Cady. She had a moment to bolt down the library stairs and try the lock, but she stayed.

"Are you taking medication?" she asked.

"A cabinet full." He paused. "It was my sister." He lifted his hand to push his hair back away from his eyes. "I didn't hurt her." He paused again. "That's not true." He looked confused. "It was an awful thing I did to her. She's gone now."

The momentary interest Cady had taken in Jonathan's story evaporated and she remembered the diagnosis of the man standing before her.

"I wasn't in my mind then," he went on. "She's older. Lives away. Won't come home. My parents want me to go away too. They won't say, but they do."

"Jonathan." She started to move toward him, her emotions flailing around like a balloon in the wind. He flinched and she sucked in air.

"Don't make me," he flared. Then more calmly. "Here," he put down the knife on the table. "I'm not going to hurt you. I just needed someone to listen. If they take me in, nobody's gonna listen." She stood where she was, not knowing whether to lunge for the knife or to try to barrel past him. She knew she'd never get the screen open before he grabbed her.

"My mom said they think I have a poker chip from the casino. She said the blood on the chip will prove I attacked Mr. M'Clintock. You. That I killed Ms. M'Clintock."

He slumped down into a chair at her table. "I have no idea what they're talking about," he said. All the nervous energy had drained from his body. "I've never even been to a casino. I don't earn no extra money to throw it away gambling." He looked at her. "I don't think I've ever done anything fun in my whole life."

"Wait," she stepped toward him, ignoring the knife less than a foot away from him. "What did you just say?"

"I've never done anything fun." Tears welled in his eyes.

"Jonathan," she moved to kneel in front of him. Hero slipped through Cady's legs. "Think carefully now. The poker chip. Who said you had a chip covered with blood?"

He drew his attention back to the urgent story. "My mom said it was Mr. Peterman who said that detective told him. I don't know. She was kind of screaming and crying when she called me. Just said to get. I didn't know where to *get* to but I knew you would listen to me." He turned his head to look into her eyes. "You always listened to me. Like I was always saying something smart, you know?"

Cady was reeling. "Jesus," she said, ignoring his last professions of gratitude. She stood up and grabbed her keys. She grabbed him by the shoulders and stood him up. Holding his shoulders, judging his shape so concretely confirmed it. "I know it's not you. I am listening. I know it wasn't you. More than that. I know who it is."

CHAPTER 24

CADY STOOD UP and turned away. "You're not safe here. Do you have some place you can go?"

"I don't know. They've already been to my parents' house," Jonathan said. "Where else is there? I've been driving around all day."

"Friends? Jonathan, think!" She was nearly screaming, holding in her rising hysteria.

"Don't worry about me." He stood up and started for the door.

"Wait, I didn't mean to yell. I can't let you go unless I know you're going someplace safe."

"You can't keep me here either," he said, standing firm, standing tall for the first time since she'd known him. "You know I didn't hurt anybody. If they find me here, I'll go to jail and that will be it. I'll be fine. You'll be fine?"

Cady was shaking. Jonathan was a grown man standing in front of her but he was still such a child. She couldn't hold him. She couldn't protect him. She nodded and he ran down her deck stairs two at a time and into the vacant grassy lot behind the library. She stood and watched him run.

Cady moved as though through water to reach her bathroom where she had set down her cell phone while she had washed her hands. She dialed the phone and he picked up on the eighth ring.

"God, where are you?" she said. "I thought you wouldn't pick up."

"I'm just finishing. Where are you?"

"Look. I'm freaking out here. You need to change tactics. I know . . ." she trailed off as she heard Hero yowl. She turned around, again as though through water. Eric was sliding open her screen.

"Thanks for that. Yep. K." She tapped her call off and slipped her phone in her pocket. "Hey," she said to Eric. "I'm so glad you're here."

"Are you okay?" He came toward her. He had added a light jacket to the same T-shirt and cargo pants he had on when he left the library this morning, the same clothes he'd slept in on her couch.

"Me? I'm fine. It's been a quiet day for once," she said.

"Are you sure? You looked rattled. Who was on the phone?" he asked as he came to her and put his hands on her shoulders, scanning her eyes.

She drew her arm across her body and patted one of his hands and moved off. "That was Blue. He was telling me that he finally got Jonathan at the farm. He confessed to everything. What a relief, huh?"

"Of course. We've been looking for that psycho all day. I was on my way home for a quick shower and thought I'd stop in and check on you. Why don't you come sit down. Can I pour you another glass of wine? What are you drinking?"

"No. Mine's still full," she indicated her dinner sitting on the table on the deck. "I'm not feeling too well, though. I think I'm just going to take a bath and turn in early. It's been a long week."

"You're not okay," he said standing back and looking at her. "I knew it. What can I get for you? Aspirin? Maybe something better to eat than cheese? A glass of water?"

"Water would be good. Okay," she said as he moved her to the kitchen bar stool.

Eric drew her a glass of water. "I heard you say 'I know' to Blue. What's new on the scene?"

"I know?" Cady took the glass of water.

"On the phone. You said, 'I know' right as I was walking in the door."

"Oh. Yeah. I was just telling him I know it's such a tragedy that a kid so young could be in such hot water." She was having trouble steadying her hands so instead of taking a drink, she put the glass down.

"You mind?" Eric pointed toward her glass. She smiled. Eric drank the entire glass of water. "It's starting to get really hot again."

"Yeah," Cady stood up. "I'm going to call it a night. I'll see you tomorrow?" She started to turn toward the sliding glass door.

"Cady."

She stopped. Even in the heat, goose bumps raised on her arms. She turned around, faced him.

"I wouldn't make another move, if I were you," Eric said. He moved toward her and put his arm around her, like they were on a date. "Why don't you just come and sit down like I said in the first place."

"Eric. I'm tired. I need to rest," she said.

"What you need to do is tell me what you told Blue. I saw Jonathan leave your apartment. I know Blue didn't catch him at the farm."

Eric tried to lead her to the couch but she shook him off.

She stood toe to toe with him. "Then you know what I know. You know Jonathan got away. You know . . ."

"What do I know? Do I know that you're getting brave all of a sudden? Do I know that you let a murderer go free when you let Jonathan leave here? Do I know that you'd rather make love to Blue and hang out with those teenagers of yours than be with me?"

"What?" She was caught off guard. "This has nothing to do with Blue."

"It doesn't?" He started to play coy.

"This isn't about Blue or about Jonathan." She stood up straighter. "You know that only the person who attacked me and put Ron in a coma would know about the poker chip next to his bloody and beaten body. That chip nearly dug a hole into my knee. You know that the attacker took that chip after I lost consciousness. You told Jonathan's parents that he had a poker chip on him that implicated him in the attack. Were you planning on planting it on him when you found him?"

The blood drained from Eric's face. She could tell he had been feeling cocky because he thought she knew nothing but she saw all the realization flash on his face in increments.

"What?" she said. "Do you need a glass of wine now?"

Her sarcasm snapped him back into focus. "Who the hell do you think you are? You know so much? You ought to know by now who you're dealing with."

"Who's she dealing with?" Blue said as he slipped the screen door open in its tracks.

Eric turned and faced Blue.

"Blue, thank God," Cady said and started toward him.

"You okay?" he asked her as he stepped further into the room.

"Hold it," Eric said. "Everybody just hold it. Cady, sit down like I told you before."

"What's going on here?" Blue said.

"It's him," Cady said. "It's been him all along. Rosalind, Ron, me."

"What are you talking about?" Blue asked Cady.

"She's smoking crack is what she's talking about," Eric said.

"Blue, listen to me," Cady went on. "Mulligan, Kiery, Jonathan. None of them had anything to do with the violence we've been experiencing this week. It was all Eric."

"Cady," Blue said. "Haven't we been through this before? With Delaney? Are you going to accuse Mollie next? Aunt Jessica?"

"It's true," Cady said. She looked at Blue and begged him to understand she was not making wild accusations. "Eric went to Jonathan's house this morning after you both left here. You told him not to go up to the house, right? I was there when you said it. But he did anyway. He told Jonathan's parents the police were looking for him. They're the ones who called him at the farm and told him you were coming."

"I was just trying to apprehend the fugitive," Eric said.

"Okay, so he's not the smartest cop. He's not trained in . . . fugitive apprehension." He looked at Eric on this last.

"He's not a cop at all." Cady was ice cold. She was starting to get hysterical but she was containing it for the moment. "He told Jonathan's parents about the chip."

"What chip?" Blue said.

"The chip I saw at Ron's house the night I was attacked. There was a poker chip lying next to Ron's body. I didn't think anything of it at the time."

"Blue." Eric was trying to steal his attention. Cady started talking faster.

"No. Don't listen to him. The chip. There was no chip found at the scene, right?"

"No. No poker chip on the crime scene log," Blue said.

"Exactly. I knew you would have mentioned it as out of the ordinary. No one knew about the chip except Ron, who is still in a coma; me, because the damned thing stuck to my bare knee with Ron's spilled blood; and the person who attacked us. I have the perfect chip-shaped bruise on my knee to prove where it dug in." She turned to Eric then. "But he told Jonathan's parents about the chip and asked if they knew if he'd been to the casino lately. Jonathan showed up here after his parents called his cell on the farm. He tossed off this comment about a chip and the casino and right then I knew that only the killer would know about that chip. It all clicked. The killer took it with him when he left us both there to bleed to death. Blue, I nearly gutted him with a wine bottle. You check his ribs. There *will* be a bruise."

"Eric?" Blue said. Cady saw a calmness wash over Blue. She imagined this was the face of resignation but she couldn't be sure. She was so scared her knees started to shake. Her mind was spinning and she wanted to get out of there. Eric was between her and the door and Blue was still standing nearly in the doorway. She could make a break for the library, but if she were in real danger she would never even make it to the stairwell.

"Eric," Blue said again.

"What?" Eric flung his hands in the air. "What do you want from me?"

"I want the truth," Blue said.

"You can't handle the truth." An old line they quoted to each other often.

"You. Me. Now," Blue said, not amused.

Eric's face started to crumple. The familiar sign of needing Blue to come to his rescue. "I fucked up, Blue. I shouldn't have taken the chip." Cady felt sure this wasn't going to end well but she breathed a heavy sigh of relief at hearing these words.

"I realized the second I said it out loud that I shouldn't have mentioned the chip. As soon as I heard the words come out of my mouth with 'Turning Stone,' I wanted to kill myself for my stupid mistake. I heard them telling Jonathan as I walked around the house to my car in the driveway. Their windows were open. Another back-ass house in this town without air conditioning." He wiped the back of his hand against his forehead. "Theirs and this one. They had dialed their son the second the door was shut. I heard them mention the chip. Your boys arrived just as I was turning the corner. They never even saw me there."

"Rosalind?" Blue asked. He was standing now in his trooper stance. Legs set apart and rooted to the ground. Arms at his side. Ready.

Eric looked at the floor to the right of Blue. He chewed his lip and nodded once.

Blue said, "Why, Deuce? Did she catch you gambling? Did they catch you at Turning Stone? As bad as that has been for you, it's not a crime, you son of a bitch."

"No." Eric folded in on himself, almost imperceptibly. "They saw me. With someone. He wasn't someone I wanted to explain. She'd snapped a picture of us. She was going to tell."

"Tell what?" Blue said.

Eric's eyes went dead as he stared into the eyes of his life-long friend.

"You're such a dumb fuck," Blue said.

"I told her to meet me under the bridge." Eric was still chewing his lip. "I just wanted to talk to her. She told me Ron was with her that night at Turning Stone. She said I should tell Cady. Not lead her on. Said I should tell you. Come out. She was so fucking accepting. I didn't want her acceptance. There was nothing to accept." He was exasperated. Cady was witnessing a full confession. She could see him justifying it all in his mind. The tone of his voice. It was all so sane to him.

"I told her there was nothing to accept. She had it all wrong. Stupid bitch thought I was gay. She thought I couldn't come out and she was going to ride in and save me from myself. She was always so thick-headed. Always thought she was right. I'd been worrying myself gray all week about her and she's thinking I'm gay. Even in this dumbshit town, people don't have to hide that. What fucking year did she think this is?" His voice was rising. He calmed himself again. "I couldn't talk to her. I couldn't let her continue to think I was gay because she'd tell Cady. I needed to not have to explain that picture. Fucking cell phones.

"She turned away from me. She held up her hand and said, 'The truth will set you free. Everybody should be free. It's part of my mission in life.' I snapped. She was going to tell. I'd have to explain." He implored Blue with his eyes. "I picked up a rock and smashed her head. It didn't even make a sound. Just a dull thud. She staggered back and fell onto the sidewalk. She just sat down like she was dizzy and needed a rest. I reached down and grabbed her phone out of her pocket. Then she tipped over and slid into the water. I panicked, man. I got out of there. I wanted her to die, for my secret to die with her, but I didn't mean to kill her."

"You left her there to drown," Cady said. The scene of Rosalind's body being dragged out of the water came rushing back to her. Her friend's life had ended in the course of less than a minute.

"I didn't mean to! I didn't know what I was doing," Eric said.

"And was it panic when you went to kill Ron, too?" Cady said. Blue was standing stock still. Cady was flinging words at Eric.

"I just went there to find out what he knew," Eric said.

"With a ski mask?" Blue said.

"And his face fell into the wine bottle in your hand?" Cady said.

"He was in the wine cellar when I got there," Eric said. He ignored her sarcasm this time. It didn't even seem to register with him. "I wanted to see if she had printed the picture she took. She had taken a picture of us from across

the goddamned room. We were hidden in the hallway behind the stairwell. I knew that second that it would end up
in her infernal scrapbook."

"Enough," said Blue. "What didn't you want to explain?" Blue's interrogator terseness was taking over.
"Who else is in the picture?"

"He's a nobody. Just like me."

Blue waited.

"I got in bad, man. I got in deep and when I couldn't
get out, I sold my soul. It was over for me with that first
bet. I just didn't know it then. I was theirs. I did whatever
needed doing. He was the guy who told me what needed
doing. As soon as Rosalind walked over and showed us
that stupid picture, I could tell it would be the death of
me. I played it cool. Had to come up with a plan to get
that picture. I could tell she hadn't figured it out yet.
That must have happened later. What she thought she'd
figured out.

"When I got her phone, I could tell she hadn't forwarded it to anyone, but I had no way of knowing if she'd
printed it yet. He knew it was me. Ron. He was riffling
through his Turning Stone bag of the pictures they took
and the couple of chips and bingo cards they'd saved. He
wanted to find evidence before calling the police. We were
both looking for the same thing. He knew it was me." Eric
was wringing his hands. He started to pace. Two steps one
direction. Two steps back. "Rosalind had sent him a text
when she was on her way to meet me under the lock
bridge."

"Why didn't he say anything when we went to see him on Sunday?" Blue said. Cady could see that Blue still wasn't completely believing what he was hearing. He wanted an out. He wanted anything but for his best friend to be who he was confessing to be.

"He didn't know then," Eric said. "He said he hadn't thought to check his cell phone because he'd been home all weekend. He said she was usually tech-free during the Convention but she had just gotten her new phone and was playing with it. By the time I got there on Monday night, Ron knew I was the last one to see her alive. He had our texts. He knew the time of death. He put it all together. I wasn't even thinking about regular texts. Just if she'd forwarded that picture." He looked square into Cady's eyes. "He wasn't even afraid of me. I was dressed all in black, for God's sake. In the middle of the summer. He didn't even flinch. He came at me with the wine bottle. I had to defend myself."

"And me? Was I just collateral damage?" Cady said.

"Yes," Eric said. Calm now. "Actually you were. I never wanted to hurt you. I never wanted to hurt you in any way." He spoke tenderly to Cady. Like they were alone, like he was breaking up with her and didn't want her to hurt. "I never wanted to hurt you in any way. I tried to make you happy so you could forget. When I found out, I wanted to help you move on and be happy. I did it for you. I heard them talking about Victor and the way it all went down."

Cady felt Blue look at her but her eyes locked on Eric. "What about Victor?"

"They talked about it in front of me because they thought I was theirs. I was." Eric focused on Cady.

"Who?" Blue said, ready to move in toward Eric.

"Telling you who makes you theirs. I'd never do that. You don't need to know who. It wouldn't help you if you did." He looked into Cady's eyes. "Just know it's over, okay? I wanted to help you with that. He told me about the acid, about the barrel, about the label. There is no trace of him left, Cady. I wanted to help you through that. Let go without having to know. Can you do that?"

Cady's mind was seizing. "Why?" she asked with a throat as dry as cinnamon powder.

"I don't know why. Maybe he was theirs, too. You said you went to Turning Stone all the time. Victor was a high roller. These guys aren't even Indian. They run everybody. Maybe he got in to them, too. You'll never know. You don't need to know. It's not about you. They know that. Now you know that. Let it go. I never wanted to hurt you in any way. I just had to get out of there. I put the mask on when I heard you calling downstairs. I was halfway up the stairs when you blew past with the apple core. I was sure you knew it was me." The wild emotional swing swung again. Eric's eyes started to dance. "When you allowed me to spend the night here, I realized you didn't and I was sure I'd be able to let you live."

"Deuce," Blue said, "don't make this worse."

"Worse?" Eric snapped his attention back to Blue. "How is this not going to get worse? After today I get to live with the fact I am a mass murderer." He paused. "But I will get to live. We all know what happens to guys like me in prison." Calm. "I am not going to prison."

"I can help you," Blue said.

"How? You cannot." Eric ramped up again. The whites around his pupils were clearly visible on all sides. "This ends here."

Eric pulled his gun hidden under his jacket in the back waistband of his pants. In the same moment, Blue drew his gun from its holster. Cady gasped. They stood there pointing their guns at each other. One blink from either of them and the other would have a clear shot. From the floor, Hero growled like an attack cat out of a horror movie, the suddenness of all the movement in the room inciting him. Eric turned his head at the noise. His gun went off. Blue fired his gun at the same time. Cady covered her ears and dropped to the ground. The room was filled with the sound of Eric screaming, gunfire. It felt like it happened in slow motion. Then total silence, except for the low guttural growl Hero was emitting from the edge of the room. He was crouching and all his muted-gray fur was standing on end.

Eric stopped screaming. He was lying face up on the floor, staring at the ceiling. Blue had also dropped to the floor. Cady looked up and there was blood everywhere. She fumbled her cell phone out of her pocket and dialed 9-1-1. She was screaming her address at the top of

her lungs. The air around her was still. There were no other sounds in the room but the piercing of her screaming.
"Officer down! Officer down! Come quick!" The operator
told her to hold on while help was dispatched. In a daze,
she tapped End because it was all finished.

Blue edged his way over to Eric. He was dragging his left
leg like a heavy piece of luggage at the end of a vacation.
There was a pool of blood under Eric. Blue had shot him
in the chest.

Eric's breathing was shallow. His eyes were searching
the room. They came to rest on the ceiling fan turning
slowly, blade over blade. Blue edged his arm under Eric's
head and cradled him, resting on his elbow.

"You were never satisfied," Blue said in his friend's ear.
Blue winced as the pain ripped up his leg in spasms. He
spoke haltingly. "Nothing was ever good enough. And
nothing I could ever do helped. Always the next score. I
need to know who. No more secrets."

"The secret just made it all easier."

"Easier for who?" Blue said.

"For everyone." Eric's breathing turned labored.
"Victor was respected. Maybe he still would be. I don't
know the why. I just wanted to help Cady. I tried so she
wouldn't have to know." Blue touched his forehead to
Eric's.

"I'm sorry, Blue," Eric said as he tried to turn toward his friend. "You too, brother. I wanted to protect us all. Tell them I'm sorry."

"Sorry," Blue said. "Do you realize how much paperwork I am going to have to fill out? That's what you ought to be sorry about." Blue was crying. His ache was as big as all the years he'd known Eric and all the pain his friend had caused. All the pain his friend had suffered. Every spit ball they had nailed each other with and every video game they had mastered together and every beer they had shared. It all meant everything and it all meant nothing.

Eric smiled. His eyes closed as a tear ran down from the corner of his eye onto Blue's arm. Eric shivered and Blue held him while he died.

Cady had moved over to Blue and was holding a blanket to his bleeding leg as the sirens came blaring down the street and police cars of all stripes screeched up to the back of the library. Hero jumped out the cat door in the window and leapt to the ground without taking the stairs that were quickly filling with officers with guns drawn.

CHAPTER 25

STANDING IN FRONT of her bedroom dresser mirror, Cady found herself lingering. Not to gaze but to see what was looking back. Her eyes read stoic. Blank. She looked closer. Stepped closer. *Where are you?* she asked herself.

The trauma of Eric's death was being hammered away in her living room. Mulligan and his team were there the following morning to pull up her blood-soaked floor boards and begin rebuilding with new material.

I need new material. I need to rebuild with clean floor boards. She had begun to loosen her grip on her emotions. She'd taken them out for a spin with Eric. They never got farther than the driveway, though. Rosalind's death threatened to sideline her permanently. She looked closer. If there was one thing Rosalind was, it was bald emotion. She ran hot and cold and every temperature in between. She engaged with her world. Cady wanted that.

She twirled her ring, slightly looser now since she'd not eaten much this last week. She held it up to the mirror. A solid band of white gold. She looked down at it. Reflected or directly, it was the same circle. Never ending, always beginning again. She slipped the ring off her finger.

"Let's just go with this one," she said out loud. Hero trilled from her pillow, tucked his head into his circle of body and paw, and fell asleep.

In the mirror, her eyes glinted off the late afternoon sunlight streaming in through the bedroom sliding glass door. She tucked the ring into the slot in her jewelry box next to her engagement ring. It was the old jewelry box her mother had given her for her 7th birthday. The ballerina twirled and *Ode to Joy* twinkled out from the little speaker in the back. She ran the pad of her index finger over them both. She closed the jewelry box. The music stopped. She heard the sawing out on her deck.

Cady came through the double doors from her apartment into the library holding a basket and a little paper bag folded over at the top. Hero waited in the stairwell as she opened the door and then led her into the corridor of the library.

"Thanks for getting started," Cady said to Natalie, who was powering down the computers and running the final register tape. Cady had gone upstairs to freshen up as the Friday late afternoon sun was edging over the library. She'd slipped off her wedding ring. She'd washed her face and rewrapped her hair in a loose coil and fastened it with a wooden clip. She had changed her shoes to the T-strap sandals she'd worn on her birthday but she did not change her dress. To work, she had worn a cap-sleeved faux wrap dress that gathered at her side in soft folds and accentuated the shape of her toned arms. She had spritzed herself with a light ginger-grapefruit scented body spray, grabbed her basket and returned to the library to help Natalie close up for the week.

"My pleasure," Natalie said. "This has been the longest week in the history of all weeks that ever existed since the beginning of anything resembling a week."

Cady laughed. "Agreed."

"What have you got there?"

"I baked." Cady looked at Natalie. "I know. It's not something I do. Well, not normally. The guys are back upstairs. I'm taking muffins to Detective Emerson at the hospital." She blushed deeply.

Natalie brightened. Cady smiled even though she tried to screw her face so that she would not.

"For you," Cady pushed the small paper bag toward Natalie. "For you, too."

"You didn't." Natalie grabbed the bag and opened it up. She inhaled the fruity blueberry scent mixed with the rich smell of cake and butter. "Oh," she groaned, "you did."

"There's one for your mother too," Cady said.

"She'll like that," Natalie said. "You know," she continued, "ever since last Saturday," their eyes met and Natalie looked away to the cash register clicking and whirring, "my mom has been acting a little bit more like a mom."

Cady leaned an elbow on the counter, her eyes asking Natalie to go on.

"It was hard there for a while." She paused, looking back at Cady. Cady could sense she did not want to talk it out. She felt like Natalie was telling her that Sara was all right as much as she was telling her that she herself was all right.

Cady's smile warmed. "That's good. Mothers are important."

The front door opened with a soft click and Cady stepped out of the circulation room into the corridor to tell whoever it was that they were closed. Jonathan stood in the corridor. Cady's body went rigid. He started to speak as soon as he saw her.

"I heard," he said. He had heard on the news that Eric Peterman had been killed and that he had confessed to killing Rosalind M'Clintock and the attacks that sent Ron and Cady to the hospital. He knew he was no longer a wanted man.

"Where have you been? We've been trying to reach you."

"I'm at the farm now. Thorpe is letting me rent a room in his big farmhouse. I'm not coming back here. I wanted to tell you."

She came closer to him in the hallway. "Are you going to be all right?"

"I'm on my meds."

"I'm sorry, Jonathan." They both knew she was apologizing for having believed him guilty of murder. He didn't know she was also apologizing for whatever was disturbed in his chemistry that would resign him to the lonely fate of living apart from the world, at eighteen years old. Whatever she had read in that report, she felt true emotion from Jonathan. Both now and during the time he was in her apartment. She had no idea if medication would right what was wrong with him. The doctor thought medical science didn't seem to have an answer. She hoped he would find one.

He nodded. He gave her the gift of accepting her apology. Without a handshake or a hug or another word, he left the library.

Cady walked back around the corner to the circulation room and found Natalie on the near side of the circulation desk. She was hovering, her cell phone in her hand.

"I wanted to make sure there wasn't trouble."

Cady took her hand and started walking her toward the front door. "You have been through too much this week. I want you to go home, enjoy your weekend."

"Wait." Natalie jogged back to the desk to grab her muffins. "Can't forget the best part of the week," she said. "It wasn't all bad," Natalie said as they reached the door.

Cady puzzled her a look.

"I'll never stop being sorry about Ms. M'Clintock, but I felt sort of useful this week. You needed me here. My mom." She stopped there.

Cady looked at Natalie and did notice a certain maturity that had developed, more like an adult than a teen playing adult. She stood a little taller, seemed a little older.

"I couldn't have gotten by without you this week, Natalie."

"I like that feeling. Thanks," she said as she started to turn to leave. She turned back. "Please tell that hunky detective that we're all grateful to him."

Cady smiled.

"And that we're all sorry."

CHAPTER 26

"FIVE MINUTES. The patient needs his rest," Ruby said to Cady as they passed each other in the doorway of Blue's hospital room.

"Not a minute more, I promise," Cady said. Ruby winked at her.

"Mollie and Aunt Jessica have been here all day," Blue said. "Ruby wants me to rest. I want to go home. We don't see eye to eye."

Cady smiled. "And aren't you a sight for sore eyes?" Cady said as she moved closer to the bed.

"I'm having a bad hair day." He shifted up in the bed. They both stifled a broad smile.

"How are you feeling? Tired?" she asked. Without waiting for him to respond, she said, "I brought you muffins. Baked them myself."

"I am a little tired. Of this place. You didn't happen to bring any of your coffee in that basket, did you?"

"Sorry." She handed him the muffins. He pulled back the yellow and white towel covering the blueberry muffins in the basket, breathed in deeply. "The first thing that hasn't smelled like hospital in two and a half days. I'm indebted." He inhaled deeply again. "Ruby was just telling me that Ron is still in a coma."

"Yes. I checked on him before coming in to see you. You probably know more than I do."

"His vital signs are improving," Blue said, "but still no sign of waking up."

"They are holding up the services for Rosalind," Cady said. "Maybe it's best that he sleep for a while. The grief will surely be there for him when he wakes.

"How are you? Really?" she asked.

He looked down at the muffins in his lap. He tilted his head. "He's been my best friend since first grade. How did I not know he'd gotten in so deep?"

"You can't know what people go to such great lengths to hide," Cady said still standing next to his hospital bed. "I dated him and I didn't know. I'd heard rumors about his gambling but nothing about being mixed up in anything like that."

"I'd known he'd been in trouble before. He'd started gambling when we turned eighteen. We spent a weekend in Atlantic City and I saw something change in him. It was like a fire had been lit. When he moved into my garage, I knew he was on hard times. But he held down that job. He'd been there for years. I thought he just needed a respite. A place to crash. If he'd have just told me."

"It seems he wanted to handle things himself." They both knew she was including herself in what Eric wanted to handle himself.

"Dean was by this morning." Blue shifted focus. "He sent a team to my house. They focused on my garage, of course. I told them they better not leave a holy mess." He twisted his mouth into a smile. "They found a second cell phone in Eric's duffel bag. They put a tracer on all the numbers but they're all disconnected. Burner phones. But they did find Rosalind's phone. In his duffel as well. The picture was still on it. Unfortunately, all you can see is the guy from the side, at a distance. She hadn't mastered zoom yet."

Cady's eyes glazed over. Tears started to well up.

"Hey." He shifted up in bed a little taller. "This is a good lead. We're not giving up. We'll find this guy. And when we do, we *will* crack him. You know that, right?"

Cady did not fidget or look away. All the years of searching. He'd been gone from the first. She knew that as simply as she knew her name. Had he been in the wrong place at the wrong time? Had he borrowed money from the wrong people? Had he gambled more than he could afford to lose? She might never know. But she knew now that he would not come back into her life. He would not knock on her door and take her into his arms. The weight of six years in lockdown lifted in the single second that Eric disclosed that Victor was gone for good. She hadn't yet felt the full freedom that is supposed to accompany such a revelation but she felt sure it was seeping in.

And the police would now take over the case. There was now a case. Finally. She'd spent all those years trying to convince them Victor hadn't simply left her for another woman. There was now a lead and someone would know something about people who ran book in the local casinos, maybe beyond the local.

She let out a quivering sigh, halting, letting all the air escape, holding in the tears. "I don't know what he'd done otherwise, but it was sweet of Eric to try to help me." She paused. "Sweet? Not the right word. And it wasn't right, which is why we could never truly connect. But he *was* on to something. Moving on without having to know. I believe I can officially resign as the police's shadow." The mystery was no longer hers alone to solve.

"You never know. You've got a sharp investigative mind." She said nothing in response.

"How is that cat of yours?" Blue let her off gracefully.

"Hero? He's fine. He's settled down. He didn't come home for a whole day."

"He is a real hero. Maybe we could be the first police-feline unit. Hero doesn't sniff out drugs. He sniffs out danger. That could be useful to me in my work." He paused. "I might have taken him in. He trusted me."

"I was there. Eric wasn't going gentle into that particular good night. As much to protect you as himself." They both let the silence fall.

"Blue," Cady said as she put her hand on the rail of the hospital bed. "I am so sorry."

He looked deep into her eyes. "I know you are. I am too." He put his hand gently on her hand. Cady did not move hers away.

ABOUT THE AUTHOR

Susan James writes from the lush landscape of the Finger Lakes Region of upstate New York where she lives with her husband, son (when he's not away at college), and two literate cats (they must be literate after so much time spent lounging all over her books).

Connect with Susan James at SusanJamesWriter.com.

57282618R00186

Made in the USA
Charleston, SC
11 June 2016